STRENGTH

Strength

CAT AUSTEN

DEDICATION

This book is for you. Something resonated with you to get you to book three. Maybe the spice, maybe it was Emily, maybe it was the pepperoni and the marinara. Whatever got you here, I love you for it. Thank you.

And to Tasha, who was here even in the beginning.

As always, until the day I die, this book is for the stay at home moms. This book was written while potty training my second born during the sickest winter I've ever known. That's all I gotta say about that.

Content warning/ Author's Note

This book contains adult content and is not suitable for minors under the age of 18.

Content includes but is not limited to torture, death, violence, violence with weapons, alcohol use/abuse, marijuana use, discussion of human trafficking, drug distribution. Pregnancy (NOT EMILY), mentions of pregnancy complications (NOT A MAIN CHARACTER).

Dubious consenting exhibitionism and voyeurism, consenting exhibitionism, and voyeurism, use of BDSM bondage, blindfolds, blood play, knife play, spanking, gagging/choking, primal play, fear play, and anal. Male/male sex, male/ female sex, male/ male/female sex AND FINALLY male/male/female/male sex.

This book contains scenes of BDSM that may not adhere to safe practice standards. I encourage you to research safe ways to play if you are inspired. Let's leave the unsafe practices for the fictional characters, babe.

All efforts to keep a detailed content warning list have been made and any missed triggers are solely the author's fault. If content that needs to be listed is found, please contact me at cataustenauthor@gmail.com and don't report to Amazon.

PREVIOUSLY IN THE SERIES

If you're anything like me, you forget what you read five seconds after you finish reading it. We're here for the vibes, ya know? Anyway, if you forgot what happened in book 1 and 2, I gotchu.

Book 1: Solace

Plot: Emily, a suburban kindergarten teacher, catches her mayor husband Gregory cheating with his secretary tied up on the work conference table. He claims Emily wouldn't be into BDSM, so he had to stray. Gregory is a general piece of shit and says he wants to make their marriage work because it would look bad for his career in politics to divorce his high school sweetheart for his secretary. Emily says, "fuck that" and divorces his ass anyway.

Emily feels ostracized by the town, her job, and her family after her divorce. During her post-divorce hair style change she is approached by a woman who gives her a business card with a phone number on it. Desperate to get away she calls the number and gets herself kidnapped. Excuse me, "forcefully hired" by a mafia they call the "family business" and is decidedly Not Only Italian Anymore. It's 2023, baby.

Luckily, her kidnappers new bosses are three hot mafia bosses named Sterling, Milo, and Devon. She struggles to feel safe in their home until they start to respect her and give her responsibility in their business operations. This happens after she kills a dude who tried to kill them.

They find out their leaders, Devon's dad and Milo's uncle (Anthony and Matthew), are getting involved in human trafficking with a mafia from out of town (leaders are Giovanni and Taz).

As a part of a deal with the out-of-town mafia, the guys have to be a part of an MMA fight. Sterling and Milo win but Devon loses. But he was a total asshat about training, so he deserved it tbh.

They plan to confront their leaders about the trafficking, but Emily and Milo are in a car accident and then taken to a basement. They're tortured for information on their mafia operations by Giovanni and Taz. The other mafia believes that Anthony and Matthew are making political connections, and they feel threatened by it. It's a whole Thing.

Sterling and Devon are told that Emily and Milo are dead, and they spiral. But Sterling has a drunken epiphany and sees their Air Tags located in a mechanic shop in town. They sober up and check it out and end up busting the place down and killing everyone to get to Their Babes. Emily and Milo are rescued, and Emily is a bad ass and helps kill Giovanni and Taz.

But not before Giovanni and Taz tell them that Anthony and Matthew are responsible for Milo and Sterling's parents' deaths and paid for Emily and Milo's deaths. It's a sad story, dude.

They finally get to confront Anthony and Matthew and be like "Hello we're not dead, fuckers!" and Devon demands control over the gangs. Surprise! Gregory the Douchebag Ex-husband is in that meeting as well as other local politicians. Devon announces to the room that Anthony is a terrible person who killed his friends for power. Matthew is like "Omg, you killed my brother?!" and ends up getting shot by Anthony. RIP.

Devon kicks Anthony out and is like "I'm king of this town now. GTFO."

Solace ends with him asking his mom, and other oldies of the family business "Are you with us or against us?"

Romance: Sterling makes videos of him masturbating and role playing for a video service called Personal Cameras, and Emily finds it. Milo catches her just after she touches herself while watching Sterling. It's awkward. Then Milo gets involved and makes a video with Sterling and they go viral.

There's unresolved sexual tension between Sterling and Milo. Sterling is very confused by his feelings for Milo, but Milo is obvs in love with Sterling.

Emily starts to have spicy feelings for her captors and there's a slowish burn until she finally hooks up with Sterling. It's pretty hot.

After they are reunited after being kidnapped and

tortured, Sterling and Milo admit their feelings for each other.

Emily has nightmares about being kidnapped and Sterling comforts her with BDSM. He helps her reclaim her body after the torture. Sterling ties her up with ropes and her cries of pleasure call in Milo who thinks something terrible is happening. When he sees what's happening, he says, "String me up, Rope Daddy" to Sterling and he is also tied up. Sterling puts in the work and gets them both off. It's hot, it's therapeutic.

Emily realizes she might not be so vanilla after all.

Book 2: Spite

Plot:

After the big confrontation with all the oldies of the Family Business (where Matthew was killed by Anthony), Devon asked if they were with him or against him. They all said they were with him but he now has *trust issues* so he sent them into hiding.

Milo let Marie know that he was not dead and found out she was pregnant. Stress from finding out her brother was dead had her experience some bleeding (some irritated placenta previa) and was on bedrest.

They meet with all of the gang leaders that Anthony controlled to try get them on their side. Everyone said no because Anthony is paying them more and they couldn't suffer a pay cut for their men. They were nice about it, though?

They went clubbing and Emily ended up running into one of Giovanni and Taz's guys outside and she got to use the torture chamber in the basement to beat the crap out of him. A cute bonding moment, I'm sure.

Milo and Emily started cyber stalking Gregory to figure out how he could lead them back to Anthony and found out he's been getting money from Anthony and sending it to his secretary. Remember, she's the one who hooked him up with Anthony to begin with.

Emily, Milo, and Devon go to a bookstore for a cute lil afternoon and then get attacked in the street on their way to dinner and after a dramatically ominous phone call from Anthony. The attack was aimed at Emily and Milo because Anthony believed they were the reason Devon was not loyal to him anymore. Devon got shot, but it was not serious. He stitched and bandaged it himself because he's a badass.

Then they got attacked at their house in the middle of the night. Milo had bombs rigged to go off in the woods behind their house, and they had security cameras set up. It got messy, and kinda scary, but they survived. It was gang members that used to answer to them but now only answer to Anthony that attacked. So, it was super awkward. But we found out they had all had their family members or livelihoods threatened to get them to comply.

The clean up effort after the attacks cost a lot of money so Devon and Emily sneaked to Anthony's house and into his safe. They stole money and gold to fund their own ventures and to pay off the gangs to at least stop attacking them.

A new house rule had to be instilled: "No orgasms while discussing business" because of Sterling.

They ended up forming an alliance with a gang run by a guy named Randy and they plan to take down Anthony.

A press conference on tv with Gregory and Emily's parents put a spotlight on her "disappearance" and named Devon, Sterling, and Milo as suspects. Everyone believed this was actually being encouraged and set up by Anthony to get them out of the picture.

Gang leader Randy found out about an upcoming meeting and where Anthony would be, so they organized a take over. The meeting ended up being with Gregory and his secretary, which sent Emily into a rage. She ended up storming the building with Sterling and a machine gun. They got Anthony, Gregory, and the secretary cornered.

Emily locked the guys out of the room and tried to cut off Gregory's ring finger. Devon crashed through the window and stopped her from killing him. They got Gregory and the secretary the fuck outta there because they aren't worth shit.

Devon gave Anthony the choice to step down the easy way or the hard way and Anthony tricked him and moved to pull out a hidden weapon. Milo saved the day and shot Anthony.

Strength begins right where *Spite* ended.

Romance:

This is Milo's book and it began with him as a virgin.

Emily and Sterling made him wait a bit longer because they wanted it to be special.

Milo and Sterling were making their Personal Cameras content still and found a way to make considerable money doing it.

Emily got Sterling and Milo to experiment with anal plugs and Sterling used a vibrating one. Emily made him come during a meeting at the table.

Milo and Emily had sex for the first time while Sterling was tied up at the end of the bed and had to watch. Which was what she promised they'd do when they were kidnapped in book 1.

After the attack on their house, Sterling and Milo had penetrative sex for the first time. This was where the terms "ass blast" and "butt nut" were used with unfortunate frequency and ease.

Devon was voyeuristic but did not participate in book 2. There was some fingers in mouth, some choking, some come-swap, and some tense moments. But nothing of *substance*.

Are you refreshed and ready?

"When you are not fed love on a silver spoon, you learn to lick it off knives."

— LAUREN EDEN, LIONESS AWAKENS

Chapter 1

Emily

Devon had roared and gone down to a crouch. The toes of his black combat boots kissed the expanding pool of his father's blood. He clutched his dark hair in his shaking fists and rested his elbows on his knees. His streaming amber eyes and plush lips were in a wincing scowl as he stared at his father's body. His father. The man that had just used his son's mercy to gain him the opportunity to pull out a weapon. Milo had shot Anthony to save Devon. Not out of the revenge he had spoken of while we planned and organized. But to *save Devon*. I knew this to be true, and deep down, I was sure Devon would come to the same realization.

I felt he may know now, crouched in his father's blood, since he had made no move toward Milo. He looked so broken, and the simmering putrefaction in my own soul reached out to his. On shaking limbs, I crawled to him. The abandoned medical lab's linoleum was dusty and cold under my hands as I made my way to him. Sterling and Milo's comforting hands left trails of warmth as I left their embrace for my cold, crumbling devil.

The closer I got to him, the more I smelled blood and death, sweat and urine. I needed to get him away from it all. "Dev," I croaked as I reached him. I placed a dirty, icy hand on his forearm, shocking him out of his trance. "Come away," my voice rasped, and I gestured toward the wall of filing cabinets.

He obeyed my plea, and we both crawled to tangle together in a clutching, desperate heap. And there we stayed for hours. Sterling and Milo organized the cleanup crew and Sonny's team to come in for the removal of bodies. They called Doc, who tearfully kissed us both on the forehead, and gave Milo a container of pills. Sterling had gently placed the pills on our tongues and coaxed us to swallow them down. Milo stayed away, his eyes worried and pleading. Devon and I remained silent and staring, clutching and holding until the pills relaxed us to sleep.

I had almost killed Gregory. I had almost killed Gregory. *I had almost killed Gregory.* It was a self-hatred and disgust filled mantra that repeated in my head for weeks. I spent the days in my dark bedroom, barely speaking to Sterling or Milo. They tried, and I loved them for it. They would coax me to watch comedy movies with them, calming baking shows, and even children's cartoons at one point. But I was rotten through to my marrow and didn't deserve their kindness or love. Milo would come and read aloud romance novels, computer manuals, and cookbooks to me. Sterling would brush my hair and draw me baths that weren't nearly hot enough to burn off my guilt or thaw the ice in my bones.

At night, I would crawl into bed with Devon. Our pain was not the same, but the phrase "misery loves company" was probably about wanting to be around someone who expected nothing and wanted nothing. He didn't care that I was too broken and rotten to comfort him, and I didn't care that he was too devastated to coddle me. We would simply be near each other until sunrise when I crept back to my bed. I knew Sterling was taking care of Devon just as lovingly as he took care of me. Devon's hair would be damp and smell clean, his new beard would smell like Milo's beeswax balm, and there'd be a sheen of oily medication around his bloodied cuticles.

It was nearing early May when the frost had finally let up outside. Doc visited us every other day to check vitals and urged us to eat and drink. But one day, he handed me a bundle of seed packets. I had blinked up at him wordlessly, and he had smiled down at me and said, "I've always thought it was a shame there was no vegetable garden in the backyard."

That night, when I crawled into Devon's bed, I turned to face him. "Doc brought me seeds," I whispered.

He jumped slightly at my words. I didn't think we'd spoken once in the weeks I'd been coming to his bed. "Seeds?" he whispered back.

"Vegetable seeds," I replied. "May I grow a garden?"

Devon was silent as he started up at the ceiling. A thin ray of moonlight was all that illuminated the room, and it reflected in his eyes. He cleared his throat. "I think there's landscaping tools in the shed behind the garage."

"Thank you," I said and rolled to my back to stare at the ceiling like we both did most nights.

"You can grow tomatoes to make me homemade marinara," Devon said in a gravelly, unused voice.

A sound like a laugh, stale and cracking, came from my mouth. It was so unfamiliar I hadn't fully recognized it. The back of Devon's hand brushed mine. We had never touched in our nighttime inner demon congregations. I turned my face back to him and watched him blink up at the dark ceiling.

Devon cleared his throat again. "I know he saved me."

"Milo?" I asked. My heart gave a kick-starting thump in my chest.

I felt more than saw Devon nod.

"Yeah," I said in a reedy voice. "And you saved me."

"I thought you'd hate me," he said.

"Never," I replied.

He scoffed.

"I was mad that you stopped me. But I don't hate you," I said after a moment.

"I need a drink," he said suddenly and got out of bed.

He was out the door and down the hallway before I could move. The light of the hall made me blink in the darkness.

I recognized that the way we'd been living the past few weeks was not healthy. I knew it, but I hadn't felt ready to do anything about it. Maybe tonight was the night we moved aside some of our rot. With a deep breath, I hefted myself from the bed and followed him.

In the kitchen, Devon was pouring himself a double of bourbon, neat. "Make that two," I said when I entered.

"No, you drink chardonnay with two ice cubes," Devon grunted as he pulled an unopened bottle from the refrigerator.

I scoffed. "I haven't drunk that-"

"Since you decided you were one of us. I know," he said and poured some into a rocks glass. He plopped in two ice cubes.

"What does that mean?" I spat, realizing that working through our issues was going to get ugly.

"It means-" he stopped to exhale sharply and look up at the ceiling before settling his eyes back on me. "It means that you've spent so much time trying to *be* us, you've become an entirely different person."

"No," I argued. "I'm still the same person! I just...."

"Changed."

"Everyone changes. Especially when they're in a

new environment," I retorted and crossed my arms over my chest.

He shook his head and glared at me. He sipped his drink slowly. "How many people did you kill when you were a teacher?"

"None," I huffed.

"And how many have you killed since coming to us?" Devon shouted.

I swallowed and shifted on my feet. I took a drink of the wine. It was cold and oak heavy on my tongue. "I don't know," I mumbled.

I had lost count. That realization startled me. I blinked at Devon.

He nodded solemnly.

"I did it to protect us," I defended weakly. I had spent weeks mulling over my actions and decisions backward and forward. It was not foreign to me to feel like the scum of Hell for what I'd done. But I wasn't acquainted with having it under someone else's microscope.

"Absolutely. Except for when you didn't need to," Devon said slowly.

"That's not fair!" I shrieked.

He watched me intensely as my tears threatened to fall.

"You can't make me feel bad- you can't tell me I'm a bad-" I stumbled through gasping breaths.

"No," he cut my rambling off. His amber eyes were sad and regretful. "I failed you."

"H-how?" I asked, shocked by his words.

"I was supposed to protect you. It was my job the moment you came into my life, Emily. And I let you get into a situation where you had to take a life. Many lives, actually," he said and braced his hands on the countertop. "I let you get to a place where you see your kills as signs of your strength when each one of those kills is a sign of my weakness as your leader."

"Weakness? Devon, you handed me the knife!" I gasped out. And he had, indeed, handed me the knife down in the basement cell the night I killed for the first time.

"I know, and I'm sorry," he said and hung his head.

"You handed me the knife!" I repeated in a cracking shriek. "Devon, you made me feel like I was unwanted and untrustworthy until I killed him! What else was I supposed to do?"

"I KNOW!" he bellowed and rounded the counter to be face to face with me. "I KNOW, EMILY!"

"YOU TAUGHT ME TO BE STRONG!" I screamed right back at him, squaring up to him toe to toe. I wanted to hit him. I wanted to scratch him. I wanted to beat him until he understood just how scared I was that I was ruined forever.

He tipped his head in a warning and growled, "There is no strength in taking someone's life."

"Well, you should have told me that before I almost killed my ex-husband," I scoffed as an angry tear rolled down my cheek. I did my best to blink the rest away.

"I'm sorry," he whispered as his eyes tracked the falling tear. He swallowed.

I shook my head. My chest ached, and I didn't think I was actually mad at him. Sure, we'd both made mistakes. We'd both fucked up. But nothing either of us did was intentionally malicious toward the other. He was watching me so closely that I remembered how his father had watched me. Anthony had watched me try to cut Gregory's finger off with the same intense gaze and had praised my viciousness. He had praised the demons that Devon had tried to protect me from.

"I'm sorry I ruined everything," I whispered back and looked down. He was standing so close to me. His black silky pajama pants and white undershirt were clean and smelled like laundry soap. The scent of his cologne was faint in the air, like it clung to the fibers of his clothes and not his skin. I breathed in his scent and pulled on that like a tether to who we were when this all started. "I'm rotten now."

"Aren't we all?" he said, just above a whisper. I heard the tilt of his smile.

"You're right. I'm not the same person as I was," I said and tugged at the hem of the oversized shirt I was wearing.

"I shouldn't have said that," Devon said. Soft regret laced his tone.

"No, you were right. I'm rotten. I let my demons take the wheel. The Emily that was worth saving is dead." Tears flowed freely now.

His hands clenched at his sides. The veins in the

backs of his hands and up his forearms bulged. It was like he was fighting his urge to hold me. He didn't want to touch the disgusting creature I'd become.

"You're wrong," he rasped. "You're not rotten. You are worth saving."

"I think it's too late," I mumbled, still not looking at his face.

"No. I'll show you," he said. He unclenched his fist and lifted his hand to my chin to tilt my face up to his.

"How?" I asked. "How could you convince me that almost killing-"

"By loving you," he breathed.

"L-loving me?" I asked, my voice cracking with nerves.

He nodded and swallowed as he looked over my face. His face had softened from an angry scowl to a more relaxed expression. Like telling me I wasn't destroyed was healing him, too. Like making me feel like a person again gave him a purpose as a leader. But... also like I was a distraction from his own pain.

I closed my eyes. "Devon," I breathed out, sounding like a rejection.

"Please," he begged in a whisper, and his thumb tugged on my bottom lip.

My body flushed with heat for the first time in weeks. I opened my eyes to see his eyes like warm honey on me. His pupils dilated and fixed on my mouth. If I let him love me, and heal me, then maybe he could heal, too. Or bury his own pain. And as much as I wanted to take that chance and let us heal together, I didn't want our successes or failures to be enmeshed. Our pain wasn't healthy, but that wouldn't be healthy either.

"I can't- you can't be what heals me. And I can't be what heals you," I said even though my body was bowing towards his. My hand gripped his forearm as he held my face.

He gave a slow, understanding nod. "I know, baby. I know. Loving you would be a sort of light at the end of the tunnel. We've been barreling towards this moment since you hit me in the head with a pepperoni in Harold's deli." We both grinned at the memory. "I've denied myself you for far too long."

"You said I wasn't ready for you," I reminded him.

His eyes flashed, and he fluttered them closed for a moment, like he was gathering his control. "Do you trust me?"

"Yes," I said immediately.

His eyes opened and were hooded on mine. I bit my lip, unsure where this was going.

"Your trust is all I need."

"What am I trusting, though?" I asked, my eyes darting between his.

A corner of his mouth lifted in a smirk, and his eyes burned wherever they landed. He leaned down so his lips brushed my ear. I shivered. "You can trust that I'll make you scream. I'll scare you, hurt you, chase you. I'll make you come harder than you've ever come before. I'll take you to your limits. But most of all, baby, you can trust that I'll never let you feel like you're rotten ever again. If you're mine, you're *mine* and I will not let you feel you're not worthy of love."

My mouth was open in a gasp when his lips trailed to mine. His warm, plush lips sealed around my bottom lip and tugged until I looked into his eyes. He let go of my lip, waiting for my answer. A liquid warmth settled on my hips and anticipation surged through my limbs. Need and desire were written all over his face, and I was sure I mirrored the expression.

"The guys-" I started to ask. I wasn't giving them up for Devon as much as I wanted this moment.

"They're mine, too," he blurted. "Just differently. I want you with them as much as I want you."

"Then I'm yours. Devon, I've always been y-" I started, but he cut me off again. This time it was with his lips on mine.

His kiss was hard and fierce, but still controlled. He backed me against the countertop and boxed me in with his body. I snaked my hands up to tangle in his thick, dark hair as I moaned into the kiss. One of his hands gripped the back of my head and the other pressed at the small of my back. He made a sound like desperation when I tugged at his hair. Our tongues explored and tasted and caressed. He led our kiss like he led our family- with emotion and precision and the ability to make me feel both protected and empowered. I rolled my hips against him, feeling the hardness in his pajama pants against my lower abdomen. He let out a growling breath as his lips unlatched from mine.

He kissed down my neck, sucking at my pulse point. I whimpered and clenched my thighs together.

A throat cleared from the other side of the room. We jumped away from each other and into defensive postures. Both Sterling and Milo stood grinning in the doorway.

"It's two in the morning. You should be sleeping," Devon tried to scold them, but his voice rasped.

"This weird sound woke me up, and I realized it was hell freezing over," Sterling joked.

"Yeah, and a pig flying past the cameras set off a perimeter alarm," Milo added.

I bit my lip to keep in a laugh as I looked up at Devon. His jaw feathered as he glared at Sterling and Milo. It was his anger that sent me into a fit of giggles. It felt like a rush of ecstasy.

"Bambi!" Sterling said cheerfully and rushed to me. "You're back!" He picked me up and twirled me in a circle before turning to Devon. "Devon!" he said in the same tone before hefting Devon up in the same spinning twirl.

"Watch it, he still has a boner," Milo warned Sterling with a laugh.

Sterling spanked Devon on the ass. This resulted in Devon and Sterling wrestling on the kitchen floor, while Milo pretended to referee. I laughed until tears streamed down my cheeks. Things were going to be difficult, but for the first time, it seemed like we were going to be okay.

Chapter 2

Emily

The late-night giggles hadn't completely broken the ice between all of us in the house. It would have been ridiculous if it had, honestly. Milo had murdered Devon's dad. In front of him. Moments after Devon had shown him mercy. It wasn't like Milo had stolen one of Devon's knit sweaters or ate the last of Devon's favorite croissants. Though, I *had* witnessed both incidents ending in minor bloodshed in my time in this house. While our relationships were not healed, we could all be in the same room together.

Milo and Devon still didn't speak other than simple conversations when either Sterling or I were present. It wasn't as if they hated each other; it was like they were afraid the other hated them. I saw their sad, worried glances when the other wasn't looking. I saw the way they gave each other plenty of space but didn't run away. I didn't know what would break the seal and lead to their healing, but the rift ate at me.

After that night in the kitchen, Devon and I didn't

talk again for a few days. I didn't go to his room for two nights, afraid that I'd fall into him before I was truly ready. I was afraid we'd wrap together so tightly that I wouldn't put the pieces of myself back together without pieces of him woven within. I wanted him. I wanted this family. But I wanted myself whole more. I would not allow a man to put me back together like a leather pants and lingerie wearing Humpty Dumpty. I had allowed myself to crumble, and I needed to be the one to clean it up.

It was early one morning, or rather, early for someone who had done little more than rot in bed for weeks, when I ran into the new housekeeper. Mrs. Golding was a plump, older woman, who had worked for the Bilals for years. While we hadn't seen or heard from Stephanie, Doc had informed us she was back in town and he had apparently apprised her of the information that we were struggling. Doc had shown up with Mrs. Golding in tow the next morning. I didn't know she was there for the weeks I'd stayed in my room. She had respectfully left me and Devon alone. Sterling had informed me of her presence now that I was "joining the land of the living" and moving about the house again.

"I've made eggs, if you're hungry," she said in a soft, motherly voice as she put away the ingredients she'd used.

I had wanted to be mad that she was there. Mad that it seemed like she needed to be there. Because what good was I as a woman if I couldn't keep house?

Or so my suburban housewife programming had instantly kicked back as a reflex. But Doc had been right to suggest that we were struggling and needed help. Nothing about our situation was normal and our grief was to be expected. Why not accept help? Especially when that help made amazing food and folded the towels the correct way.

"Thank you," I said and helped myself and sat at the island.

"I got a message from Stephanie this morning," Mrs. Golding said lightly. "She said Marie and Brendon are back in town. They want to come visit this morning."

"Milo will love that," I said and sipped some coffee that she placed in front of me. "Is Stephanie coming?"

"No," Mrs. Golding said in a quiet, sad voice. She looked down at the granite countertop. "She hasn't left the house and doesn't want to see anyone yet."

I nodded in understanding.

"She has asked about each of you," Mrs. Golding said.

I looked up. "Me?" I was nothing to Stephanie Bilal.

"Of course," she said, like it was obvious. "You got swept up into... well, you know." She waved her hand dismissively. Mrs. Golding had worked for the Bilals long enough to know way too much.

"Good morning, beautiful," Sterling's voice boomed as he entered the kitchen. "Oh, and Emily." He kissed Mrs. Golding on the cheek, and she swatted him away, a little blush to her face.

Sterling plopped down on the stool next to me

and pulled my seat closer to him. He moved me like I weighed as much as the bowl of fluffy scrambled eggs he was scooping from with his other hand. "You okay?" he asked me. "You haven't gone to Devon's room in a few nights. We figured you two would be inseparable."

I glanced up at Mrs. Golding, but she didn't react to his words. She went back to work to brew more coffee. "Um, I just feel like jumping into things with Devon would just make everything more complicated."

"You know Milo and I are cool with it, right?" he asked around a mouthful of eggs. His gray eyes were wide and worried.

I nodded. "Yeah, I know. I just want to get right with myself first."

"Okay," Sterling said with a shrug, but his eyes still studied me.

"Mrs. Golding said Marie and Brendon want to visit this morning," I said to change the subject.

"Milo's going to freak," Sterling said with a grin.

"Is he still sleeping?" I asked and finished my coffee.

Sterling's grin turned salacious. "He's exhausted this morning."

I snorted a laugh.

But it was moments later that Milo was entering the kitchen, with Devon not far on his heels. They both took eggs and coffee to their seats at the island and Mrs. Golding folded a pile of kitchen towels at the counter.

Milo shifted in his seat and stood to pull his pants up with an annoyed expression.

"You good?" Sterling asked him with a bemused expression.

"Yeah, I grabbed a pair of underwear from the basket outside my door and they're falling off of me," Milo grumbled.

Everyone leaned back to look Milo over as he ate his eggs. He looked exactly as he always did. "Did you lose weight?" I asked him.

"No, I think I've actually gained weight," Milo said with a shake of his head.

"Check the tag, dear," Mrs. Golding said.

"The tag?" Milo asked.

"Yeah, I think the only person who has had their own underwear in their hamper has been Devon. Everyone else had underwear in every room of the house. I was very grateful to see that someone had already written 'S', 'M', or 'D' on the tag of each pair of men's underwear in the house," Mrs. Golding said.

I tucked my lips into my mouth to hide my grin. Mrs. Golding and I made amused eye contact as Sterling jumped up from his stool and pulled back the waistbands on both Milo and Devon's clothes. Devon swore at him about personal space, but Milo let his fork clatter to his plate. "Please tell me I'm not wearing Devon's fucking underwear!"

"Hey, my underwear would not be bigger than yours," Devon shot back defensively.

"Nah, you're wearing mine," Sterling said and let both waistbands snap back. "Devon's got his own on."

"Should I check you?" Milo grumbled.

"Not wearing any," Sterling said dismissively and sat back down on his stool.

"Should I assume you were the one to vandalize our clothes, Emily?" Devon asked in a calm but almost threatening tone.

I rolled my eyes. "Assume all you want. Your ass is wearing your own undies."

"Why is my sister here?" Milo asked, excitement ringing in his voice as he looked at his phone.

Nobody was quick enough to explain, and it didn't matter, because as soon as Brendon had parked the car, Marie was flying up the front steps. Her petite frame had been overtaken by her pregnant belly and she was like a bowling ball flying toward her brother.

Hugs, tears, handshakes, and loud voices tumbled from the foyer to the hearth room. Mrs. Golding brought in coffee and tea and cookies before quietly leaving. Milo gripped Marie's hand next to her on the couch. He couldn't take his eyes off her belly, and it warmed me to see it. I sat on Sterling's lap in one of the wingback chairs and he stroked my back, slowly and absently, as we listened to Marie and Brendon talk about their time in New York like it had been a vacation.

It was clear Marie had been told everything about what had happened and how Milo and Devon weren't really talking yet. She steered the conversation away from heavy topics after checking in that we were all eating and drinking and bathing again. She reached up and fingered the ends of Milo's hair. It had started to curl a little at the ends and he was constantly flicking it out of his eyes.

"You all look terrible," she laughed. "I mean, you all look *well*, but completely terrible."

I looked at Sterling and Devon. I guessed I hadn't really noticed, but their hair had grown out as well. Sterling's hair was straight, but the black strands stood up at the back of his head and looked like there were actual knots. Devon's hair was slicked back more than usual, but looked like it could curl around his ears.

"The beard is a big no. It looks like-" she said to Devon, but stopped and her mouth snapped shut. She winced.

"It's okay, Marie," Devon said with fondness in his eyes. "I look like my dad when he grew his beard out for our trip to Pakistan."

Sterling let out a snort of a laugh. "I wasn't going to say anything. But you look like someone who is about to realize that he hates Pakistani food, despite his heritage."

"You look like someone who went nonverbal for the entire trip home," Marie said with a giggle.

"Alright, alright," Devon said with a huff of a laugh.

I didn't know what they were referring to exactly, but I gathered enough to paint a picture. Devon looked at me with the "I'll tell you later" expression.

The laughing at Devon's expense led to Marie offering to cut everyone's hair. Brendon had been quiet, but he made Marie promise to take breaks. "Actually, I have some business to discuss with you, Devon," he said. "I guess now is as good a time as any."

"Emily, you're first. I'm dyeing your hair back to your natural brown," Marie said without room for argument as the guys stood.

Brendon and Devon went into the office, and Sterling and Milo carried in all of Marie's supplies that were conveniently in the car. She mixed the dye in my bathroom as the guys carried the rest of her stuff up. "I was hoping none of you went somewhere else for your hair," Marie said as I brushed through my hair.

"We were busy for a while and then... well, our hair was kind of the last thing we were thinking about," I said, avoiding her eye contact in the mirror.

"Do you have any matted spots?" Marie asked without judgment.

"No, your brother and Sterling brushed my hair every day. And washed it a couple times a week," I mumbled. My depressive episode wasn't exactly something I wanted to discuss.

She stopped mixing the dye and looked up at me, face to face and not in the mirror. "Hey, I'm not shaming you. I have a hair oil that's good for detangling and wanted to know if we needed it. That's all," she said, her wide eyes and her tone emphasizing her words.

"I know, I'm sorry. It was just a... rough couple of weeks." I didn't know what to even say. I wasn't healed. I wasn't all better. But I was standing again. I was speaking again. I even laughed a few times. Maybe I was making progress, sure, but I wasn't ready to talk about it.

"No kidding, your roots looked like this that whole time," she said and looked in the mirror at my reflection. A glimmer of humor in her eyes now.

I smiled.

She looked back down at my hair and did the hairdresser assessment. She felt my hair and flopped it about with a thoughtful look on her face. Then she snorted suddenly. "Wait, Milo brushed your hair?"

"Yeah, he and Sterling would do it," I replied.

She made a face like she was impressed. "Hm, never thought I'd see the day Milo Holden simped for a girl."

I giggled.

"Did anyone do Devon's hair? I'm just worried about what I'm in for with him. He's a picky client," she said with a raised eyebrow.

"Yeah, Sterling did. He always smelled and looked clean when I saw him. Sterling even used Milo's beard balm on him," I said, remembering how he would smell like beeswax and soap.

"Wait, so Sterling and Milo had to bathe both of you?" Marie asked.

My heart jumped in reaction. This revealed too much of our relationship and our trauma, and I wasn't sure if I was ready, let alone the guys. I swallowed and fidgeted with the cape Marie had swung over my clothes. "Um," was all I mumbled before she continued.

"No, don't clam up! I'm just trying to figure out who is dating who because I'm getting mixed messages and don't know how to ask the right way," Marie exclaimed, sounding the most like her brother I'd ever heard.

"I- uh- we-"

"No way!" Marie stood in front of me now, her big belly in my direct eye line. "All of them?"

I stared at the indent of her belly button on her shirt instead of her face. "Um, sort of," I mumbled.

"Can you not accost my girlfriend?" Milo drawled from somewhere behind me.

"Yeah, what he said," Sterling's voice followed.

I fought a giggle at Marie's shocked expression. But then I looked in the mirror at the reflection of the door and saw Sterling with his arm around Milo in a possessive, intimate embrace. Not an arm slung around his shoulders like a casual friend, but in a way that clearly said "Mine." The giggle I'd been holding burst from me now.

"I'm so confused," Marie said and set the dye down on the counter.

"I'm with Sterling and Emily," Milo said simply.

"Both?"

"Both."

"Oh."

"Yeah."

"That's cool," Marie said blankly and picked the dye back up, a furrow between her brows.

"That gonna be a problem?" Sterling said, his voice deep.

"Don't threaten my sister," Milo scolded with a slap to Sterling's chest.

"I did no such thing!" Sterling defended and rubbed at the spot Milo had hit.

"'That gonna be a problem?'" Milo mimicked in a deep voice with extra aggression than Sterling had used. "Might as well fucking bark at her."

"*Woof.* No, Marie, I didn't mean to sound... threatening," Sterling said softly, like he was overcompensating for his aggressive tone.

Marie's eyes bounced between all of us with a puzzled expression before she burst into laughter. "Good fucking luck," she said to me before she started sectioning off my hair.

She shooed the guys out of my bathroom so she could concentrate. I sat quietly in my chair, waiting for the onslaught. Was she going to be protective of Milo? Would she think I was the third wheel and should leave? Would she be accepting? I shifted in my seat.

"So," she said.

"So," I replied just above a whisper.

"When did this all start?" she asked. "I mean, I would ask how you all met, but I already know that."

"Um, well, me and Sterling hooked up around the time of the fights just after Christmas. And then Milo and I talked about it when we were… taken. I talked over my feelings for Milo with Sterling after we… came back. I knew they liked each other before they admitted it out loud, and I encouraged them to act on it. And, well, here we are," I explained awkwardly. I wasn't exactly going to give the dirty details to Milo's sister. "What about Devon?" she asked as she worked.

"Uh, Devon is complicated," I replied.

"No kidding. But I mean, where does he fit in with you three? Or not at all?" she asked.

"He and I have feelings for each other, but I'm not ready to jump into a more serious relationship with him," I said.

"I was under the impression that Milo and Devon haven't spoken?" Marie whispered.

"No," I replied sadly.

"Okay, so again, I'm not sure how to ask delicately: is my brother dating you, Sterling, *and* Devon?" Marie asked with a huff.

I giggled. "No, just me and Sterling. Devon isn't interested in guys."

"Are you sure?" Marie asked and stopped her work to make eye contact in the mirror.

"Um, I'm pretty sure," I said. Because that was never a conversation we had.

"And everyone is okay… sharing?" Marie asked.

"Yeah," I replied.

"Okay, because I grew up with them and they've never been good at sharing anything. Toys, snacks, you name it, and they fought over it," Marie scoffed and shook her head.

I smiled. "Well, it hasn't happened yet."

"Good luck," she said with loaded emphasis.

After my hair was dyed back to brown, cut, washed, and styled, I flounced down to the guys in the office. I was feeling lighter and more like myself after a few hours of girl talk and a new look. Sterling and Milo had pulled up the stiff-backed chairs to the desk where Brendon and Devon were hunched over paperwork. Devon looked up and saw me first. His brow relaxed from his almost scowl and a small smile curled at the corner of his lips. Sterling turned to see what he was looking at, and his stony face bloomed into a smile.

"Bambi! Look at you!" he exclaimed.

I did a little spin and Milo and Brendon looked up. Brendon was looking mildly confused as he looked between us all but said nothing.

"Do you like it?" I asked and fluffed my hair.

"You look beautiful," Devon said quietly. He had this way of speaking softly and still held the attention of everyone in the room. It was what my Teacher Voice rarely accomplished in the classroom and he had it naturally. His eyes held mine and simmered with a promise. A promise of both bliss and ruin.

"Very beautiful," Milo said and held out a hand for me to come to him. My eyes broke from Devon's gaze to settle on Milo as I approached.

"Marie said you're next. She's in my bathroom," I said to Milo.

He sighed and stood up, offering me his seat. "They need you anyway," he said before kissing my cheek and leaving.

"Need me for what?" I asked as I took the seat, still warm from Milo's body.

Brendon cleared his throat before speaking. "All of Anthony's legitimate businesses were in his will to go to Devon."

"And I'm not taking them unless I can put all of your names on them," Devon insisted.

"Wait, me too?" I asked, shocked.

"Yes," Devon said with a nod.

I sat back in the seat and looked at Devon and Sterling. They both had the same expressions, a questioning smile, and raised eyebrows. Were they for real? I had no business knowledge and no experience in any sort of management other than classroom management.

"You don't need to sign today. But I would be sure to look it over and decide within the week," Brendon said. "We can only push it off so long before we get attention from the authorities."

I let out a breath. That was a huge decision to make in a single afternoon. "Good, because I need time to think it over."

Devon's eyes shuttered and turned back to hard copper and not the warm honey I was used to seeing. I swallowed. I hadn't meant to upset him. Brendon shuffled the paperwork and said something about checking on Marie.

Chapter 3

Devon

S he was sitting in front of me looking the healthiest I'd seen her since she came into our lives, and she wanted to leave. She didn't want to be here with me, and my blood boiled with the urge to drag her up to my room and lock her in. To wrap that silky brown hair around my fist and-

"Devon, I didn't say no," she whispered. She bit that plush lower lip of hers and her wide blue eyes stared at me. She looked every bit like the doe eyed character Sterling had taken to calling her.

I *tsk*ed and sat back in my seat. If I didn't get my body to relax, I was sure I'd make a terrible decision. Sterling shifted in his chair, and I refused to look at the man who was my brother in every sense of the word but blood. Pain spiked in my thumb, and I realized I was tearing at my cuticle with the nail of my index finger. Clutching my hands into fists with my thumbs curled in, I quelled the nervous habit.

My mother still hadn't contacted me since the

death of my father. Was I so abhorrent that I couldn't get a parent to love me, let alone a woman? My chest ached with the acutely remembered pain and grief of the past few months. I cracked my neck in a vain attempt to expel some of my anger.

"Dev," Sterling said, drawing my attention from the intense focus I'd had on Emily. "Let's just all talk about it together later. We need to have a planning meeting like we did before."

I grunted in agreement and looked back at the paperwork in front of me. Brendon had assured me that the businesses had been unmarred by my father's corruption, but I still felt like they were dirty. Other than being used for money laundering, they were legitimate businesses that provided incomes for good people. I couldn't fold them. Our options were to keep the businesses or sell them. And then, do we keep up our drug and weapon sales? Do we keep up the liquor sales, the gambling rings, the gangs? These provided livelihoods the same as our legitimate businesses.

My anger and frustration at my growing responsibility had stolen my attention from Emily and Sterling. But a soft, breathy giggle snapped my focus back up to them. Sterling was kneeling in front of Emily's chair, between her knees, and kissing up her neck. "I like this smell. What is it?" he mumbled against her skin.

"Hair spray," she replied, her eyes sparkling with humor.

"Mmm," he practically moaned.

I rolled my eyes at them and pretended not to be affected by their display. I put the papers into a meaningless pile on the desk and sprawled back in the chair, spreading my legs. The leather of the seat creaked beneath my shifting weight, and Emily's eyes fluttered to me. She bit that lip again and the rage that lived coiled up in my stomach stretched languidly like a cat before settling into a dull burn instead of its usual volcanic ache. She was a balm, a relief, for my pain and my rage when she sighed like that. I wasn't the one giving her pleasure, but her bliss was all that I wanted, even if it was another man giving it to her. I couldn't give it to her. I would only burn her up in my fury.

So, with her eyes on me, she relaxed into Sterling's hands and mouth. I watched every breath she heaved as it expanded her chest in reaction to Sterling's caresses. He was mumbling, whispering to her and I couldn't hear his words. They weren't meant for me. The cadence and tone were reverent, desperate. Something I'd never heard from the man before. He had always been anger wrapped up in a steely package. He'd always been closer to Milo than me, showing him his heart and humor. But she had broken through that anger. She had controlled his demons easier than I had ever done.

His hand gripped her throat as he nipped at her jaw. She sighed at the rough contact and my cock sprung to action. The office door was open and any of our guests could walk in, but they didn't seem to care. I monitored the door, but most of my focus was on her. Sterling's hand that wasn't around her throat was down the front of her leggings. Her eyes rolled and fluttered, a soft whimper escaping her.

She had been in my bed every night and not Sterling or Milo's, and they spent their days bouncing between both of our rooms caring for us. I knew she'd been untouched since she'd hurt Gregory and my father died. Now, her need reverberated through the room like a drumbeat with every breath, palpable and hypnotizing.

The muscles in Sterling's forearm shifted repeatedly as he touched her, and her whimpers got louder. He chuckled, and I stood up and leaned over the desk, covering her mouth with my hand. Her eyes flashed with irritation as she looked at me.

"Be quiet, we have guests," I said darkly.

Sterling chuckled again, and his hand moved faster. Emily's breath puffed over my hand as I stifled her whimpers and moans. I felt it when Sterling squeezed her throat tighter. I felt the moment she lost her ability to breathe. My cock surged in my pants, and I was impressed that I hadn't come on the spot. Her eyes were closed, and her body writhed beneath our hands. The scent of her arousal met my nose as I leaned over her. She was intoxicating. The way I knew she responded to roughness, to aggression, had me hooked. Addicted.

Her body stiffened and vibrated with shivers as she came. Sterling let go of her neck and she gasped a breath of euphoric oxygen as I uncovered her mouth. Her eyes squeezed shut and she let out a low moan as she exhaled. Not loud enough to be heard down the hall, but enough to make my cock leak pre-come in my pants.

Sterling sat back on his heels and adjusted his erection in his pants with a grin at Emily. I returned to my chair and leaned back, watching her cheeks bloom with a blush and her chest continue to heave for breath. Her blue eyes bounced between us and she licked her lips. I wondered if she was thinking about crawling under my desk and pleasuring me, but I cleared my throat. "That was a beautiful performance, Emily." My voice still rasped as I spoke.

"Um, thank you," she said, her voice rough and quiet.

Sterling licked his fingers loudly and obnoxiously, like a child with a popsicle. "Delicious."

A person darkened the doorway, and I looked up. Milo returned, looking well groomed and mildly irritated. Typical for him after seeing his sister. The scent of Marie's products filled the room as Milo plopped into Sterling's abandoned chair. He looked at Sterling on the floor and me in my seat before settling his gaze on Emily.

"Nuh-uh," he said dejectedly. "That's not fair!"

Emily giggled and straightened her clothes.

"Sterling, it's your turn with Marie," Milo grumbled.

My phone rang as Sterling stood to leave. "Mom"

was displayed on my screen. It was the first time she had reached out. I took a deep breath and answered.

Three hours later, Mrs. Golding was nervously putting the finishing touches on a platter of sandwiches in the kitchen. She and Emily were flitting back and forth, gathering items they needed. The two of them worked well together, dancing around each other like they'd worked in the kitchen together their entire lives. They looked more like mother and daughter than employer and employee. Though, I figured it was likely because Emily didn't view herself as the employer.

I smoothed a hand over my shirt, pressing out any nonexistent wrinkles. My mother was coming for lunch. I was going to have to recount my father's death to her. Sure, she knew the happenings since Doc had explained it to her after Sterling and Milo told him. But she was going to want to know what I'd done. What I'd experienced. And what drove Milo to ultimately take my father's life.

Emily slid a rocks glass of bourbon toward me over the granite island. I smirked at her and she lifted a brow in expectation. "Chug it."

I scoffed. "Emily, this is not a liquor that one can just *chug*. It costs almost three hundred dollars a bottle."

She rolled her eyes. "Aw," she said short and mockingly. "Sad story. Chug it. Your hands are bleeding from your nervous picking, and I don't think you want to meet your mother while literally red-handed."

I looked down and almost every cuticle was bleeding. My hands looked like a cat had shredded them. Mrs. Golding clucked disapprovingly. She'd been around most of my life and knew my nervous habits well. I spared her a glance when she clunked a small first aid kit on the counter from under the sink.

"I'll help him," Sterling said as he entered the room. He couldn't help himself from posing in the doorway, flexing his muscles, and giving Emily his best bedroom eyes.

Emily fluttered her lashes at him, still admiring his new, shorter, and cleaner looking hair. I lifted the bourbon to my lips and chugged. The liquid burned on its way down and stifled the jealousy that I refused to acknowledge. Emily looked back at me as I lowered my glass and a little innocent smirk played on her lips. I knew trouble before she even spoke. "Good boy, Devon," she said lightly, but a slight whispering rasp in her words left little to my imagination about her intentions.

Praise was not my kink, but I understood the bid for play. Sterling's hand slapped down on my shoulder, queuing me into my tensed body. My muscles were coiled like I was about to fly over the counter and show her just how *good* I was.

"Let's go clean you up," Sterling said loudly and jovially as he forcefully steered me out of the kitchen. He set my empty glass on the table as we passed, gesturing to Emily to refill it as he picked up the first aid kit.

I allowed him to steer me to the bathroom upstairs. Part of me barked to shrug him off to maintain my composure and to not show weakness. But the larger part of me recognized Sterling did not begrudge my vulnerability and had, in fact, encouraged it. "Dude, you almost ripped her to shreds," he said in a low laugh.

"I would never hurt her," I insisted. At Sterling's pause, I rolled my eyes. "I would never seriously hurt her. Especially not without consent."

"Oh, so if she consented for you to stab her, you would?" Sterling nagged.

"You know what I mean," I grunted as I washed my hands in my bathroom.

Sterling shrugged and looked like he thought he wasn't so sure about that, but said nothing. He opened the first aid kit and got out the antibacterial balm and liquid bandage container.

"Emily and I will greet your mom, but we'll leave for you two to talk," Sterling said as he blotted on the liquid bandage a few moments later. I could do the bandages myself, but Sterling had taken to caring for these wounds when I was... indisposed, and I found I liked the act being done by someone else. Someone who cared about me.

I nodded.

"We won't be far. If you need us, Dev, we're here," Sterling said and then blew cool air over the drying bandages.

"And Milo?" I asked in a whisper, my eyes on the top of his dark hair as he blew on my hands.

"He's here. But... he knows he's not welcome today," Sterling said, not looking at me as he gathered the supplies back into the container.

My stomach clenched, and I didn't know what the feeling was. It was a jumble. A mess. I couldn't find the loose end to unravel it, so it made me angry. "Sterling, I-"

"It's okay, he gets it. We get it. Um, he's actually looking to get an apartment at the end of the month, so you won't have to see-"

He would take Sterling and Emily with him. I knew it. He would leave and they'd choose him over me. "No," I blurted. I sighed. "Let me have some time, Sterling. I just need... time."

Sterling nodded and faced me. His eyes were intense, like he wanted to hug it out or say something mushy. "Dev," he said in a murmur. One syllable loaded with emotion. He wanted a heart to heart and to tell me he was still my brother and he still loved me.

No. Not right now. Not when my mother was on the way to my house to talk about my father's death and betrayal. *God*, not right now.

"Are you gonna kiss me? Because I could really go for a blow job instead," I said sarcastically. My voice was laced with more venom than I meant to spit at him.

His eyes flashed with annoyance. "Fine. Fix your own boo-boos next time." He left me alone in the bathroom. I exhaled a laugh at his words, but that sickly feeling returned to my stomach just after as the doorbell rang.

Chapter 4

Devon

Mrs. Golding greeted my mother like an old friend at the door. I watched them as I crossed the balcony to the stairs. They were, in fact, old friends. Mrs. Golding had worked for my family for decades and ended up a close friend to my mother. As my mom handed Mrs. Golding her coat, I saw she was thinner than I remembered. Her face was gaunt and there were purple smudges under her eyes. My stomach lurched seeing her like that. She looked up as I descended the stairs into the foyer and her eyes warmed and welled up at the same time.

"Oh, Devon!" she wailed before throwing herself into my arms as I reached the bottom stairs.

"Hi, Mom," I said in a tight whisper as I stroked her hair. Her tears wet the front of my shirt and I took in a shuddering breath filled with her perfume.

She pulled away and looked up at me with concern. "Hi, baby," she said softly and petted my newly shaven face. Mom looked around and saw Sterling and

Emily standing in the doorway. "Sterling," she gasped and reached for him.

He went to her easily as I stepped back. They embraced tightly and she petted his hair and murmured to him. I frowned. My mother had never been... motherly to Sterling. His body was stiff as she embraced him as though he were her own.

"Emily," she said warmly as she pulled away from Sterling.

The two women embraced before we separated, me and my mom to sit in the hearth room and Sterling and Emily to wait in the kitchen. Mrs. Golding had an actual fire in the hearth today despite it being the middle of May. But my mom's hand was icy on mine as we sat on the couch.

"I don't know where to begin," my mother whispered with a watery look out the window.

"We can start with some tea," I said and reached for the teapot.

Mom scoffed and waved a dismissive hand.

"Whiskey?" I offered.

"That's more like it," she said with a smile.

Once we were settled with drinks, she spoke. "It's my fault."

"What?"

"It's my fault Anthony..." she trailed off and sighed. "I should have spoken to you about the changes I'd been seeing in him near the end. I should have told you that something was up with him. When he didn't let me in on the dealings with Giovanni and Taz, I knew something was terribly wrong, but I didn't speak up enough."

"No, it's my fault," I said with a sharp shake of my head. "I let him get away with too much and it got too far. Everyone else knew. Everyone else saw it but me."

"Oh, baby," Mom soothed. "No, this has gone on much longer than you've been aware. There's so much more than you could have seen or controlled."

"Do you mean the stuff with the Hawthornes and the Holdens?" I asked, referring to Sterling and Milo's parents.

"Partly. Even I didn't make the connections until I learned he was guilty of their murders," Mom said and took a slow inhale like she was steadying herself. "I thought his newfound coldness after their deaths was how he was managing his grief and the added responsibilities of managing the businesses alone before Matthew. I had you and Sterling to tend to, so I wasn't so involved in those days. I think... I think if I'd been more involved, things would have been different. But more changes happened in him slowly over time and I just... waved it away until it was so big, I didn't know how to address it and not ruin my marriage. I didn't jump in each time he changed his plans or his mind on things because I thought he was just being creative or- or he'd thought of something new. I didn't know about the trafficking until it was way too late. You knew before I did, and I'm ashamed I let him take all the control."

"He must have known you'd be against it if he kept it from you," I said and finished my whiskey.

"I think he was very aware of what he was doing," she said coldly. Her ice was not for me, it was for my father.

"He never came home after Matthew's death," she breathed after a moment. "That meeting was the last time I saw him."

"He knew."

"He knew," she agreed. "Is Milo here?"

"He is," I said after a hesitation. I didn't know how she would react.

She looked puzzled. "That sounded troubled."

"Milo and I... haven't spoken," I confessed.

"Why?" her eyes were wide.

"He killed Dad and we haven't addressed it yet. It's complicated," I said finally.

"He saved your life, Devon," she said, like I was an obstinate toddler.

I didn't respond to her. My body froze, but my resolve thawed. My determination to hold steady to my family and maintain loyalty to my one blood family member remaining had hardened me to my chosen family. To Milo. I had been so sure that my mother would be resentful of Milo's actions. That she would feel betrayed by him for killing her husband. So, I had iced him out. He wanted to move away; I had done such a proficient job.

"I know," I said, my voice a reedy whisper.

"Get him," she said and shooed me away.

"Are you sure?" I asked, poised to stand.

She gave me a scolding look, and I went to the stairs. "Milo!" I called up to him.

Sterling, Emily, and Mrs. Golding were staring, wide-eyed, from the kitchen. Sterling approached me with a cautious, questioning look.

"My mom wants to talk to him."

"Should I be there?" Sterling asked quietly, his head bowed towards me. My stomach churned for a moment. He was asking as though his presence as security was needed. As a bodyguard. But for who? My mom or Milo? Who would he protect?

"If you want," I said with a shrug. I felt a prick of pain in my hand as I subconsciously picked at my cuticle. I shoved my hands into my pockets.

Milo came down the stairs, an unsure expression on his face. "What's up?" he asked.

"My mom wants to talk to you," I said.

He blanched. He was already pasty as fuck, but he looked almost vampiric as he looked toward the hearth room. My mom was looking out the window and sipping her whiskey. She appeared older than I'd ever seen her despite the same hair and make-up as always. There weren't more lines on her face to make her seem older. It was the way she held her body. Like she was curling in on herself.

"Me?" he asked.

"Yeah," I said and guided him by his elbow toward the hearth room.

"Hello, Stephanie," he said and stood awkwardly near one of the stiff-backed chairs.

"Milo," she said in a whisper as she stood and walked to him. She held his face in her hands and sniffled as she looked at him.

He looked worried and pale. Tense, like he was concerned she was about to snap his neck. I didn't blame him one bit.

"Thank you for saving my son," she said in a tight and tearful voice.

Milo's shoulders relaxed, and his eyes closed behind his glasses. It was like he had been a balloon of anxiety and she had just deflated him.

"Thank you," she repeated, shaking him a little in her fervor. "And I am *so sorry* about Matthew."

He opened his eyes as she let go of him. "I didn't want to do it," he said.

"I know, baby, I know," she soothed. She reached out for me, and I went to her. She put my hand in Milo's and wrapped both of hers around ours. Her hands were ice cold still, but Milo's was warm and clammy from nerves against mine. "Please, you two are as good as brothers. No more silence."

Milo's blue eyes were on me, unsure but steady. I nodded at him before looking back down at my mom.

"All three of you," Mom said and gestured to Sterling, who was standing in the doorway. He came over and she put his hand around mine and Milo's. It was a little like a slightly homoerotic football huddle, but I understood her meaning.

"I'm not going anywhere," Sterling said. "At least not without these guys."

"This. This right here is what- oh- what we all wanted in the beginning." Mom hiccupped a sob and stepped away. "Before everything. Before everyone...."

"Mom," I said, going to comfort her.

"No, no. I'm alright," she said unconvincingly. "Your mothers and I were very close and before you all were born, we had wanted you to lead together. To be as close as brothers. To be a family. Anthony tore that dream apart as best as he could. He tried to ruin it. But here you are. You're still so strong together. I am endlessly proud of the three of you."

"Thank you," I said.

"I- I need to go, boys. I'm feeling unwell," she said after another barely held in sob.

Mrs. Golding came in swiftly and helped my mother to get her coat.

"Mrs. Golding, could you spend the afternoon at my mom's house? Maybe call Marie and see if she's available for a manicure or a pedicure," I said conversationally, but gave Mrs. Golding a loaded expression. She nodded once in understanding.

"Oh, sure, Devon," she said lightly. "I've finished up here, anyway."

My mom gave Mrs. Golding a watery smile. "It'll be nice to have you around for the afternoon. There won't be much work. You know how I've been lately."

"Hm," Mrs. Golding said. "In that case, I think I could use a nice sit in the rose garden with you."

Mrs. Golding helped my mom into her jacket and shoes and out to the car.

The house was silent as we watched my mom drive away.

"Hey, could we maybe *not* call each other brothers anymore?" Sterling broke the silence.

Milo snorted.

Chapter 5

Emily

"Emily, can I talk to you?" Milo asked a little while after Stephanie left.

"Sure," I said from where I was looking through the seed packets Doc had given me. Some were to be started indoors, and some were to be put right in the ground. I was making a list of supplies I'd need for indoor starters in the empty office. I stood up from my seat at the desk and followed him out. "What's up?"

"Come with me," he said and led me up the stairs.

I had left them all alone after Stephanie went home in case they needed to do some talking, but it had seemed like they'd all gone into their rooms. Milo and Devon needed to talk their differences out and do some soul searching after everything that had happened. The rift between them was large and dark, and I was afraid I would get swallowed up in it.

He led me to his room, and I willingly followed him in. He shut the door behind me, and his lips were on mine. Hard and insistent. *Oh.*

"They had you before and now it's my turn," he said when he pulled back for air.

"And Sterling had you while I was recovering, so now it's my turn," I retorted with a challenging grin up at him.

He smiled down at me, his eyes molten behind his glasses. "Take your clothes off."

He didn't need to ask me twice. I stripped quickly and heard his clothes dropping to the floor behind me as I walked towards the bed and shed my clothes. I was wearing just a pair of plain white cotton briefs when his body pressed against mine from behind. His skin was smooth and warm. He hooked a finger in the waistband of my briefs and kissed my shoulder.

"These are nice," he said, his voice rumbling against my skin.

I giggled. "They're just plain granny panties."

"No, they're hot. They're normal, comfortable. There's no show and no expectations. It's just... Emily. Emily almost naked for me," he explained in a hushed voice as he slid them slowly down my legs. He kissed my hips, the globes of my ass, the seam where my thighs met my glutes, the backs of my thighs. I shivered as his beard tickled the backs of my knees.

"Just Emily," I repeated in a breathless whisper.

"Just perfect," he clarified as he stood up. His

erection pressed into the small of my back, and I shivered again. It had been weeks since I'd had sex.

"Tomorrow is my birthday," he said with a hint of shyness.

"What?" I said and whirled around to face him. My hair hit his chest as I spun. "Why does nobody ever tell me?"

He smiled and shrugged. "All I really want is to spend it with you and Sterling."

"Doing what? Shopping for computers? Playing video games?" I asked eagerly, planning in my head as I spoke.

Milo laughed, tipping his head back. "No."

"Um, building computers? Cyberstalking people?" I giggled. "What do you want to do, Milo?"

"You. And Sterling," he said simply. "All day."

The door swung open and banged against the wall. Milo and I both jumped and shouted in alarm.

"I heard my name," Sterling said, his eyes raking over our naked bodies.

"Jesus, Sterling!" Milo scolded.

"Just 'Sterling' is fine," he said as he approached us.

"You scared me!" I said angrily and with a pout.

"Aw poor baby," he said insincerely. "On the bed. Face down, ass up."

"Which one?" I asked him.

He looked at both of us contemplatively. "Emily."

I obeyed immediately. Both men stood silently behind me. I shook my ass in the air. More silence. I peeked over my shoulder. What were they-

Rock, paper, scissors.

They were playing rock, paper, scissors. Presumably to see who would get to fuck me.

"Really?" I asked.

"Would you rather us fist fight?" Sterling asked me with a cocky grin.

"No, please. I don't think my nose can be broken again before I need plastic surgery," Milo groaned.

I giggled. "Okay, the winner of two out of three gets me." I stretched and arched my back sensually. An idea occurred to me. "Wait, don't tell me who wins."

A pause before two deep chuckles. "Alright, Bambi. We'll play the guessing game."

"Not like it'll be hard. I'm much bigger than S- *oof*!" Milo began, but a sound like a punch to his stomach stopped him.

Silence surrounded me except for the soft sounds of them moving as they played their little game. While they played, I took a moment to check in with myself. It had been weeks since I'd been intimate with the guys. Other than earlier today in the office, I hadn't even had an orgasm. There had been a voice in my head in those weeks saying I wasn't worthy of pleasure. I wasn't worthy of these men. Yet here they were fighting- um, rock, paper, scissoring- to get to be with me first. Milo wouldn't have come looking for me, and Sterling wouldn't have come bursting into the room if they didn't want to be with me. I needed to put it into explicit terms in my head to believe it. If they didn't want to, they wouldn't.

A tongue met my pussy and shocked me to jerk forward with a little yelp. Rough hands grabbed me and yanked me back to place. Sterling? He was usually rougher than Milo. But the hands felt longer and thinner. So, Milo? I didn't have time to think about it much more because the tongue was back. I wanted to analyze the technique to decipher who it was, but my brain was going fuzzy.

The guys were unusually quiet behind me as I panted and moaned into the mattress. I felt my core clench as it desperately tried to pull them into me. I needed *more*. Arousal slid down my thighs as whoever was behind me pulled away to breathe.

"More," I whined.

Two chuckles again and a sharp slap to my behind. I shivered and my body felt feverishly hot. I breathed through it, hoping that someone would fuck me soon. Just as I was about to snake my hand down to take care of it myself, I felt the bed shift and then pressure as one of them pressed into me. He slammed into me quickly, and I bucked back to meet him. Our skin slapped in the quiet room, and I heard a muffled moan behind me while I cried out. It had been so long since I had one of them inside me I cried out in pain at the stretch. It was overwhelming, and I gasped in a breath.

Hands soothed over my skin. Both touched me now. "We've got you, baby," Milo whispered from behind me. His whisper was thick and breathless. Was Milo in me?

"You're doing so well," Sterling praised. "Show us how good you can take it." He was behind me, but to the right.

As I adjusted to the stretch, I thought more about the feel of the man inside me. No piercing, very large.

"Milo is in me," I moaned.

"That's right, Bambi. Milo's big cock is stretching you out," Sterling said reverently. Like he was watching a picturesque art exhibit. "Your perfect pussy has him drugged. He has his head tipped back and his beautiful chest is heaving. You have him lost, Bambi."

"Fuck," Milo gasped. "I just want to fuck her hard and fast, but I don't want to hurt her."

I craned to look over my shoulder at him. "Do it," I said, a slight rasping growl to my voice. "You won't hurt me."

I had adjusted to his size and could feel my body fluttering around him, desperate for more. He would not hurt me. I needed him unchained and lost to his pleasure.

"Suck his cock while I fuck you," Milo moaned.

Sterling kneeled before me and pulled me up with my hair. I opened my mouth eagerly for him. He fisted his cock twice before positioning himself just in front of me. I was about to move forward to take him into my mouth when Milo pulled almost all the way out and slammed back in, pushing me forward onto Sterling's cock. His piercing clacked against my molars twice before settling deep in my throat. I took a gasping breath as he pulled back a fraction and unblocked my airway. As he plunged back in, I exhaled and closed off my nasal airway, ensuring I'd gag less. It didn't stop my eyes watering and drool leaking down my chin, though. He fucked my mouth with the same ruthless pace as Milo in my pussy.

It was so much sensation, so much pleasure, that I had almost missed the sound of them praising me and talking me through it. I focused on their words as they grunted and moaned. It was my favorite sound in the world.

"We're so deep in you we could meet in the middle," Sterling joked through a moan.

"I want to come so far up this perfect pussy that you leak for days," Milo said and tightened his grip on my hips to a bruising hold.

"You take his cock so good, Bambi," Sterling grunted as he fisted my hair tighter. "Just watching his huge cock disappear into you has me about to come. You're going to take our loads so well. You're going to-oh, god- you're going to swallow me down like I know you can. You take us so good."

My eyes blurred from lack of oxygen, and I tapped lightly on Sterling's thigh. He was usually good at knowing when I needed to breathe, but today was an exception. He pulled out to rest on my lips immediately, panting, "Fuck, fuck, oh fuck, I'm close."

Milo's thrusts stuttered behind me and his moans turned desperate. His hands gripped so tight I swore his nails were biting into me. I didn't care. I wanted it. I wanted him to lose control. I wanted the pain. I deserved the pain.

"Wait, she hasn't come yet," Sterling said breathlessly to Milo.

Milo smacked a hand down on my ass. "Ladies first," he grunted and reached around to my clit. He rubbed clumsily as he thrust into me. When Milo was about to come, his thrusts always took on a rocking, rounded motion. Like his inexperience hadn't loosened that animal instinct to breed and direct his seed into my womb. And his clumsy touches to my clit showed his desperation for me. I craved it. I craved his wildness.

The sound of kissing above me while I had a cock in my mouth and my pussy sent me off. Knowing that they were taking pleasure in each other, as well as me, had me coming. The orgasm ripped through me hard and had my limbs locking up. It made the one I had with Sterling and sort of Devon in the office pale in comparison. My eyes screwed shut as I rode it out, screaming around Sterling's cock. Milo shouted out his release, and Sterling tapped my cheek in warning as his balls drew up. Their gasping breaths and moans echoed slightly, like they were still mouth to mouth above me.

Sterling's orgasm had me sputtering and gagging. It had been a while, and I was out of practice in taking his huge load. He pulled back, and the rest landed on my face.

Two more snapping thrusts and Milo's orgasm

receded, and he pulled out of me. Our combined come slid down my trembling thighs as he collapsed on the bed, watching as Sterling milked the last of his come out onto my face. Sterling gave one last relieved sounding moan before sitting back on the bed.

I flopped onto the bed to catch my breath.

"You could have joined us," Sterling said, breathless and rasping.

"He likes to watch," Milo's voice mumbled sleepily in response.

My head shot up and my eyes locked on Devon's. He was standing in the open doorway. Sterling hadn't shut the door when he came in earlier, leaving it open for Devon. I was covered in come, but Devon didn't seem to mind as he stared at me like he wanted nothing more than to join and finish me.

"How was the show?" I asked in a bratty tone.

His eyes flared. "Acceptable."

"Yeah? What would have made it better? Another cock?" I asked in challenge and lifted a finger to swirl in the come on my face.

Devon smirked in a way that spoke of trouble. It was a warning, and my senses were on high alert. He approached the bed, and Sterling shifted out of the way. Devon kneeled before me and picked up Sterling's discarded t-shirt from the floor. He wiped the come from my face and where it was about to drip into my eye. That smirk remained on his face as he grabbed my throat and dropped the shirt.

"We had spoken about healing separately before we came together," he said and held me in his firm grip.

I tried to nod in agreement, but he held me firm.

"My mother has been the biggest hurdle in my healing. I thought she would never forgive what I've done," he said and glanced quickly at Milo. "What we've done. And I hated myself for it. But she holds no anger for my actions. Our actions. And I'm feeling much better about our arrangement. Emily, your time alone with them is limited."

I shivered as he let go of my throat. He stood up.

"Are we good, too?" Milo asked from his place on the bed behind me.

"Yes, Milo, we're good. I'm sorry for my behavior toward you. I was having a hard time managing my emotions on the matter," Devon said, his hands in his pockets.

"It's understandable," Milo said with a wide-eyed shake of his head.

"I owe you. You saved my life," Devon continued.

"No," Milo said and shook his head again. "We're even. You saved my life with Giovanni and Taz."

Devon considered this for a moment before nodding once and leaving. He closed the door behind him.

"Oh... my god," Milo said after a moment.

"He never apologizes. Ever," Sterling said with awe.

"Nuh-uh," I said as I stood up and stretched. "I've heard him apologize before."

"Eh, life or death situations, sure," Sterling explained

and gathered our clothes and put them in Milo's hamper. "But not emotional ones. Or with us."

"Maybe he has a crush on you, Milo," I joked as we headed to the bathroom.

Milo made a face and tilted his head like that was a possibility as he turned on the shower. "You know, that's funny you say that. We've had a moment or two."

"What?!" Sterling yelped.

We crowded Milo into the shower, hoping to bully and intimidate the information out of him. He laughed and held up his hands to defend himself from us. "Stop it! All I know is that he has considered joining us long before we asked him to."

Chapter 6

Devon

Emily, Milo, and Sterling sat at the dining room table with me and our planning supplies. Admittedly, we did our best work when Emily ran the meeting with her big paper and smelly markers. I slid the pack of markers over to her, and she grinned at me.

A plate of pastries and a carafe of coffee sat before us on the table and Sterling grabbed a large, glazed apple fritter. He took a huge bite before speaking. "Alright, let's talk about our five-year plan."

Milo and Emily laughed. I stiffened. Planning out our lives was not a joke to me. What was so funny about a plan? Unease prickled the back of my neck. I cleared my throat. "You laugh, but that's half of our meeting today," I muttered irritably.

Emily instantly quieted. Milo and Sterling exchanged loaded, wordless glances.

"Okay, sorry, Dev," Sterling said and swallowed his pastry before repeating with less sarcasm. "So, uh, what is everyone's five-year plan?"

"I want to stay local," Milo supplied. "With Marie having a baby, I don't want to go far."

"Of course," I said with a nod. "Marie and her baby are a priority."

"What do you think about the business?" I asked him. "Do you want to keep working... with us?"

"Uh, well, I haven't started looking for other jobs yet. I thought about a resume, but most IT jobs want to know who your previous employer is. How do you put 'The Mafia, employer deceased' on a resume?" Milo said with a scoff.

"Wait, you're not going to do some dark web shady shit?" Sterling asked.

Milo shrugged. "That was Plan B."

"So... you're staying?" I asked, my eyes locked with his.

"Yes. For now. I'm not promising forever, or even five years, though," Milo replied.

He had already signed to be part owner of the family's legitimate businesses, as had Sterling, but we hadn't decided about selling them going forward. And Emily hadn't given me her answer about joining us. I curled my thumbs into my fist to resist the habit of picking at my cuticles. If she left the business, they'd follow. If she left me, they would leave me. They were a package deal, and I was on the outside. As I was meant to be. I was not worth being in their... unit. I was meant to use my coldness, my ruthless training, to lead them. Because if I was not leading them, not controlling them, then they would leave me. I would be alone.

"Well, you all know I want out of the mafia bull-shit. I'll stay on for the legitimate stuff. But in other news, I bought a cabin," Sterling said. This must have been news to Milo and Emily based on their shocked expressions.

"A cabin?" Milo said with a disgusted look. He was an indoor guy.

"Yeah," Sterling said with a smile. "Thought we could use a vacation spot."

"And you chose *camping*?" Milo continued, looking appalled.

"That's great, Sterling. But are you staying in the family business?" I asked, my heart pounding with anxiety.

"Emily, are you staying?" Sterling asked by way of his answer.

"I have no part of the family business," Emily said. "But I'll go wherever you guys go. I think I'm the only one with a transferable job."

"You can be our sugar mama," Sterling suggested with a waggle of his brows.

"My tastes are far too expensive for a teacher's salary," I drawled, but smirked at Emily.

She giggled.

"I'm asking everyone's intentions because I got a call," I said after a moment. "And I wanted to know where you all stood."

"What kind of call?" Milo asked.

"There's someone new in town giving our gangs a hard time," I said. "Interrupting shipments and starting fights."

"Fuck," Sterling sighed and sat back in his seat.

"They must think we've moved out," Milo said. "I haven't seen anything come up in police reports, so they must be going after our people specifically and not civilians."

I nodded. "I suspected as much. I told Randy I would meet with him this weekend to at least give some guidance," I said, referring to the leader of the River Blades that had helped us take down my dad. "We owe him at least that."

"At the very least," Emily said with a shake of her head. "We owe him and his gang our lives."

"Are we all in agreement, then?" I asked the guys.

"I don't know what I'm agreeing to. Can we keep it to the meeting to gather more information?" Milo asked as he typed on his laptop.

"Yes," I said as Sterling nodded his agreement with Milo. "I mean, are we in agreement to see what we can do for Randy? We will discuss it again with more information."

"Devon," Emily said softly as I picked up a croissant. "What is your five-year plan?"

The pastry went extra dry in my mouth and I sipped my coffee. Sterling and Milo also waited for my answer. They waited like they were looking for any reason to abandon me. Any reason to take Emily and leave me alone.

"I want to stay here. Continue the family business," I said finally.

"Why?" Emily asked. She didn't ask in a judgmental way. She seemed genuinely curious to see if my reasoning had changed.

"It's what I know. It's what I'm good at," I said. "I've been trained to lead my entire life-" *by a sadistic psychopath* "-and I want to continue." *Because if I'm not controlling everyone and everything, I have nobody and nothing.*

Emily's eyes narrowed like she suspected there to be more to my statement, but she didn't call me out on it.

"Always about being a leader," Sterling sighed exasperatedly.

I didn't respond. It was easier that way. It was easier if they thought I was a controlling asshole for the sake of the power and not so I could keep them. It was easier if they thought me to be power hungry and not hungry for the devotion they had, and I didn't deserve. It was easier if they thought I was predictable.

"So, what am I writing?" Emily asked and uncapped a marker.

"Nothing until Devon meets with Randy." Milo shrugged. "We're keeping hold of our legal businesses for now as an income source. Devon's going to see what's going on with the gangs and maybe help a little, and Sterling bought a tick infested rabid raccoon shack. The rest we'll figure out as we go."

"It's not tick infested. And there are no raccoons

inside," Sterling defended and kicked at Milo under the table.

Milo spun his laptop around and showed us a picture and records of a cabin. It looked well maintained and like a nice hidden getaway. I bit the inside corner of my lip to keep from smiling. Milo's scowl was pronounced and looked almost more like a pouting toddler.

"It looks nice, Sterling. It looks like a vacation rental," Emily said as she peered at the screen. She was right. He bought it for an impressive amount of money if the document Milo had pulled up was accurate.

"Thanks, Bambi," Sterling said defensively while glaring right back at Milo.

"It's in the middle of the woods. Does it get internet? Cell service? Running water? Did you even tour it?" Milo groused.

"Yes, I toured it. My cell worked fine, full bars. And there is a well with a new electric pump and softener. So, suck it," Sterling shot right back. "It also has a six-person hot tub and a pool table."

Milo's glare turned suspicious as he spun the laptop back to him and resumed typing.

"And *maybe* it would be good for *some of us* to get out in nature and away from computers for a while," Sterling said pointedly.

Emily and I shared a humorous look. She tucked her lower lip into her teeth to fight a grin, and I pressed a fist to my mouth. This was a fight we've had with Milo on a semiannual occurrence ever since we were kids. Our parents would force us on camp-outs, beginning in tents in our backyards, and then later in the local Metroparks and state parks. Sterling and I would sleep and eat junk food, while Milo snuck out Gameboys, took apart radios, and sulked. As teens, Sterling and I drank and smoked and invited girls. Milo never relaxed the way we did, and we loved him for it and despite it.

"We'll have to go over security and features," Milo grumbled, giving in to an angry and stubborn defeat.

"It features your ass sleeping for eight hours straight and not fucking with any computers," Sterling nagged.

"*I don't need eight hours; I do my best work with five!*" Sterling, Milo, and I chorused. While Milo was defending himself, Sterling and I mocked him. It was a well repeated Milo sound bite. A personal meme.

"Yeah, well, you won't be working at the cabin and that's a rule," Sterling said while Milo's face scrunched in anger.

Emily leaned over and whispered something in Milo's ear. His face relaxed its anger instantly, and his eyebrows shot up. He looked at her. "Really?"

"Yeah," Emily said and fluttered her lashes up at him.

"Okay, I'm in," Milo said to Sterling.

I rolled my eyes.

"Folded like a napkin," Sterling laughed.

Chapter 7

Emily

We celebrated Milo's birthday with Marie and Brendon on Friday night with pizza, cake, and beer. It was surprisingly... normal. Milo had said Matthew used to take him to strip clubs and out drinking, but it never was a good time for him. Now that Matthew was gone, pizza and video games were his chosen activities outside of the bedroom.

Saturday found me having a peaceful shower after a workout. I washed my hair slowly and left the conditioner on while I shaved my legs. Marie had told me to use a specific product line, and I was luxuriating in the scent. It had been a nice afternoon, and I was looking forward to the meeting with gang leaders later that evening. Randy had helped us a lot, and I was hoping to see him again to thank him.

Movement in the yard below caught my attention. Devon, Sterling, and Milo were dragging tools out of the shed behind the garage. I peered down and watched them pull out a rusty wheelbarrow and some long-handled gardening tools. The tools looked old, but they would probably work just fine for a beginner's garden. Doc was right, we had such a big backyard. It was a waste to not grow at least a couple of vegetables. I'd never had a vegetable garden before. Every summer I thought about it, but I always found a reason not to. Gregory and I had rose bushes and peonies, but nothing edible.

Devon, Milo, and Sterling pulled out a long wooden table. It was taller than a typical table. One for potting, perhaps? I watched them bicker back and forth like usual as I finished shaving. Devon had disappeared from the yard while I was looking away, and I figured he was going to get ready for our meeting. Sterling and Milo continued to look over the tools from the shed and stood looking out into the yard as they talked. It looked like they were planning where to put the garden, and I smiled.

When I came out of the bathroom to get dressed, clothes were draped over my bed. Devon must have dropped them off. There was a pair of high-waisted, soft, black pants. Nicer than a legging but not quite a jean. A long-sleeved black crop top, and a leather jacket. I made a confused face at the clothes. They were not what I pictured Devon to choose for me. But I put them on, nonetheless. My phone chimed with a text from Devon instructing me to wear my black boots.

"Bossy," I typed back.

"You have no idea," he responded immediately.

Devon and I met at the door, and I looked him over. He was wearing jeans and a leather jacket over a maroon button down. "Are we a motorcycle gang now?" I asked him.

He smirked, but said nothing. He led us out to the garage, and I reveled in the late afternoon sun. It wasn't warm enough to make me sweat in my leather jacket, but it was enough that the chill of winter was gone. In the garage, the smell of oil and gasoline was heavy. I walked to Devon's vehicle and tugged on the passenger door. It was locked. I tugged again.

"Over here," Devon said from the other side of the garage.

He was standing near an all black motorcycle. Oh. I must have looked confused because he chuckled as he picked up a helmet.

"We're riding tonight. It's perfect weather for it," he said with a remaining grin and handed me the helmet.

"I've never ridden a motorcycle before," I said excitedly as I shoved the helmet over my hair. "I didn't know you had one."

"It's been in the garage this whole winter," Devon smirked as he opened my visor and pushed away a few strands of hair.

"Hm, I never noticed it," I said with a shrug.

He put on his own helmet and opened one of the garage doors. He straddled the bike and looked over at me with a jerk of his head. I hopped on behind him, not sure what to do with my hands. If anyone had asked me which of the guys was most likely to ride a motorcycle, I would have said Sterling. But Devon? That was a pleasant shock.

"Arms around me," he said, and I jumped. It sounded like he was speaking directly into my ear. "The helmets have microphones."

He started the engine, and I wrapped my arms around his middle. Just as my hands were around him, he had us rocketing forward and out of the garage. I gasped, and his dark chuckle reverberated in my helmet and under my hands.

We shot down the driveway and through the open gates. Our road was empty of traffic, and I giggled breathlessly at the feel of the air against my body.

"I figured you'd have a good time," Devon said warmly. I couldn't see him but I thought for sure he was smiling.

"When did you learn to ride?" I asked.

"I signed up for lessons on my twenty-ninth birthday," he explained.

"So, a one-third life crisis?" I teased.

"You could say that," he laughed.

"I can't wait to see what you have in store for a midlife crisis," I laughed as we sped through the city.

His chest and belly expanded with a deep inhale just as I realized what I'd said. I'd admitted my commitment to him. To them. While I'd said as much to Sterling and Milo, I'd not talked to Devon like this. Instead of expanding on it or taking it back, I squeezed my thighs around his and settled in to enjoy the ride.

We pulled into a bar in Randy's gang jurisdiction and got off the motorcycle. I took off my helmet and shook out my hair. Devon raked his hand through his hair and stowed his helmet and took mine from me. He gave a friendly nod and warm greeting to a younger man who stood at the door, smoking a cigarette. I didn't recognize him from our previous interactions with the gangs. He didn't seem like he was just having a quick smoke, but was watching the parking lot.

We entered the dingy and loud bar and Devon took my hand. He led me back past the patrons and bar. A few people nodded toward us, and Devon returned each of them. Past the bar looked like a party room. We entered the doors and the sound of the bar cut in half. Randy was inside. He was alone and looking down at his phone. This wasn't a party room, it was clearly an office. A desk stood in the middle of the room and chairs were placed around it.

"Devon, Emily," he greeted us fondly. "It's good to see you."

Randy stood up and shook our hands before he gestured to the rickety wooden chairs in front of his desk.

"It's good to see you, too," Devon said as we took our seats.

"You're both well?" Randy asked and looked us over.

"Yes, thanks to your men and your help," I said.

He waved his hand dismissively. "Something needed to be done."

Devon nodded, and I gripped his hand tightly. "And indeed, it was done," he said, his light tone belied his grief.

"Now," Randy said with an exhale. "There's more work to be done."

"I'm sorry we've not been as present as we usually conduct business. I've told Emily and the guys about the issues you've been facing. Have there been any updates?" Devon said. I wanted to text Milo and Sterling and let them know Devon had apologized again, but felt it would be unprofessional.

"No updates," Randy said. "We've had a shipment of guns go missing, two drug deliveries gone, and some girls out on the street are asking our guys for protection. They're getting roughed up out there."

"What are your theories?" Devon asked.

"A new gang," Randy replied. "Must be a lot of guys, judging by how much has happened."

Devon nodded his agreement. "I think you're right. With Anthony and Matthew dead, they must believe us to be gone. Emily?"

I straightened in my chair. He wanted my input as though I was experienced in gangs. "We haven't been active and seen in weeks. They must think we've taken off after the deaths of Anthony and Matthew. Even Stephanie, Marie, and Harold were all out of town for weeks."

"Well," Randy shifted uncomfortably. "Are you back? Are you guys still in the game? I mean, I've been paying my guys out of our earnings. I'm keeping records in case you ask for our dues."

"There's no need to pay dues for the time we had not collected," Devon said. "For your people only. Don't spread the word."

"I wouldn't," Randy said earnestly. "Thank you."

"As for our status, I'd say we are active," Devon said and chanced a glance at me. I dipped my chin in agreement. We couldn't leave these people with nothing.

"What do you want us to do about this new gang?" Randy asked, his eyes bouncing between me and Devon.

"You need to prioritize the safety of your people," I said, surprising myself. "Have extra men at deliveries and keep someone trusted near the women on the street. I would assume any time there is a large exchange of merchandise or money, there is going to be an attack. Even if there's not, it's best to be prepared. Safety is the top priority, and we will discuss more with Milo and Sterling to come up with a plan for you."

Randy exchanged an impressed look with Devon. I suppressed a giggle. I had honestly shocked myself with the clarity I had on the situation. Randy and his people were probably our most loyal gang members. It would be a true loss to lose them. And while I didn't know what to do about the new gang just yet, I was sure we'd be able to figure something out to at least help Randy. Maybe we wouldn't remain in the business, but we couldn't leave our gangs with nothing.

Devon stood up and reached to shake Randy's hand. Randy raised his eyebrows as if to question if what I said was accurate. Devon gave a professional but friendly smile as he extended his hand. He smoothed down his shirt with his other hand. "We will talk soon, Randy."

Randy stood to shake Devon's hand and then mine in agreement. "Alright, I look forward to hearing from you."

Devon and I turned from the room and walked side-by-side back through the bar. Heads turned and watched us walk as we left. I felt powerful. I felt important. The feeling rushed through me for the first time since our fight with Anthony. This time it didn't corrupt. It didn't take hold of my body and make me crave more. The feeling was a rush but didn't consume me whole. It felt like progress.

"Are you hungry?" Devon asked me as he donned his helmet.

"Starving," I said with a smile. It had been weeks since I'd had a real appetite. I tugged on my helmet.

"Let me take you to dinner." His voice was smooth and silky in my ear through the helmet headset.

"Okay," I said, a little weak in the knees as we got on the bike.

"Are you in the mood for anything in particular?" he asked as he started the engine.

You. In the leather jacket.

"No, I'll eat anything," I said and wrapped my arms around his middle.

"Hm," he hummed in a teasing tone. "Well, I could use a good steak."

"Sounds great," I agreed. "And an enormous glass of wine."

"Chardonnay, two ice cubes," he said, and it sounded like he was smiling as we sped through the streets.

"Perfection," I sighed and nestled against his back.

He rubbed a hand, cold from the wind, over my hands on his stomach. I thought about moving my hands lower. Or sliding my hands under his shirt to feel the warm skin of his stomach. Or down his thighs. Cupping him through the denim. After dinner, I would do it on the ride home. Now, I was hungry for food. The way I wanted him would need fuel.

Devon pulled up to the sidewalk in the center of the city. Lights and music and traffic filled the air. It was a Saturday night, and the weather was finally nice. We dismounted the bike, and Devon secured the helmets. I shook out my hair and used the rearview mirror on a car to check my makeup. The restaurant he'd chosen was just a block away from our lucky street parking, and he clasped my hand in his as we walked.

The host's eyes bulged when he saw Devon and me walk in. "Mr. Bilal, I didn't know we'd be seeing you this evening."

"I didn't call ahead. I'm sorry. It was a spur-of-the-moment decision. If my usual table is not available, we will take a table in the dining room," Devon said.

His voice wasn't unkind as he spoke, but he offered no room for the young man to refuse.

"Sure, um, let me see what we have available," the host said and scurried away.

I cocked an eyebrow at Devon, and he rolled his eyes at me in response. "I own the building."

"Oh?" I asked and looked around. "The whole thing?"

"Yes," he replied with a cocky grin. "It's this restaurant and the café next door, and then all twenty floors above us."

"What's up there?" I asked.

"Three floors are offices for some start-ups, and then the rest are apartments. I think one is storage and maintenance right now," he replied and pulled out his phone. "Don't let him seat us near the bathrooms."

I waited while Devon called Sterling and filled him in on what we'd talked to Randy about. Milo joined the conversation and talked about getting better cameras near where the prostitutes typically hung out to better protect them without the looming presence of men. I listened to Devon's quiet conversation while standing proudly at the host's stand. Devon owned this building. I needed to look like the woman who would be on the arm of the man that owned the place.

We were eventually seated at Devon's usual table. The table in question was in the softly lit back corner with a private, plush booth. It was incredibly romantic.

"You take a lot of girls here?" I asked after we ordered drinks.

Devon smiled. "Actually, I think I've taken Milo here most of all."

"And he never put out?" I fake gasped.

"I know. Frigid bitch," he chuckled.

Our drinks were delivered incredibly fast. I took a long sip of my chardonnay. It was perfect and buttery, not too oaky. I moaned into the glass. Devon's eyes flashed with interest as he sipped his Manhattan.

"I hope what I said to Randy was okay. You haven't really said anything about it," I said and toyed with the napkin on the table. We had eaten our meals mostly in silence after the waiter delivered them. We had shared bites from our respective meals, but mostly remained in congenial quiet.

Devon was quiet again as he considered what I asked. It wasn't an angry silence, so my worry eased a bit. "You have become an integral part of this family. You recognized the heart of what I hoped our business to be from the start. I believe you saw the heart, the center, of this business before you even decided to stay with us. With Randy today, you made the right choice to direct him to ensure their safety while we planned."

"Oh," I said with a blush and looked down into my second glass of wine.

"Now you're feeling shy?" Devon asked with a smirk.

"It's not shy. I had just felt... powerful in that

meeting. I've never felt powerful before. At least not in a way that didn't feel... dangerous," I explained. I sipped my wine again despite the alcohol fueled heat that was creeping up my neck. "I was ready to feel bad and get into trouble with you for the direction I gave Randy."

"The feeling of power is often like standing on the edge. You can remain on your feet, or you can fall. Or jump. Or be pushed," Devon said. He looked at me and tapped his fingers on the table. He looked like he was considering saying something. "I want to show you something."

"What is it?" I asked.

"An opportunity," he said and stood up.

Our waitress, a trembling but pretty woman, rushed over. "W-would you like me to-"

"Please see that our bill for this evening is added to my tab," Devon cut her off and handed her a wad of cash for a tip. Her eyes went wide, and she squeaked out a thanks.

Devon took me by my hand and led me through the back of the restaurant. My legs were slightly shaky after the wine, but I felt clear headed and relaxed. I trusted Devon because, apparently, he trusted me.

Through the back doors of the restaurant, there was what looked like a lobby that led out to a parking garage. The buzz of fluorescent lights and a ticket machine for hourly parking filled the area. Devon led me to the elevators and pressed the up button.

"Do you have an apartment here or something?" I asked as we waited for the doors to open.

"I did for a time before we all moved into Sterling's house," Devon replied. "But not anymore."

The doors opened, and we stepped inside. Devon used a key on his keyring to unlock and press a button that said "Roof Access."

"What's on the roof?" I asked.

He smirked at me instead of answering. As we went up floor after floor, my anticipation escalated with the tension in Devon. The higher we went, the faster he breathed, and his eyes sharpened. His shoulders tensed and pulled back, and he stood, his profile to me, not speaking and not looking at me. What was going on?

"Are you afraid of heights or something?" I asked him.

He didn't answer me.

The doors opened onto the roof, and my stomach bottomed out from anxiety.

Chapter 8

Devon

I gripped Emily's hand and pulled her out of the elevator after me. She stumbled slightly on her feet as she followed. "Devon, what are we doing up here? It's just a roof?"

She was right, there was nothing up here. The HVAC units stood on the roof, with exhausts and chimneys, but no other features. A few birds fluttered in the dark as we moved across the space. Light from the city street below was thin and offered little guidance as we walked. The edge of the building had a low brick guard wall about waist height, but no other protection against tumbling off the edge.

"Devon," she said my name again, anxiety thick in her tone.

She wanted to know what power felt like and if she could be a good person with it? Who better to show her than me? I let go of her hand and leaped up onto the brick guard wall. She shrieked like I knew she would. My blood pumped hot through my body. I could hear it rushing in my ears.

"Get down!" she shouted. She reached out like she wanted to grab me, but didn't know how to do it without knocking me over to my death.

"Power, Emily, is like standing on the edge," I said, repeating what I'd said earlier. My voice was calm as I spoke, even though I was anything but relaxed.

"Okay, I get it. Come down," Emily said gently and made grabby hands at me like I was a small, misbehaving child.

I felt out of control. The adrenaline spiking through my body was sharp and addicting. It had been so long since I'd felt in control of my own life. While I was physically on the edge of the roof, an inch from death, it's how I'd felt for months. Maybe years.

"You have the power right now," I said and spun on my feet. Bird shit crunched under my shoes as I spun towards her. I put my hands in my pockets and smirked down at her. I hoped she wouldn't see my heavy breathing in the dim light.

"Devon, please," she begged, a terrified tremble in her voice.

"Do you feel it?" I asked her.

"The urge to puke? Yeah. Come down," she said, a bite of anger with the terror now.

"You have the power to push me. You could take over the business. *You* could lead. Sterling and Milo would give you their shares in a minute if you asked for it," I said and walked along the edge like a balance beam.

"Devon," she gasped out in a sob.

"Emily, this is what power is. What control is," I said.

Her fear fueled me. I could taste it in the air. It was sweet and sticky like marshmallows. My cock stiffened in my pants. She trusted me and here I was, scaring the life from her. She could push me, she could run away, but instead she followed me along the edge of the roof, her hands out like she wanted to save me. As if she hadn't saved my life every single day since I was assigned to kidnap her as fucking collateral.

She gritted her teeth and reached out to me. I saw her coming, so I didn't lose my balance. "That's not what I meant, Devon," she ground out as she grabbed my arm and pulled me down onto the roof. I landed on my feet in front of her. "I meant I want you. I want power at your side. *With you*. Not stolen."

Her teeth chattered with the cool wind and fear. I had hardly noticed the gusts of icy wind this high up. Her fingers gripped the leather of my open jacket tightly at my chest. Relief and unease blanketed her face now that I was standing in front of her.

"You want me?" I rasped, looking down my nose at her.

She nodded. "Yes."

"Take me," I growled. It wasn't an invitation; it was a threat. I spun her roughly, her hands breaking their hold on my jacket. With her facing the edge of the roof, I bent her over it. She gave a brief shriek of panic as her hands gripped the brick. The mortar holding the brick in place crumbled slightly as I pressed into her hips. Her shriek echoed back to us and down the city block. I wanted to hear her screams of pleasure echoing throughout the city.

"Take me," I repeated through my teeth as I ripped down her pants and panties. They tangled around her shaking knees as she arched her back.

"Devon!" she cried out as I crouched and licked her. I plunged my tongue into her, getting her wet and ready for me.

The sound of my name on her lips was like music to my ears. I had heard her cry out Sterling and Milo's names so many times before. It was my turn. It was *my name* she was going to scream for the entire city. Mine.

She was *mine*.

I stood up as I unbuckled my jeans and pulled out my cock. There had been enough foreplay in the months we'd known each other for her to be aware of what was about to happen. I wrapped a hand around her neck to keep her steady and to prevent her from careening over the guard wall with the first thrust. I felt her swallow against my palm and my cock leaked as I lined myself up. She was shivering in the cold and fear. Her knuckles were white against the brick where she gripped it as if I'd ever let her fall.

With the first thrust in, I saw stars. She was hot and wet, clenching around my cock. I felt her walls flutter with pleasure. Her pulse pounded against my hand around her neck as she screamed.

"Devon! Oh my god!" she screamed partially in pleasure but mostly in fear of falling off the roof.

For the first time, I chanced a look down. It was a long fall. My heart skipped a beat at the sight. Her hair swung forward with the second hard thrust and I gathered it up in my fist. With one hand around her throat and one in her hair, I widened my stance to keep a good steady base. While I wanted her to be scared, I didn't want her dead.

I fucked her hard and fast then. Her pussy felt like coming home and I realized I'd been homesick for a place I'd never been. Now that I'd gotten a taste, I never wanted to leave.

"You're mine," I growled and stood up straight. Her back was arched and her shirt and coat were bunched up around her tits from my thrusts. Seeing her smooth skin against the rough and dirty brick with the backdrop of the city was enough to make my balls draw up. I felt the signs of my orgasm grow near and I yanked on her hair. She cried out and bucked back against me.

Squeezing her throat tight in my hand had her moans cut off from echoing. With a shout, I let go of her neck. I wanted her to scream. I wanted to hear her. Instead of choking her, I smacked her ass so hard it echoed. She jerked forward with a scream, her hips driving into the brick.

Her muscles tightened as she came. I joined her just

after, emptying myself into her hot pussy. A groan left me as I rode out the orgasm with deep, slow thrusts. I pulled out of her after I stopped spilling inside her tight heat. Letting go of her hair, I pulled my pants up from where they'd fallen around my knees.

She turned around as she pulled up her pants with shaking hands. "Devon," she breathed.

"Emily," I said and lifted her chin to look at me.

She looked unsure. Worried. I leaned down and kissed her lightly. She relaxed against my lips.

"See? When you're given power, you can make good choices. You're capable," I said and kissed her again.

"You could have said so without scaring me," she said when I pulled away. A slight pout to her lips.

"But you were so wet because of it." I smiled.

She rolled her eyes. "I was wet at dinner, thinking we'd go home and have sex. Not that you'd scare the shit out of me on the roof."

I chuckled as we straightened our clothes and headed towards the elevator. "No, you liked it."

"Yeah, but only after you were off the ledge," she said and punched me on the arm. "Don't fucking do that again."

"I guess I can promise that," I said with a sigh as the elevator doors opened.

Chapter 9

Emily

Monday morning, I was invited to have coffee with Stephanie and Veronica. The guys had said it would be good for me to spend time with the women. They could offer me guidance on being a woman in the family business. Devon, Milo, and Sterling came along to empty Anthony's office of any paperwork they needed or wanted. I felt better knowing they weren't far.

Mrs. Golding met us at the door and led me to the rose garden and waved the guys up the stairs. "She's in a good mood today," Mrs. Golding informed me quietly. "She's been eating, and Doc gave her a new sleep medication that seems to do her some good."

"I'm so happy she has you to take care of her," I said with a hand on Mrs. Golding's arm.

"This family may have its faults, but they've always taken care of their staff. Always. And now it's my turn to take care of her," Mrs. Golding said as we walked through the kitchen.

The sunlight was soft and had dipped behind clouds, leaving the air cool that morning. The rose bushes were peppered with young blossoms and scented the space along with coffee and cigarettes. Veronica and Stephanie were already in the gazebo with the big fluffy blankets we'd used the last time I was out there. A tray of coffee and pastries sat on a round coffee table between the chairs. Both women smiled as I approached.

"Emily, I'm so glad to see you," Stephanie said warmly.

"You look lovely," Veronica said with a smile. "The boys must be treating you well."

I blushed as I sat in the remaining chair.

"Oh, stop it V," Stephanie laughed. "You know she and Devon are meant to be."

Veronica looked me up and down with a sly look. "I think the girl has all three of them wrapped around her little finger."

I gulped. My plan in coming here wasn't to out our odd relationship to Devon's *mother*. But not saying something felt like lying. And I had been, semi unfortunately, raised to never lie to parental figures. "Well," I said timidly. "Actually, I am with the three of them."

Veronica let out a cackle. Stephanie looked confused for a moment. "So, my Devon, Sterling, *and* Milo?"

I nodded and tucked my hair behind my ear.

"Oh!" she exclaimed softly before she tipped her

head in a contemplative expression. "Alright. As long as everyone is happy and nobody is fighting."

I thought back to a recent fist fight in the house. Granted, it was over pizza and not me, but still.

"Well, Emily here is certainly happy," Veronica cackled again.

"I always thought Milo was in love with Sterling," Stephanie said, and her laughter joined Veronica's.

I was silent again. I knew the guys didn't care if I told Stephanie and Veronica. They'd told me as much that morning. But I didn't know how the women would react and I was out here without backup. My silence was answer enough, though.

"Well, that's just interesting," Veronica said, awe in her voice as she sipped a coffee.

"They're together, too?" Stephanie asked, her eyes wide.

I nodded and accepted a coffee poured by Mrs. Golding.

"It's about damn time," Stephanie said and took a pastry from the tray.

"So, I take it you're staying?" Veronica asked.

"With them? Yes," I replied.

"In the business?" Stephanie asked.

"I'm not sure yet," I said with a shake of my head. "I didn't grow up in this life, so I don't want to insert myself where I'm not qualified."

"You have three of the most powerful and attractive men in the city in your bed. You're qualified," Veronica droned with a wave of her long, delicate hand.

"What she means is that it's not just about experience in the business, it's about instinct and common sense. And you have it," Stephanie explained. "Those boys were raised in this business, and they know good sense when they see it. They see it in you."

"Great sex alone wouldn't get all three of them agreeing to give you the keys to the castle. They know better," Veronica added.

The guys could tell me all day that I was smart and could run the businesses with them, but it wouldn't have meant as much as these women saying it. They'd been around for decades. They'd built this empire with men by their sides.

"Thank you," I whispered and sipped my coffee.

"They were raised right, and they'll never do to you what Anthony did to me," Stephanie said. "Those boys will never hurt you."

My mind flashed back to all the ways those "boys" hurt me on a regular basis. But I liked it.

"I know," I said and then remembered a question I had for Stephanie. "Before I agree to join the business, I wanted to ask you if there was a reason you are no longer involved? Do you want to have your share of it back? I don't want to step on your toes."

Stephanie smiled at me. "No, I officially passed my remaining shares of the business over to Devon when he turned thirty. I retired then. Though I was the heir, not Anthony."

This was news to me. "Oh? I thought he was the leader."

"The official leader, yes, but that's only because he took that power from me," Stephanie replied. "He slowly took power from me over the years."

"You don't have to tell me. I understand this is difficult," I said, feeling bad when I saw her eyes get misty.

"No, it's important for you to know. Because I know Devon is terrified he will turn out like his father. He won't, but I know it to be his greatest fear," Stephanie said and set down her mug on the table. "My father ran the Italian mafia for my entire life. I was his only child. My mother couldn't carry any more children after I was born, so I became his only heir. Anthony's biological father was an immigrant new to the city and worked for my father. When Anthony's biological father was killed in a gang attack and his mother died in childbirth, one of the other families in our business adopted Anthony. His wife couldn't conceive, and Anthony's biological father had been a dedicated employee."

"The people who adopted him were wonderful people," Veronica interjected. "Romana was a sweet little woman. She gave Harold the recipe for his carbonara that he uses to this day in the deli."

"Did you know that Veronica and Harold worked for our parents?" Stephanie asked, in clarification.

"I did. Though I think Sterling only gave me the smallest bit of details," I said.

"Typical. Well, Anthony and I grew up together in the business and I inherited it after my father passed.

Anthony and I worked side by side for years before we married. We joined forces with two local gangs ran by Sterling and Milo's fathers. They'd helped us overcome a different war for resources and control in the area, and we had mutual respect. Milo's parents and Sterling's parents were newlywed couples like us who had worked hard to get where they were. Together, we joined forces and rebranded from the Italian mafia into a family business. And we *were* family. We were all very close. The Holdens and the Hawthornes both led with us for years before we started families at the same time. We wanted heirs together. A new generation of leaders." Stephanie stopped to wipe her eyes. "Until they had their babies, and they decided they wanted out of the dangerous business we were in. They were selling off their shares to our legal businesses and giving over control of their gangs to me and Anthony. And then they died. I did not know it was because of Anthony. It had never even occurred to me he would have been responsible for the deaths of people we considered our brothers and sisters."

Veronica reached over and held Stephanie's hand for support.

"I was taking care of two precocious little boys, one of which had just lost his mommy and daddy, and I took a step back from the business. I was grieving for my sisters and caring for these babies. Milo and Marie had Matthew, but they were always here with me, too. I love them all like my own, and it was no burden to care for my best friends' children. But it gave Anthony the opportunity to... kill me off without ending my life," Stephanie continued. "I had given him all my trust until it was too late. When I finally realized that he had all my power and my control, it was too late for me to do anything. But I didn't think I *needed* to do anything. I relaxed. I knew Anthony had changed, but I didn't know the extent. I did not know what evil he was doing until that meeting where he killed Matthew. And I don't know how involved Matthew was in the deaths or the corruption, but I know he had nothing to do with the decision Anthony made about you and Milo."

I lowered my head, remembering that meeting. Matthew's shocked realization that Milo was alive would live forever in my head.

"Anthony never came home after he killed Matthew and everything came to light. He knew I would have killed him," Stephanie said, her voice laced with venom and rage. "He had strayed so far from what we had planned for our lives. There was no coming back."

"Devon is struggling, knowing that someone who had inflicted terrible things upon his family taught him everything he has learned about running the business," I said with a quiet respect for all that Stephanie had endured.

"Seeing what his father did and how it affected everyone from us at the top to the gangs at the bottom will prevent that from happening. He has a good mind and an even better heart. It won't happen. Besides, he has you and the other boys to level him out,"

Stephanie said and accepted a refill on her coffee from the silent Mrs. Golding.

"Knowing what I know now, I won't let him get away with it," I said with a small smile.

"You better not," Stephanie said with a confident grin, not unlike her son's.

Chapter 10

Devon

It had been days since I fucked Emily almost off the roof. She wanted to cuddle up to me after we got home, but I denied her. I was still feeling keyed up. Ready to fight. Ready for her to get hurt and then turn away from me. Then the next morning, she watched me with those big blue Bambi eyes like I'd kicked her puppy. I'd hurt her by choosing not to hurt her. It was fucked.

During those days and nights, Sterling and I worked with Randy to get his guys back into shape. Sterling whipped up a curriculum of fighting techniques for them and walked them through the moves. I helped them acquire more guns and even recruit more people from some of our other gangs. Many of the leaders had said their numbers were still crippled by my father, but they had suffered the same recent losses and attacks as Randy's men.

A few of the guys were skilled enough that Sterling felt comfortable leaving them with the curriculum and only showing up every other day or so to check in. Sterling spent most of his time working with our legal businesses on some infrastructure issues that had fallen to the wayside during my father's last few years of control.

I, however, had enjoyed fighting with these gang members. I sparred with them to hone their skills, sure, but mostly to get rid of some of the tension and anger that roiled like a living, breathing entity under my skin. Every strike to their skin made the anger in me sing, and every hit to my body had the self-loathing sated.

The guys in the gangs respected me. They listened to my direction. They bowed to me. Nobody in the house let me control them anymore. The power felt good. It felt like what I'd been prepared to have my entire life. As much as I didn't want to, I liked it. I craved it.

"If we want these cameras above the train station, then you're going to have to pay off the yard guards. And prices of the stuff I use have gone up," Milo was telling me as I iced my knuckles in the office.

I grunted in irritation. I was exhausted after hours of fighting with our men last night and well into this morning. The last thing I needed was Milo griping at me.

"It fucking sucks, I know. But if we want it done right, we need the right tools," Milo continued.

"Figure out how to do it with the ten I allotted," I droned.

I had given him ten grand to set up a security net-work of cameras and surveillance around where we get train, boat, and truck deliveries. Not all our merchandise came that way. Most were by drivers, but larger orders required larger means. And our larger orders were the ones being fucked with. Other than ordering in smaller and more frequent batches that can be driven less conspicuously, we wanted to set up a clear channel to watch over our guys.

"If you'd listen to what I was saying, you'd hear me telling you it's not enough," Milo said in an irritated and bratty tone.

I quirked an eyebrow at him. "I hear you and I'm telling you I'm only allowing you ten."

"Sure, and I'll hang some shitty ass cameras too far away with outdated server tech and spotty connec-tion. Fine. So, when we lose thousands of dollars in merchandise and Randy loses dozens of guys, we can look their families in the eyes and say 'Sorry, there were *budget cuts.*'" Milo mouthed off.

I stood from the desk and slammed my hands down on the wood. Everything on the surface jumped with the reverberations. Milo narrowed his eyes at me in a challenge. A dare.

"What the fuck is wrong with you?" Milo asked. "I thought fucking Emily would-"

He didn't get any further. I was around the desk and had him pinned against the bookshelves by his neck in a second. His head rocked back against the books and knocked some of them over. A decorative paper weight rolled off the shelf and hit the ground near our feet. "Don't talk about her," I growled in his face.

His clear blue eyes flashed with anger and disbelief at my aggression. "Fuck. You." He gasped out around the pressure I had on his throat.

He was challenging me and my leadership. Even though we were supposed to be leading together. I knew it in my heart, but my head was screaming for control. My father's lessons shouted in my head to eliminate him. If there was anything I had learned from my father and his failures and successes was that control came from taking out anyone who challenged it. He would have killed Milo right here and now. Hell, he had already tried before his own demise. He was even going to kill me in the end. Why did I think I was any different from him?

It would have been so easy to keep squeezing Milo's throat....

He dared to challenge me and then brought up Emily. He'd known I'd had sex with her because she had told him. Confided in him. She was closer to him than she was to me. Closer than I could ever hope or deserve to be. I squeezed harder and Milo's eyes filled with panic.

She would be so upset that I'd killed Milo....

"Dev," Milo tried to say, but he only mouthed my name. He punched desperately at my sides, his lips tinged with blue. His knee came up to push me away, and I let go of him.

Milo gasped for air, and the sudden, dizzying intake

of oxygen made his knees buckle. He went down and coughed, holding his throat.

I didn't stick around to make sure he was okay. I bolted from the room and met Emily in the kitchen with Mrs. Golding. Before I could say anything, Emily gasped. I must have looked a mess. "Devon, what happened? Are you alright?"

"Milo's in the office. He needs you," I said before I stormed out the front door.

Hours, a bruised rib cage, and ten bruised and busted knuckles later, I was calm. I shook out my hands and rolled my neck while stopped at a stoplight on my bike. I looked over and saw a car full of college age girls gawking at me. Behind my black tinted visor, I was annoyed. I lifted my black Henley shirt and flashed them with my flexed abs just as the light turned green. They all squealed in excitement, and I sped off. That shit used to give me a high, but today it just left me feeling homesick and guilty.

While heading home, I made up my mind to apologize to Milo and then take Emily for a ride. I needed to tell her I was struggling. The post-fight clarity was a lot like post-nut clarity and I realized I'd fucked up. Big time.

I parked the bike in the driveway and pulled off my helmet. The front door slammed open, and Sterling's hulking form stood on the doorstep. I fought the urge to roll my eyes at my adopted brother. But he was right. I'd hurt Milo, his boyfriend, and pissed off Emily, his girlfriend. If he didn't hand me my ass directly, I would be a lucky son of a bitch.

"I know," I groaned as I approached him.

He crossed his arms over his puffed out chest. "He's fucking bruised, dude."

I wanted to mention that Milo was so pale that a butterfly could bruise him, but I figured an insult wouldn't be the best thing to say if I didn't want to get my head pounded in. "I'm going to apologize to him... if you'd move out of the way."

"Again?"

"Again what?"

"You're going to apologize to him again? That's what, twice recently?" Sterling asked as he turned to the side to allow me a few inches to squeeze past him.

I scoffed. "I'm not exactly counting." A lie, but I wasn't ready to talk about how hard it was for me to admit when I was wrong.

"Sure, okay," Sterling huffed.

"Am I allowed to go talk to him, or are you obligated to beat my ass first?" I asked Sterling. "I don't know the etiquette of choking out my brother's boyfriend."

Sterling's nose curled up in disgust. "Dude, I've seen you come in your pants. Let's drop the brother shit."

I pushed past him and went up the stairs. "Is he in his room?" I asked Sterling who was following like a fucking Saint Bernard.

"With Emily," Sterling replied.

"She playing nurse, or are they fucking?" I asked, ignoring the jealousy in my voice.

"They're watching a movie," Sterling said as we reached Milo's room.

I knocked.

Milo answered the door wearing only a pair of gray sweatpants with his chest and neck bruises on full display. I looked him over, taking stock of his injury. It was just some bruising. Nothing serious. Dramatic fucks.

"What do you want?" he spat, his eyes narrowed behind his glasses.

"To talk to you. Alone," I said before my eyes raked over Emily, who was wearing only one of Milo's t-shirts and a pair of cotton panties. A paused movie was on the laptop on the bed and a bowl of popcorn was mostly empty on the nightstand.

Emily slid out of the bed and padded over to Milo. She stroked his waist as she slid out of the room. I avoided looking at her as she passed me. "Emily, I'll talk to you later," I mumbled to her.

"I'll be in my room," she said and went across the hall.

"And I'll be waiting out here," Sterling said and leaned against the wall outside Milo's room.

Milo smirked as he stepped back for me to come in. He shut the door behind me. I stood in his room and looked around. I had not been there very often. In fact, I could have probably counted the times I'd been in Milo's bedroom on one hand. It was messy, and computers and tech littered every available surface. It smelled like his soap and the beard balm Sterling had used on my beard before Marie shaved it off.

Milo leaned against his desk and looked at me. His face was relaxed, but his eyes were hard with anger.

"I'm sorry for what I did earlier. I shouldn't have hurt you," I said and forced myself to maintain eye contact.

Milo let out a harsh exhale. "We fight all the time, Devon. It's that you lost control. You almost choked me out."

I nodded solemnly and ran a hand over my face. He was quiet as he looked me over. I knew I looked like shit. I'd seen the hollows under my own eyes and the ashen complexion. It wasn't a very well-hidden secret that I was a mess.

"Do we need a safe word?" Milo joked finally. "Is this going to happen again?"

I gave a small, relieved chuckle. "No."

"You okay?" he asked, looking at me seriously.

I was being presented with the opportunity to tell Milo that I was struggling. I hesitated. "My father taught me everything I know about this business, and he was a piece of shit. I'm... having a hard time finding where his corruption ends, and good business begins."

Milo was quiet again while he blinked at me. I was about to turn around and leave when he spoke. "I think maybe even you can tell the difference between hurting someone and helping someone."

I scoffed. "Sure."

"Well, did you intend to kill me today?" Milo asked.

"No," I said, not telling him I'd thought about it.

"Okay, well, that's what's important. You didn't mean to hurt me and when you realized you were, you stopped," he said with a shrug of his pale shoulder.

I nodded. Sure, that's what had happened. I swallowed.

"You're going to have to talk to Emily, though. She's pissed at you, and she was already hurt when you never talked to her again after you guys, you know, fucked," he said, a little of a defensive boyfriend tone had crept in.

I looked away from him and towards where they had been watching a movie. The blankets were bunched up where they had been curled up, cuddling, and watching the movie together. Not fucking. Spending soft and cuddly time together. I was not a soft and cuddly man. Bitterness filled my mouth and soured my stomach.

"She has you and Sterling. She doesn't need me," I said.

"Uh, dramatic much?" Milo laughed. "She's torn up about you. She thinks you rejected her again."

I shook my head. "I'm... too rough for her."

Milo's eyes bugged. "Did *she* tell you that?"

"No, I-"

"Then don't assume what she thinks. Remember, that's what her ex-husband did," Milo said. "Maybe don't choke her as hard as you did me, but she likes it rough." He rubbed a hand over his purple bruises.

"Thanks," I grunted and left him chuckling to himself.

Sterling watched me go from Milo's room to Emily's. Maintaining glaring eye contact with Sterling for the two steps to her door, I knocked and waited.

"Come in," she said, and I opened the door.

She was dressed now in a pair of jeans and an emerald green long-sleeved shirt. Her eyes were light and free of anger as she looked me over.

"Did you apologize to Milo?"

"I did. Want to go for a ride?" I asked her.

"Are you going to choke me?" she asked, a bratty challenge in her voice.

"Only if you ask nicely."

Chapter 11

Emily

We donned our leather jackets and helmets down in the driveway. "Is leather a rule when riding a motorcycle, or just a fashion statement?" I asked as I heard the beep of our Bluetooth helmets connecting.

"There's function to it. No wind goes through leather," he said, his voice directly in my ear. "And it does better with road rash than some other materials. Now, get on."

I got on behind him and settled my thighs around his muscular ones as he revved the engine. What would my mom and dad think of me now? The thought was startling and hilarious, considering all the other stuff I'd been up to since leaving their house. Murder? Polyamory? Didn't faze my sensibility. Riding a motorcycle? Scandal! What would my mother think? I snorted a laugh at my own ridiculous thoughts.

"Something funny?" Devon asked as we took off down the driveway.

"Just thinking about what my mom would say if she saw me on the back of a motorcycle," I shared.

"Want to go pay a visit?" he asked after a moment.

"No," I replied sharply.

"You know we're not actually keeping you away from your family, right? If you wanted to invite them over or go see them, we'd be perfect gentlemen," he said earnestly.

I wasn't ready to think about this yet. Anger raced through my veins like a shiver.

"You could have Mrs. Golding make a nice dinner and we can have them over," he continued and rubbed a hand over my knuckles that were clenched in his jacket around his stomach.

"Stop," I said, my voice tight.

"Alright, but I don't want you to feel like we're holding you back," he said as we sped through the city.

"What if I like you holding me back?" I asked in a soft and sensual voice. I hoped it sounded like a sexy whisper in his helmet. It wasn't just seduction and a topic change. There was a double meaning if I thought about it. It had been so much easier when it wasn't my choice not to talk to my parents. Now that control was mine, the decisions were solely my responsibility, and the fallout would be entirely my fault.

His helmet twitched like I'd shocked him with my seductive words. I smiled.

"Even after this morning?" he asked, his voice carrying a tight rasp, as if he had clenched his jaw.

"You apologized," I said and slid my hands down from his stomach to the tops of his thighs.

His muscles jumped and clenched under my hands. I heard his breath stutter in the helmet, sounding like he was gasping in my ear. With a grin and a soft giggle, I raked my nails up and down his thighs.

"Fuck," he whispered with a harsh exhale. His breath rumbled like a growl in his chest as I squeezed his muscular legs. The microphones must have been close to our mouths, which made every breath feel more intimate.

I was so wet that I was shocked I didn't slip right off the motorcycle. His head tipped back and knocked his helmet against mine gently. I slipped one hand under his jacket and shirt and traced over his stomach. He was panting now, and I could feel it under my fingers. The expanding of his belly and then the shuddering release of breath under my fingers and in my ear felt like we were wrapped up in sheets, naked and skin to skin, not flying down a public road in the golden glow of sunset.

"But I could hurt you," he said finally, his voice rumbling.

"Like with Milo?" I asked.

"I lost control. I could lose control with you," he explained.

"You don't scare me, Devon. If I told you that you were hurting me, you'd stop. I know it," I said and raked my nails over the soft skin of his belly.

"What if you couldn't speak?" Devon ground out through his teeth.

"Then we could have a... safe movement and a safe word," I reasoned. This didn't seem like that much of a hurdle. His hesitation made little sense to me.

"You have no idea what-" he said before cutting himself off with an angry growl. He leaned forward slightly and accelerated us faster. We were weaving in and out of cars, going much faster than was necessary. I pulled my hands out of his shirt to grip his jacket in a death grip.

"Devon," I warned, my voice wary.

Car horns blared around us as we sped through an intersection on a stale red light.

I squeaked in fear and buried my helmet in his back. I breathed as steadily as I could. He was trying to scare me off. He was trying to show me he was dangerous. If I showed him that he scared me, then he would win. Kindergarteners did the same thing. Would their teacher still talk nicely to them and play with them if they threw a chair? Would their teacher still love them if they used bad words? Devon was testing my boundaries like a child. While I couldn't yell at a small child in my classroom, I could surely yell at a grown man.

"Pull over now!" I shouted angrily. A crack of fear was still audible in my tone despite my best efforts.

We had come out the other end of the city and were in a larger suburban area. Devon stiffened when I shouted and brought us into the parking lot of a local park. The sun was setting and there were no people in the chilly, tree-lined park. Devon stopped the bike, and I jumped off. I ripped my helmet off as he swung his leg over the bike.

"What the hell?" I shouted at him as he took off his own helmet.

Despite my anger, my knees were wobbling with fear. I stomped to where a picnic table rested between two trees.

"I told you I was dangerous," he said cooly. But the rapid rise and fall of his chest told me he was just as amped up as I was.

"Oh, fuck you, Devon," I spat, and leaned against the side of the table. "You were in complete control. You were just being an asshole."

"Well, I am an asshole," he bit out.

Here in the shaded seclusion of the park, with the sunset hiding behind some gray clouds, he looked devilish. The shadows cast on his face made the angles even sharper, his eyes darker, and his angry expression more threatening. He looked just as scary as he claimed to be. But I knew better than to give him that satisfaction. I rolled my eyes at him.

That snapped him.

I had a singular millisecond to have the thought, "I think I girl-bossed too hard" before I was spun and pressed into the trunk of the tree that shaded the table. A *whoosh* of air left my lungs at the contact. My head bounced a little at the force and rested against the rough bark just as my eyes caught the flash of silver. Wait, *what*?

A knife.

The asshole had a *knife* to my throat!

I took in a gasping breath and my eyes met his, shrouded in shadows. I was sure I was gaping up at him. What did he think he was doing?

"Do you like that I could hurt you?" he asked, his voice silkier than I'd expected. It clued me into his power play more than an actual threat.

"Y-you're a man, of course you could hurt me," I whispered through a dry throat. I knew I was safe with him, but it didn't stop my fear at the sight of a weapon.

"No," Devon said with a deep chuckle. "I'm more than a man here. I have your life in my hands. Literally. I can see your pulse right... here."

"Do *you* like having my life in your hands?" I countered.

"Still a fucking brat with a knife to your throat," he gritted through his teeth. He pressed the knife until it bit. "Mmm, pretty," he purred and dipped his mouth to my ear. His breath was hot as it puffed over my skin. "I like the sight of your blood on my blade. And you like it, too. Don't you, baby?"

"N-no," I whispered. The electric fizz of fear had my knees locked and my body primed for a fight. He wouldn't kill me. I knew it. But my body didn't have the same confidence.

"Yes, you do," he purred in my ear, a grin audible

in his voice. "Your hands are pulling me towards you, not pushing me away."

He was right. My hands were fisted in the sides of his leather jacket and pulling his body towards mine. What was wrong with me?

"Do you want to play?" he asked in a quiet, dark voice.

I paused.

This was Devon. I trusted him and I cared for him. If this was what he needed, I could at least try it once.

"Here?" I asked, my voice barely a squeak.

"Here."

He trailed the knife down to my collarbone and I looked down at it. There was a bead of blood on it already. Had he really cut me?

"Is that-?" I questioned.

"Your blood? Yes," he said before bringing it up to my lips. "Clean it."

I tentatively licked my metallic tasting blood off his knife. His eyes flared and his mouth fell open like I'd licked along his cock. Before I could pull my tongue back into my mouth, he roughly gripped my face and sucked my tongue into his mouth. The flavor of my blood was wiped away and replaced with coffee and smoke.

"Delicious," he murmured as he pulled back, only to lower his mouth to my neck. He licked a long, slow line across my neck. I felt the sting of where he'd cut, but mostly the sensation shot directly to my clit. It wasn't a deep cut based on how I'd barely felt it and the amount of blood.

I whimpered, high and pitiful. My thighs pressed together and felt like I was one touch away from coming in my pants. How he had wound me so tightly so fast was purely Devon. Suddenly, I wanted nothing more than his cock in me with his knife at my heart. The danger of it, the almost forced submission, was something I didn't know that I liked.

"Devon," I crooned as he pulled away from my neck.

"Needy little slut," he growled as he ripped open the fly of my jeans. My body felt empty and as needy as he'd said. I needed... I needed him. I needed to feel him fill me up and cut me to pieces with that silver blade. I needed his anger to consume me and whittle me down to find my guilt and cut it out. Just like how I'd let Sterling's rage and Milo's need consume me.

Just like I said, we shouldn't do.

This wasn't healthy. This was what I had wanted to avoid. But as he shoved down his jeans and I kicked my pants off one leg, I didn't care. We were molten sugar. Sweet, sticky, and burning.

He lifted me in his arms, my ass scraped against the tree behind me, and my legs enveloped his hips. I wrapped my arms around his neck as he pressed into me. I had been so wet that he met with no resistance as he filled me to the hilt. His eyes flashed with a warm softness as we both gasped. But his eyes hardened again, and he leaned some of my weight against the tree so he could trail the knife along my skin again. Everywhere the metal touched felt hot and cold at the same time. I looked down to see he was scratching me, but not drawing blood. The welts looked red and angry in the dim light. We didn't move other than our rapid breathing and his knife on my skin. The air was chilly around us, but my body felt hot wherever he touched. It didn't matter that he was holding a knife to my throat. It didn't matter that he'd made me bleed. I felt safe in his arms and with him inside me.

I tugged at his dark hair at the nape of his neck. His teeth shone in the darkness as he hissed and tipped his head back. A rumbling growl followed the hissed breath, and he slammed the knife into the tree above my head. I felt the shake of the tree and bark fell into my hair. I didn't care as long as he put his hands on my body.

He gripped my neck with one hand, pinning me against the tree, and gripped my ass with the other, holding me up. He pulled almost all the way out of me before he slammed in again. I cried out. My pussy clenched and fluttered desperately around him. More. I needed more. I had only a little movement in this position, but I used every inch to buck into him.

"You want more?" he grunted.

"Yes," I rasped through the tight squeeze he had on my throat.

"Dirty whore wants to be fucked hard in the park," he said breathlessly.

"Please," I practically whined.

He groaned as he obliged. It was barely three thrusts before I exploded. I bit down on my bottom lip to stifle my cry as I came. Devon wasn't far behind me as he fucked me roughly against the tree. He exhaled sharply as he came inside me. His thrusts slowed to a stop.

His eyes settled on mine just as the park lights blinked on. The parking lot lamp hummed as the automatic lights came on at dusk. The spell of the dark atmosphere was broken, but our connection wasn't. Now, in the light, his eyes were sad and soft on my face.

I stroked his jaw. "Devon," I whispered.

His face shuttered, and he pulled out of me and set me down. I felt his release drip out of me as he pulled his pants back up. He turned and strode to his bike and waited, his back to me. I fixed my clothes and met him in the parking lot.

He wordlessly handed me my helmet, and we took off for home.

Chapter 12

Emily

We had a new greenhouse installed in the backyard. Every morning I went out to tend to my
seedlings before the sun had it sweltering hot. Doc
had taken on responsibility for giving me therapy
once a week. He was well meaning and often guided
me to sort things out on my own. Most of the time,
I genuinely enjoyed talking to the old man. Today,
however, he was trying to convince me to talk to my
parents.

"Reconciling with your family would be a great gate-
way to finding a teaching job," Doc said as I irritatedly
poked at a little sprout in the tomato section. "Some
normalcy would suit you. As would adult interaction
outside of this home."

"I talk to Marie all the time," I defended. It was true.
Marie and I spoke often.

Doc sighed. "Someone outside of the business."

"Marie doesn't interact with the business," I snarked
back.

He gave me a scolding, almost fatherly, look. I shook my head and turned away from him to fuss over some basil plants.

"Emily, you've spoken to me about not being sure whether or not you wanted to stay with this business. And, as far as I'm aware, you haven't given Devon any of the signed paperwork," Doc said in his quiet, doctor-y way. "Though your lack of socialization outside suggests you have already decided on staying with the mafia. You'll have to excuse my confusion."

"I don't know if I want to *own* any of the businesses. It's not my skill set. That doesn't mean I don't want to be involved," I reasoned.

Doc was quiet, and I knew he wanted me to review my own words.

"It's not a commitment thing," I said in defense with a glance back at him. I dug my finger a bit too aggressively into a potted plant to check if the soil was wet.

"What would make you say that?" he asked in a kind, curious voice.

"Ugh, Doc," I groaned and wiped my soil coated hand on my garden utility apron.

He chuckled. "You are not the same woman that you were when you were with Gregory. And these men are not even close to being like him."

"I know," I said in a dismissive tone. He took my cue as disconnecting from the conversation. He always seemed to know when he pushed me too far.

And talking about my parents and Gregory and my commitment issues all in a few minutes was too far.

"Until next week, I want you to consider talking to your parents. Maybe a meeting for coffee, nothing big," he said as we exited the little greenhouse.

"I'll think about it," I said, even though I knew I wouldn't. He knew I wouldn't, too.This was something I was nonnegotiable about.

The guys had dug a garden in the dirt yesterday, hauling away all the grass they tore up. Today we would work on tilling up the dirt with the tools we'd rented. Marie and I had lounged in the sun, sipping lemonade, as the guys worked. But today she was at an ultrasound and Brendon had promised a shopping trip for baby clothes after. I looked over the garden in progress while Devon passed by Doc with a nod as he left. Devon joined me to look at the broken-up earth and handed me a mug of coffee.

"What was Doc's sage old man advice today?" he asked.

"He wants me to talk to my parents and then eventually get a teaching job," I said, not looking at Devon.

When I brought the mug up to my mouth, I took a long inhale of the scent. Devon made great coffee, and now the rich aroma was accented by the dirt stained into my hands and packed under my short nails. The smells of coffee and dirt had become a sort of aroma-therapy for me over the time of our garden work. It calmed me almost as much as Devon's cologne,

Sterling's spring soap, and Milo's beard balm. It felt like progress.

"And none of that seems... good?" he asked and leaned against the potting table that stood outside the greenhouse. He sipped from his own mug.

"No," I said shortly.

"Do you want to tell me about it?" he asked as he absently brushed dirt from the table.

"Do you want to tell me about why you use violence and aggression to express your insecurity in your relationships?" I snapped in return. Feeling fiery and very anti-therapy this morning, I was ready to fire back.

His eyes shot to me and he stood up from how he was leaning. "No," he said, looking like I'd thoroughly chastised him. It was one of the rare moments that I realized that behind his dominant and bossy exterior, he was just a boy with a soft underbelly like the rest of humankind.

"Alright then," I said and folded my arms over my chest.

He watched me, considering for a long moment. I turned back and watched birds swoop through the yard. We needed to get some bird feeders.

"You know, we wouldn't think you were any less capable of leading our business with us if you had a relationship with your parents," he said. His voice was just louder than the calls of the active blue jays further in the yard.

I only spared a glance at him.

"I, for one, say fuck them," he continued. Now, I

looked at him fully. "Some people deserve your softness and your goodness, and some people don't. Your parents and Gregory didn't deserve it then and don't deserve it now."

"You mean I should have been meaner?" I scoffed.

"No, I mean, they didn't deserve your kindness when they were actively fucking you over. And I believe they don't deserve your forgiveness now," he said.

"So, I'm a pushover?"

"Listen," he said, his eyes showing the sincerity of his words. "You were soft and trusting of the wrong man. There's nothing wrong with being kind and good and trusting. Gregory broke your trust. But just like my father to my mother, Gregory wasn't always your villain. Your parents are the same. They weren't always bad to you. From my understanding, you were raised lovingly. Their mistreatment of you came after you gave your trust as an adult. You couldn't have known. I believe they all knew you trusted them implicitly and used that against you. That's why I say fuck them. But to be clear, I wouldn't think any less of you if you forgave them."

"Do any villains get redemption arcs?" I asked.

"I think it happens a lot, actually. I'm not sure if it sticks, though," Devon laughed. "Sterling was more into superhero comics than I was. You'll have to ask him."

"There wouldn't be a way to explain the end of things with Gregory without telling them how I... how

I almost killed him. How I hurt him," I said finally. "I'm not ready to tell them what I did."

"Okay," Devon said casually, and finished his coffee. "I'll go get Sterling and Milo up and ready to do yardwork."

"Tell them to wear their little workout shorts," I said, remembering the shorts they wore when practicing their fighting.

"I will not," Devon drawled as he walked away, not looking back at me.

I wasn't sure if Devon had told them, or they knew what I wanted without instruction, but they were wearing their loose fitting and short workout shorts when they came out to work. Even Devon's shorts were suspiciously short. I wore a loose, pale-yellow sundress. It was still the beginning of truly warm spring weather, and I was soaking up as much of the sunlight as I could get. Bare legs and shoulders were a must.

After tilling the garden with some fresh bags of dirt, we stopped for a water break. Sterling ran inside and came back with tequila, a jug of margarita mix, and a bucket of ice. I laughed as he jogged back to us, covered in sweat and dirt. All three of the guys had ditched their shirts long ago and were sweaty and dirt smeared.

"If you're thinking of having us do any planting, I'm going to need a drink," Sterling said.

"And margaritas are the drink of choice?" Devon asked with a raised eyebrow.

Sterling shrugged and made us drinks on the deck with the bar cart that Mrs. Golding had wheeled out earlier before she left for the day. The sun was bright but dipped behind clouds heavy with rain the more the afternoon continued.

"I told Mrs. Golding we'd be ordering pizza tonight," Sterling said as he browsed the pizza app on his phone. "Does everyone want their regular order?"

We all agreed as we sipped our margaritas. Devon wasn't drinking a margarita, but only sipping tequila over ice.

"You don't like margaritas?" I asked.

"I don't want all the sugar to give me a hangover after sweating in the sun," he explained and gestured to his glass of water.

"Have you ever heard of a Hurricane shot?" I asked Devon.

"Is it a rum drink?" Milo asked.

"Nope, it's whatever liquor you want," I said, feeling mischievous. I'd seen Hurricane shots ordered at a bar in college and all the frat boys loved it. It was even part of the hazing in one house. And Devon seemed like the perfect candidate. Just because he'd been nice to me that morning, didn't erase the fact that he was an all around asshole on a regular basis.

Devon gestured to his tequila and caught on to my mischievous mood. "What is it?"

I hopped up to sit on the patio table and put both of his tequila and water glasses between my legs. My sundress bunched around my hips. Sterling stopped ordering pizza to watch with interest and Milo leaned back against the patio railing like he was settling in for a show. I only spared them a grinning glance as I pulled the two glasses closer to my core and leaned back as if in invitation, making it look like this was a sexual activity.

"Take your shot of tequila," I said in a husky voice.

"Can I lick salt off your body first?" Devon asked as he stepped up between my legs. His hands ran over my thighs. The new calluses on his hands lightly scratched my skin.

"Shit, I knew I forgot something," Sterling swore.

"No need," Devon said and leaned over to lick sweat from my cleavage. His tongue dipped between my breasts. His mouth was warm and wet on me and I fought a wave of lust.

He stood up and finished his tequila in one gulp. His eyes were fixed on me and I almost chickened out. He was probably going to get mad. Well, I'd gotten this far, and I had to see it through. As he was pulling the empty glass away, I threw the ice water from his glass into his face with one hand and gave a good hard slap across his cheek with the other.

Everyone froze. Even the birds in the yard stopped chirping. A neighbor, somewhere in the distance, felt the earth shake as Hell cracked open and stopped leaf blowing. The slap had echoed off the house and birds in the woods flew out of the trees. My heart basically halted in my chest.

"She just bitch slapped him!" Sterling hissed to Milo.

"We're going to have to dig a bigger hole," Milo groaned.

I watched as a red handprint bloomed on Devon's frozen face. He was as still as a statue as water and semi melted ice cubes slid and dripped from his head. There was a steady drip off the tip of his nose that landed on my bare thigh. His face was expressionless.

Did he not think it was funny? It was only a little water... and an open-handed slap to the face. My palm stung a little now that I thought about it. Nothing on his face suggested anger. It was the way the air around us seemed to vibrate and buzz like a neon sign that cued me in.

As always, Devon's anger made me giggle. It's as if my body enjoyed signing my death warrant. A little giggle burst from my lips, and I lifted a hand to stifle it. His jaw clenched so hard I swore his molars would crumble to dust at any second.

"Oh. My. God," Milo whispered.

"Run," Devon finally ground out through clenched teeth.

"What?" I asked. Was he threatening me?

"*Run*," he repeated and his shoulders pulled back and he cracked his neck.

"What if I don't want to run?" I asked and gave him a saucy wink and spread my legs further.

"Run," he grunted a third time and cracked his knuckles.

"You can just spank me here," I said innocently and turned slightly to expose my ass to him.

"Five."

"Five slaps?"

"Four."

"Emily, he's giving you a head start to get running," Sterling said through a baffled sounding laugh.

"Three."

I squeaked in excited anticipation and slid off the table. I wasn't wearing any shoes since my gardening shoes were muddy and had been left at the bottom of the stairs. There wasn't time to grab them.

"Two."

Halfway through the yard, I could hear Sterling and Milo cheering me on as I ran towards the woods at the back of the house. I didn't dare look back to see if Devon was chasing me. A wild, breathless laugh burst from me as I sprinted.

I had been working out on the house's equipment and had built up a pretty good endurance. It felt good to run somewhere that wasn't a treadmill and my body sang with endorphins. Running from Devon through the woods was more exciting than it probably should have been. I was slick between my thighs with more than just sweat as I jumped over logs and bushes. My feet crashed through the leaves, and I vaguely hoped Milo had disengaged those bombs that surrounded the property.

I crouched behind a log to catch my breath and listened for Devon. I looked up when I heard a mechanical whirring sound. It was a security camera, turning to focus on me. I breathlessly snorted a laugh.

"If that's Devon, it's cheating!" I hissed.

The camera slowly shook like it was saying no, and I giggled again. Milo and Sterling were watching the chase on the security cameras.

"Is he close?" I asked.

The camera shook again.

"Did you turn off those bombs?"

The camera nodded.

"I want double pepperoni on my pizza," I said as I stood back up and looked around. "Wait, I meant literally, not like a dirty joke."

In the distance, to my left, I heard a crashing movement. It was too close. I took off further into the woods. My feet stung and throbbed where I'd stepped on rocks and broken branches. I wished for my shoes and was about to call the chase off when I heard Devon getting closer.

We spent the better part of an hour running through the woods. I was too competitive and loved the excitement to stop or let him find me. I knew when I came into view of a camera because I could hear it whirring as it followed me. Milo and Sterling were probably watching over pizza like it was a sporting event.

During a break in my running, I sat with my back against a tree and breathed. I was getting thirsty, and a double pepperoni pizza was sounding absolutely amazing. Both the literal pizza and the one involving two of my men. I was still, but I heard a camera move.

Was Milo trying to get a better view of me? Or was Devon close? I tried to listen, but I didn't hear any movement.

Suddenly, Devon dropped from the tree and landed on his feet in front of me. I shrieked and tried to scramble away. His hands grabbed me by my hair and yanked me towards him. I cried out at the sharp tug on my sweaty, messy braid.

He let out a wordless growl as he pinned me down on my stomach with his knees. I felt the mud and leaves of the ground pressing against my face. The smell of loamy earth filled my nose as I struggled to breathe. He pulled me back again, and the ground scraped the side of my face. I whimpered in pain. My sundress was forcefully ripped from my body, and he practically snarled at the sight of my sweaty skin.

Despite the pain of being pressed into the rough dirt, I lifted my hips to present to him. Another low groaning growl as he ripped my thin cotton panties from my body. They were soaked through and probably more uncomfortable than going commando. I heard a rustle of movement as he shoved down his shorts a split second before he slammed into me. A shriek slipped past my lips at the shock of the forceful intrusion. His hands came down hard on the ground on either side of my head. His fingertips curled into the dirt to offer leverage as he fucked me. It was brutally hard and had my body sliding up the leaf strewn ground. My shoulders met his wrists and held me in place as he thrust one bone shakingly hard thrust after the other. My teeth clacked in my head, and I ground my eyes shut against the dirt.

He was animalistic, out of control. Our sweaty and dirty bodies slid and rocked and gritted against each other. Pine needles pressed into my knees and my stomach, but I didn't care. Devon grunted and groaned above me. More vocal than I'd ever heard him, and my pussy dripped with desire as he slammed into me. Every smack of our bodies had me crying out and tears leaking from my closed eyes. I felt his forearm near my mouth, and I opened up to chomp down on him. Just as animalistic as he fucked me. I screamed through my bite as I came. Wave after wave of pleasure had me bucking against him and shaking. He screamed in pain and anger at the bite and lifted his unbitten hand to pull my mouth off of him. He pinned my skull under his palm and used it as his anchor for his brutal fucking.

Metallic blood coated my mouth as I heaved in a breath against the dirt. Leaves and soil came in with the air and I tried to spit it out. Using my skull as leverage had him hitting a different spot inside me. It had me seeing stars and my pussy flooding with arousal. I could barely stand it. It was so good. My breathing was a high pitched, whining whimper as he pounded into me. He was growling and breathless above me and I knew he was close.

I arched into him as much as I could from where I was pinned and tried to grind against him. His wild and uncontrolled thrusts had me coming again.

I screamed and my body shook hard under him, my pussy milking his cock for all it was worth. It felt like I'd been struck by lightning with how forcefully the climax claimed me. The pleasure bordered on pain and I felt tears flow from my eyes.

He was not far behind me. His thrusts slowed to hard, deep ones as he came with a low and long groan. I felt his body shuddering and shivering above me. Goosebumps arose on his arms, and I reached out to stroke them. He pulled away and out of me with a wet sound. I felt cold and empty as soon as he was off me.

Devon stood up, pulled up his pants, and left me.

It was a minute or two of catching my breath before I could move. I sat up with a cringe. I was naked except for my bra in the forest. My bra was ruined with dirt and leaves and pine needles. My soft stomach was covered with angry red scratches from the rough ground. I was shaking and feeling cold despite the warmth of the day.

I sniffled and realized I was crying. When did I start crying? Angry at myself for allowing Devon to fuck me in the woods and then leave me crying, I looked around for my dress. I found it and balled it in my fist. It was ripped and ruined beyond the ability to wear. I rubbed my face free of the tears that stung the light scratches on my cheeks. Standing up, I looked around for the way back home.

The sun was setting, and I could see it through the trees in the distance. The sun set on the back of the house, so I knew which way to walk to get back home. My trip back to the house seemed much slower. I sniffled back my tears and whimpered pitifully every time I stepped on a sharp branch or stone. The endorphins and adrenaline had left my body. It had left me in what Sterling had once told me was called sub drop. But knowing what it was called didn't make it suck any less. I felt depressed, used, disgusting, and everything on my body hurt.

The back patio door was open when I shuffled up to it. Pizza was laid out on the island, and my stomach growled as I stepped through the glass door. Milo and Sterling were quick to jump up as I came in.

"No," Devon scolded from his seat. "Don't touch her. She's being punished."

"She's hurt!" Milo snapped back at him.

Devon looked me over. I looked down at myself and saw the scratches I knew were there. Everyone's eyes landed on my thighs. Devon's come and a thin streak of blood covered them. He'd made me bleed? It hadn't felt *that* rough in the moment. A fresh wave of sadness had me gritting my teeth to fight crying.

"She's fine," Devon said coolly and returned to his dinner. "I've seen to her aftercare already. Emily, you have a bath drawn and I'll be up to give you first aid on your scrapes. I've already purchased a replacement sundress and panties. They'll arrive tomorrow."

I didn't move or speak. Was he serious?

He stood up and came to me, tilting my chin up

to meet his gaze. "Emily, you did beautifully today. Absolutely perfect."

"Wh- what?" I spoke for the first time in what felt like hours.

"Primal play," he explained and softly stroked over my cheek, pulling a leaf from my hair. "It's a way to lose control in a very specific setting. I know you don't feel great right now and likely don't care, but I haven't felt this relaxed in... years."

His gentle touch and silky tone had me leaning into his hand like a cat being pet despite the anger I wanted to hold toward him. I was desperate for his softness, for his reassurance. His eyes were warmer than I'd seen in months. Like tea with honey, surrounded by his long and dark lashes. It made the sadness and aching loneliness in me loosen its hold. Understanding filtered in and warmed me slightly. It didn't make up for the scratches and the humiliation, but it helped me understand the why and the what of Devon's actions.

"Thank you," he whispered and dipped to kiss me lightly on my dry and dirt-caked lips. "Now, would you like help to get cleaned up? I'll have pizza brought up to your room. We got you triple pepperoni."

Chapter 13

Devon

I slept. I slept amazingly. It was truly the best sleep I'd had since... God, I couldn't even remember. I used to take sleeping pills and had tried every herbal and homeopathic medicine that I could get my hands on. Apparently, all I needed to do was go full caveman and chase a pretty woman through the woods and fuck her into the dirt. The next morning, I had a spring in my fucking step. I had thought to myself, without irony or fucking sarcasm, how charming the birds in the backyard were as I sipped my coffee and looked out over the newly dug garden. I felt proud of our hard work and excited for a few fucked up looking home-grown vegetables.

I had known that woman had to have a magical fucking pussy if it had both Sterling and Milo falling over themselves. It was humorous to have thought I would be immune. I stood and looked at the disarmingly aggressive blue jays in the backyard, defending their space from some robins. Did we always have so many birds? I smiled at their brutality.

What in the actual fuck *was wrong with me?*

Instantly, I sobered my stupid fucking smile. Disgusted with myself, I turned to go back inside, but saw Emily and the guys through the sliding door. They were moving around each other with familiar ease as they made coffee and breakfast. Emily was in one of their t-shirts, Sterling in sweats and an unzipped hoodie, and Milo in only a pair of boxer briefs. They were chatting rapidly and laughing with each other. They weren't missing a piece of their puzzle. They weren't missing me.

All their soft touches, smiles, and easy conversation made that stupid happy feeling in my chest wane. Every moment I watched, the feeling trickled out of me like a poorly installed bath drain. But that's what I got for thinking I could have what they have. That's what I got for thinking I belonged within their relationship. I belonged on the outside.

Sterling smiled at Emily and Milo as they joked about something. A pang of painful jealousy and confusion rang through me like a tuning fork. He grew up under the same roof, with the same parental figures, with the same rules as me. In fact, he grew up admittedly with less affection and love than I did. My parents stopped hugging him, kissing him, and started treating him more like a house guest than a family member as soon as Sterling gave my mom a handmade Mother's Day card when we were eight. Looking back,

I regret not sticking up for him, but he had always played it off as being okay with the change. Wouldn't that fuck a person up? Wouldn't that make him more damaged than me?

Perhaps wishing emotional trauma on my adoptive brother wasn't my best form. But I couldn't help but wonder how he could move past his maltreatment and find love. Not only with one person, but with two.

Sterling looked up and saw me outside. A crease formed in his brow, and he said something to the others before getting up and coming outside with me. When he opened the sliding door, the smell of toast with jam and coffee wafted out with a sweet giggle from Emily as she played with Milo.

"Hey," I greeted him. My voice was harsher than I'd meant, but he didn't flinch.

"Hey," he echoed. "How are you this morning?"

"Just peachy," I drawled and pretended to sip from my empty mug so I had something to do with my hands.

"Thinking about running naked through the woods again?" he asked me. His tone suggested he was joking, but his brow was still creased.

"The full moon isn't for another week. I'll wait," I said sarcastically.

He smirked at that, but that crease remained.

"What's up?" I asked him. "Is everything okay with training Randy's guys?"

"Yeah. Yeah, that's all fine," he said dismissively.

"Then what's got your panties in a twist?" I asked him.

"She's all bruised up," Sterling said in a rush.

My eyebrows shot up, but I said nothing. I wasn't sure what he was insinuating. I had helped tend to her bruises and cuts last night after she bathed. There was nothing serious or lasting on her body. She'd be without a mark in just a couple of days.

"She's bruised and cut and was sore getting out of bed this morning," Sterling said, his voice laced with anger.

"Okay, but you saw what happened," I said and set down my empty mug on the patio railing.

"Yeah, and I think you need to chill out," Sterling said and crossed his arms over his chest.

"She's a big girl, she can handle it," I said and rolled my eyes.

"Sure, but you know she's just as messed up as you are right now. She's not exactly making the healthiest decisions," Sterling explained.

"And *I'm* not healthy for her?" I snapped. If I had a heart, it would have hurt.

"Not with the way you've been treating her. Dude, you fucked her while she was hanging off a twenty-story building! Then you fucked her with a knife to her throat! Don't think we didn't see the cuts. And yesterday you chased her for an hour in the woods before you fucked her and left her bleeding and naked in the throes of a nasty sub drop!"

"Don't act like she didn't like it and didn't want it every single time!" I shouted at him.

Sterling growled angrily. "I know, Dev! But she's still working through her shit, and what you're doing isn't exactly helping."

"If she felt I was hurting her, she would tell me," I insisted with a snarl.

"She wouldn't," Sterling said softer now. "That's what I'm trying to tell you."

"No, you're just jealous that she wants to be with me, too. You feel threatened," I said tauntingly with a smirk. It wasn't what I thought was happening, but Sterling had hurt me, so I needed to reciprocate.

Sterling's right hook came out of nowhere. Well, if I was being honest, I had expected it. He'd just done it quicker than I'd anticipated. I fell against the railing. My head rang like a fucking bell. Pushing myself back up, I spun to retaliate. There was a flash of regret on his face as he registered that he'd just socked me before the anger reclaimed his eyes. That flash of regret made me even more angry, and I swung on him. Hard. I'd been working out a lot with Randy's guys and had a lot of rage stored up. I wasn't the same asshole who'd been laid out flat in the underground fights for Giovanni and Taz.

Sterling was ready for the blow, but I punched through his block. He wasn't ready for the power I had behind my fist. His nose cracked and blood sprayed. I vaguely heard screaming, but it sounded like it was miles away and underwater. The rage that had lived like a demonic possession in my body had taken over. The vessel formerly known as Devon Bilal had left the building.

Before Sterling could recover from the hit and swing on me, I knocked him on his ass. He reared back to kick at me, getting me right in the soft part of my stomach. Air left me with a heave that had a taste of my morning coffee returning to my mouth. I spat and was mid launch back at Sterling when I was clothes-lined onto my back. The half breath of air that I had reclaimed was pushed back out of me and I coughed. A weight settled on my hips and hands shoved my shoulders down to the patio.

Black spots from the oxygen deprivation and bright rays of morning sunlight had me blinded. I reached up to shove off my attacker and my hands met bare skin. Panicking, thinking it was Emily, my hands fell to hairy thighs. I blinked to focus and saw Milo pinning me down, looking frantic. Another blink and shake of my head and sound returned to my awareness.

"Stop it! Just stop!" Emily was shouting somewhere to my left.

Milo was breathing heavily and panicked over me. His bright blue eyes searched mine like he was looking to see if I was conscious. I bucked against him, but he was heavier than I'd thought, so he only bounced.

"What the fuck is going on?" Milo shouted.

"He's been hurting Emily, and he doesn't care!" Sterling roared from somewhere over Milo's shoulder.

Milo's eyes went from confused to angry. I wouldn't

have been shocked if he used his position to pound my face in. "You don't care?"

"I care," I said through gritted teeth.

"Okay, that's enough," Emily said in a sharp, authoritative tone. Teacher Voice with an edge of anger.

Milo, clad only in his tight boxer briefs, got off me and my hands fell away from his thighs. He watched me warily, like he didn't trust me not to pounce back at Sterling to restart the brawl. I stood slowly, my head still aching and spinning from the initial punch, and saw Emily with her hand on Sterling's chest and examining his bleeding nose. Blood dripped freely down his tattooed chest between his unzipped hoodie and stained the waistband of his gray sweatpants. I felt the trickle of blood on my left cheekbone. I swiped at it agitatedly.

"That's enough," Emily repeated and looked at me. Her big, blue Bambi eyes looked hurt. Like I'd been the one to start the fight and hurt her *beloved* Sterling. I couldn't look at her. I turned away.

With impeccable timing, from the pocket of my jeans, my phone rang.

Chapter 14

Emily

Devon had gotten a call from the new family in town that was messing up our gangs' deals. He hadn't told us anything other than they had called and we were going. He had snarled and wiped the blood from his cheek and disappeared into the house.

Sterling and Devon spent the day in their rooms, not speaking to anyone. Milo advised me to leave them alone and let them cool off, so I spent the day with Milo. We took one of their spare cars into town for a quiet and romantic lunch and to browse through a bookstore and a used electronics store. In doing so, I saw Milo finally relax after the fight this morning. He had assured me that fights were pretty typical for them, but something told me this was different. This was bigger than fighting over the movie choice, who got to practice with the better gun, and who ate the last slice of pizza. They had been fighting over me. Or, rather, Devon's treatment of me. Our time in the woods yesterday had concerned Sterling enough to confront Devon.

Sterling, who had tied me up, poured hot wax on me, and more, was concerned about what I had done with Devon. But he couldn't see how much Devon needed that release. Devon hadn't hurt me more than I could handle or consented to. Right? Sterling's concern brought me pause. When I had told him and Milo about my experiences with Devon, they'd exchanged worried glances and asked if I was okay with it. I'd said yes, because it had been exciting and sexy and I had felt... relief. Relief from feeling like a terrible person for everything I'd done in the last six months. After Devon helped me treat my scrapes last night, I'd felt that relief potently. His words and his touches were gentle, praising. Very unlike what Sterling had seen earlier.

Spending the afternoon with Milo had a similar effect, but came about through his surprising sweetness. He was doting and kind and showered me with little touches and soft kisses. He was still grumpy and snarky, but he held my hand while he griped. I saw this as an improvement and rewarded him richly. After he had gasped and immediately purchased what he exclaimed "a once in a lifetime find, a good condition Commodore 64" at the used electronics store, we went home. Where I enthusiastically sucked him off under his desk while he attempted to rewire and hook up his new computer.

We should have met for a game plan before the

meeting. But the chances of more friendly fire blood-shed were high, so we went in blind. Devon grumbled as we got in the car about the general idea of our plan for the meeting. "We go in, tell them we're still here, and ask them to leave or stand down. If they refuse, we threaten them. Randy's guys will be in the street in case it gets ugly. But it won't unless they are very dumb."

The meeting was in the parking lot of a factory that looked abandoned, or at least not operational at night. I could hear the highway in the distance and the thump of music somewhere. Seagulls were gathered in sleepy clusters around the cracked cement. Litter scattered about the area on the gentle breeze as we pulled up.

There were two huge SUVs parked in the lot with their lights on and a bunch of guys stood around them. They had guns strapped to their backs and sides and looked formidable, to say the least.

"Visual on eight men, all armed," Sterling muttered as Devon parked us facing the gathered people. "Milo and Emily, keep eyes on the cars. Devon and I will watch the guys out here. Dev, you're left and I'll be right."

"I thought you said it wouldn't get ugly?" I asked, ignoring the tremble in my voice.

"There are a lot of guys here. It would still be a bad move if they attacked us because there would be a huge retaliation, but it's not out of the realm of possibility. They seem cocky," Devon said as we unbuckled.

I gulped.

"You can wait in the car," Sterling offered softly.

"No, I'm coming. You wanted me to be a part of this business and I can't do that from the car," I said as we opened our doors. "The safe, warm, and cozy car that doesn't have strange guys with big guns."

My guys chuckled quietly as we straightened our clothes. The air had a slight chill in the breeze, but was mostly a perfect spring night. I thought about my toasty greenhouse back home. I needed to be as cool as the cucumbers I was hoping to grow. We walked out to meet the gathered men. I tried not to lock my knees in fear. Looking like a trembling and leg locked little girl would not do us any favors.

I stood between Milo and Sterling, with Devon on the left end of our line. "Evening, gentlemen. We're here to meet your boss, I presume," Devon said in a very businesslike tone. Not unfriendly, but also not inviting.

The doors of one of the SUVs opened and a man and woman stepped out. They were dressed entirely in black, and the woman was wearing a lacy corset and a thick leather collar. Her nipples were clearly visible through the lace, and the dirty cement crunched under her shiny black leather stilettos. I wondered vaguely if I was overdressed in a black sweater and jeans with my boots. My hair was in a low bun and I looked more like an employee of a gun range than a mob boss. She looked exactly like a hot mob boss, and I felt a teensy bit jealous.

"Bosses," she said in a husky, lustful voice.

"Good evening," Devon said politely. Nobody moved to shake hands or exchange any more pleasantries. "You called for a meeting and we're here. But we'll not be discussing any business dealings. I understand you learned of the deaths of Anthony Bilal and Matthew Holden and thought you could take their place. The only problem is that *we're* still here."

"For now," the woman said slyly. Her long blonde hair was framed around her in luscious waves. The breeze blew the hair over her slim shoulders.

"What Eden means is that we're here to ask you to step down," the man spoke in an equally smoky voice. His dark hair was slicked back, and he had his hands in his pockets in a casual and nonchalant stance.

"She's Eden, and who are you?" Milo asked.

"I'm Lucifer," the man replied with a dark smirk.

I fought the urge to laugh. Eden and Lucifer? Were they serious?

"Devon, Milo, Emily, and Sterling," Devon said and pointed to each of us. "We control Cleveland and are not stepping down."

Eden let out a girlish giggle as she looked us over.

"I think you'll find that your gangs are already coming to us," Lucifer said and brushed at his clothes as if they were dusty.

I made no move to react to this news. The last we'd heard, everyone was still with us.

"They are not," Sterling said with a roll of his eyes. "They are as loyal as they come. Which is why they came to us when their shipments were being fucked with."

Lucifer gave a slow smile. "Your... family is a minor hurdle for us. You can either step aside or be wiped from the game board. It's your choice. Either way, you will fall."

"We are prepared to retaliate for the offenses to our business," Devon said harshly. "And I assure you, we are established in this town and our forces are strong."

Lucifer's smile didn't budge. "I was hoping for some bloodshed."

Eden turned to Lucifer and licked up the side of his neck, arching into his body. Gross.

"Are we done here?" Sterling spat.

"We are finished," Lucifer drawled.

Milo touched my hand gently, and we turned to go back to the car, leaving Sterling standing with his arms crossed, still facing the couple. Milo and I got in the back seat of the car and Devon stood facing the couple outside the driver's side door while Sterling turned and walked to us. I realized this was a choreographed maneuver, so all our backs were never to our enemies at the same time. It was something I'd never thought of, but my men had down to a choreographed dance.

We were silent as we drove out of the lot and back home. Milo had a laptop balanced on his knees and his mobile Wi-Fi on the seat between us. He typed furiously and the light of his computer illuminated his furrowed brow and bitten bottom lip.

"Got anything?" Sterling asked him, looking back from the front seat.

"Almost," Milo muttered after a pause. He sucked in a breath suddenly. "Got it. 'Lucifer' AKA Jared Rumple and 'Eden' AKA Cheryl Rumple are legally married and are listed as co-offenders in multiple prostitution, drug distribution, and possession crimes throughout the Columbus area."

"Jared and Cheryl? Rumple? No wonder they went with stupid ass fake names," Sterling snorted.

"According to their records in the police system, it seems like they believe she runs the prostitution rings, and he runs weapons and drugs. They've been in and out of the system for a while, even as juveniles. They both have records going back a long time," Milo said as he typed.

"Sad," I sighed.

"Sad?" Devon asked, his eyes on me in the rearview mirror.

"If they were getting in trouble as kids, they likely came from bad homes," I said with a shrug.

"A lot of people come from shitty homes, but they don't go into a life of crime," Devon muttered.

"You're just upset because he out Devon-ed you," I snarked.

"Oh shit, he *was* like Devon times ten," Sterling laughed.

"What's it like meeting your long-lost twin brother?" Milo joked dryly, not taking his eyes off his screen.

"Ha ha, very funny," Devon said darkly as we pulled into the driveway.

"Damn, who would have thought *Cleveland* would be such a hot spot for organized crime?" I asked.

"Um... many people," Milo said, like I was dense.

"It's because of our beautiful landscape, isn't it?" I joked.

"Well, actually," Milo began as he closed his laptop. Sterling and Devon groaned from the front seat.

Chapter 15

Devon

It was late when we got home but I was too wired from the meeting. It seemed like the others were, too. Everyone congregated in the kitchen for drinks, and Milo perused the pantry for a snack. I was too on edge to eat despite the empty pit feeling in my stomach. I poured us all drinks while Milo opened a package of cookies.

My hand shook as I lifted the glass to my lips. Nobody was talking other than little quips about the drinks and snacks, like they were waiting for me to begin talking as their leader. Despite the whiskey, my throat was dry and scratchy. I wondered if I could get a couple of Randy's guys together to spar. The need to hit something was intense.

"So," Emily started with both her palms flat on the counter.

"So," I echoed in a drawl, my voice reverberating in my glass. I slowly set the glass down, hoping nobody else noticed my tremor.

What would my dad do in this situation? I had thought about it the entire way home. He likely would have gone full nuclear and had every gang member of his in the area ready to jump at his word. He would have had Lucifer and Eden blown from the map at that meeting and been done with it. Anthony Bilal would have been home before midnight for a nightcap and a cigar. Not a care in the fucking world.

I cleared my throat and resisted the urge to claw at my skin. "I-" I started and cleared my throat a second time. "I think we need to consider our options." I was stalling.

Sterling and Milo narrowed their eyes at me because they knew what I was doing. They'd been around me long enough to know.

"And those are?" Milo tested.

I glared at him and vividly recalled choking him out.

Emily grabbed the paper and pen from next to the coffeepot. She flipped past the grocery list and wrote "Option One."

"I think option one would be to give over our operations to these new people," she said and wrote in her neat handwriting.

Everyone made faces of disagreement.

"Option two is to run them out of town," Emily continued as she wrote.

"Option three is to take them out," I added. "Aggressively."

"Right," Emily agreed.

"You guys know I'm not super into continuing in the family business, but damn, do I not want to see those ass hats in charge," Sterling said, and then shoved a cookie in his mouth. Crumbs landed on his chest, and he didn't bother brushing them away. How that man managed to get both Emily and Milo in his bed was beyond me. Well, it wasn't entirely a mystery. I'd seen his piercing, his muscles, and seen him in action. He could probably throw me around like a maiden, too. But the man was a pig.

Emily hesitated a moment, visibly uncomfortable. "I must ask... what would Anthony and Matthew have done in this situation? Not that I think we should do it. I'm only asking because I'm new to this and want to know."

I cracked my neck while I gave a long exhale.

"Uh, they would have shown up with heavy artillery and been done with it," Milo snorted. "Those two fucked with our shipments, stalling multiple operations and delaying payment. Once they touched our money, they would have signed their own death warrants."

I nodded.

Emily wrinkled her nose.

"Maybe it's gruesome, but it's effective," Milo droned.

I noisily cracked my knuckles against the cool granite counter.

"Are you good?" Milo snapped at me irritably. He hated the sound of joints cracking.

Sterling snorted a laugh.

"Devon never learned how to deal with his big boy emotions," Emily explained to Milo in a teasing tone.

"He's about to blow, dude," Sterling added.

"But why, though?" Milo asked and pushed his glasses up his nose. His blue eyes raked over me like he was cataloging my behavior. As if he'd never seen me lose it before. The fucker was typically the one to send me over the edge to begin with.

"Because!" I shouted. My voice cracked like I was going through puberty. "Because I'm finally in control of the family business like my father had been training me to do for my entire fucking life and I don't know what to do! He was a fucking sociopathic lunatic, and he was the one who taught me everything! How do I know if I'm making choices for this family based on his dumb ass ideas or actual business sense?!"

"I may not be the best person to say this, but I feel like it's the same as when you came to talk to me after you choked me. I asked you if you *meant* to kill me and you said no. This is the same. Do you *want* to put people in danger?" Milo said in a calm voice, like he was trying to emulate the way Doc speaks.

I shook my head.

"Okay, well, I think if we do our best to not put our people in danger unnecessarily, then we're doing good. *And...* if we remember we are leading *together* and not on our *own*, it would be even better," Milo finished with his typical bratty flair.

The urge to roll my eyes at his attitude won out,

and I tipped my head back to stare at the ceiling. Someone refilled my glass.

"I would offer to run through the woods, but I don't want to start anymore fights," Emily said with a softly sarcastic lilt.

Honestly, that was exactly the kind of release I needed. I sighed and rolled my head to look at her.

"No, we're not letting you do that again without us there," Sterling said. A note of hesitance in his voice was the only thing keeping me from knocking his lights out.

"Oh," Emily crooned. "All three of you chasing me through the woods?"

"No way," Milo piped up. "It's dark out, and I will *not* be running into a skunk or something rabid. Besides, we'd all get fucking lost."

"Just figure out where these two assholes are living or where they're working out of," I said to Milo. "Then we can make a plan and I'll feel better."

Milo opened his laptop on the counter and got to work immediately. Sterling watched over Milo's shoulder and Emily came to my side.

"Do you want me to make you a tea or something?" she asked in a soothing voice.

"No," I said.

"Want to watch a movie with me? Get your mind off everything?" she continued and traced her finger over the back of my hand on the counter. Her touch tickled and my hand twitched away from her.

I couldn't remember the last time I curled up and

watched a movie with a woman. Maybe as a teenager on a date? I snorted a laugh and picked up my glass. "No, thanks."

Her face fell before she moved to sit with Sterling.

Fuck.

I tipped my head side to side to crack my neck again, but there were no pops or cracks. No tension relief. I checked the app on my phone that allowed us to see the surveillance footage of our gangs' headquarter hangout locations. The lights were off at most of them or there were very few people there. This was their prime working time, and most were out doing their jobs. Nobody would be available for some sparring for hours unless I took them off a job.

While looking at the footage, an idea occurred to me. A car was up on a jack stand in our chop shop. Milo could see if these two new players had registered any vehicles. I didn't see the license plates of the cars at the meeting tonight, but surely, they belonged to someone.

"Check to see if they've registered any vehicles," I said.

Milo didn't look up from his work.

"Hey," I called.

Milo often got incredibly focused on his work and required a soft touch to break him out of his concentration. Unfortunately for him, I was all out of soft. I stalked around the island where Emily and Sterling were making out and over to Milo. My fingers itched to throttle him. Instead, I grabbed a fistful of his hair at the back of his skull and pulled.

He hissed in a breath through his teeth and winced. His eyes flashed with pain and anger. "What the fuck?" he groaned.

"Check for car registrations," I grumbled.

"I did!" He snapped and tried to beat my hand away from his hair.

I let go with a jerk.

"Careful there, Devon. My-My likes it rough. You might confuse him," Sterling teased me.

"Maybe he's not confusing him," Emily suggested with a giggle.

"I sure want to tie him up and beat the living daylights out of him, but you can do the fucking," I groused and returned to my glass of whiskey.

There was silence in the kitchen.

"Are you up for a tag team?" Sterling asked, like I'd just offered to get him a puppy.

I pictured Emily and Milo tied up in front of me. Could I play with them without injuring them? The thought of Emily tied up and waiting for me was per-fection. And Milo tied up? He deserved a beating for his attitude alone.

"He's considering it!" Emily gasped.

I glared at her. "I don't know," I said and trailed off.

"You don't have to touch me or Milo sexually. We aren't expecting that," Sterling said earnestly. "But you can do the... punishing and I'll do the pleasure."

"For Milo. I'll give Emily pleasure," I clarified.

She was pink and blushing already. I could see her pupils dilated and her chest heaving. She wanted this. I wanted anything that got her that worked up.

"H-how do you *know* you don't want to touch them?" she asked, her voice breathless and gasping. She wanted me to play with Sterling and Milo.

I snorted a laugh and drained my whiskey. Honestly, if we were going to do this, then I needed to be comfortable with the guys. I'd seen the three of them fuck enough to know there were limbs everywhere. We were bound to touch in some way, and I needed to not recoil in disgust or ruin the moment by moving away. I wasn't about to suck one of their dicks, but I needed to show I was ready to be a team player.

Two good sized glasses of whiskey and a taunt from a pretty girl was apparently all I needed to shove my tongue down Sterling's throat. Sterling practically gasped like a woman in reaction to my lips on his. The kiss had most certainly caught him by surprise. He had probably thought I'd deny Emily. *As if.* I took that opportunity to slip my tongue in. He grabbed me by my collar and returned the kiss. There was no heat, no spark. He tasted like cookies and whiskey. I recognized his talent for kissing, but it did nothing for me. We pulled off with a *pop* and I stepped back.

"Thanks, but no thanks," I said to Sterling. His face split into a huge smile, and he laughed and shook my hand. It was like our fight from earlier had now been forgotten. And I had, indeed, kind of forgotten about it after that meeting. Sterling had taped his bruised nose, and I had bandaged my cheek earlier. The reminder was right on our faces. God, I was a fucking mess.

I turned to Milo and Emily. They were wide eyed and slack jawed, staring at us. A blush was high on both of their cheeks.

"Now you gotta kiss Milo," Sterling said brightly, and poured himself another glass of whiskey.

Milo turned fully on his bar stool to face me and unconsciously licked his lips. His eyes were still wide behind his glasses as he glanced at Sterling. His reaction made me want to laugh, but I kept it contained.

"Oh my god," Emily squeaked. "Oh. My. God."

I took the two steps to Milo, slowly and with a steely gaze. I watched his throat bob as he swallowed. Standing in front of him, I gently slapped his legs further apart and stepped between them. His foot slipped off the footrest and he jerked in his seat. I leaned down, maintaining eye contact with him. His nervousness fed that beast that craved control inside my chest just a sip. Interesting. I slapped one hand on the cool counter behind him and snaked one to grip the back of his hair in a milder version of what I'd done earlier. He looked almost terrified, and the beast in my chest awoke with a lift of its fiery head. When I kissed him, I was pleasantly surprised at how soft and pliant his mouth felt. I wouldn't say he felt or tasted feminine. The rasp of his beard and the whiskey on his tongue were fully male, but his submission was what I needed. My tongue dominated his mouth. I felt his breath, ragged and hot, against my face and opened my eyes to see his closed and fluttering. Milo's hands moved like he wasn't sure if or where he should touch me, and it broke me out of the spell. I pulled away and let go of his hair. His lips were swollen and wet. When his eyes opened, they were hazy and dilated, but still shocked. I smirked down at him.

The beast inside my chest remained unsatisfied. It was excited at the prospect of someone else to play with. I found this interesting because I did not feel sexually attracted to Milo. But the idea of having complete control over him attracted me. His pain *and* his pleasure. I didn't know if I would ever be the one to touch him sexually in a scene, but I could control and direct Sterling or Emily to provide that.

"You okay?" I murmured to Milo, still nose to nose. I would not play with him if he was upset.

"Definitely," he rasped.

"Would you be willing to play with me?" I asked.

Milo swallowed and glanced at my lips again. I gave another slow smirk. "Hell yeah," he replied.

Chapter 16

Devon

"What's your safe word?" I asked as I stepped back from Milo.

"Um," Emily giggled breathlessly.

"Devon's polka dotted underwear," Milo recited primly.

I turned my gaze to him.

"It's what, now?" I asked, eyebrows raised.

"I figured it would be something they'd never say day to day," Sterling said dismissively.

"Fine," I spat. "Bring her to me."

Sterling and Emily exchanged glances before he grabbed her by the arm and dragged her to me. I sat her on the stool next to Milo's and she looked up at me with her large, expressive eyes. She was excited, turned on, and a little wary. As she should be. Sterling stood next to me, arms crossed over his chest and bouncing slightly on his toes.

"They like to be tied up?" I asked Sterling, my voice low and calm.

"Yes."

"They like to be spanked?"

"Absolutely."

"Any hard limits?" I asked.

"I haven't touched Emily's ass," Sterling replied.

Emily gulped audibly as I looked at her. She shook her head once.

"We haven't come across any hard limits," Sterling added, sounding impressed with them.

"Knives?" I looked at Milo for this because Emily had already shown her acceptance of my blade.

Milo gave a quick nod, but looked at Sterling. That one glance told me he was worried I'd get out of hand. That I'd lose control with the blade. The beast in my chest crowed with twisted pride.

"You will only speak when I ask you to speak," I said in the same low tone. "You will not touch me or Sterling unless I command it. You may be bound and not able to say your cute little safe phrase. If you need to safe word and you cannot speak, you will hum the alphabet song. I am not new to reading submissive bodies, but I am new to reading *your* bodies."

"I'll know when they're near the edge," Sterling said next to me. "I'll teach you."

My beast snarled at that, but I allowed it for now.

"Do you consent?" I asked them both. "You may speak."

"Yes," both Emily and Milo said in breathless and eager voices.

Their submission and consent had my beast

pounding its chest, ready to go. I took a long breath. Sterling was here in case I lost control and I felt comfort in that. I let go of my hesitation and let the beast that craved this take the reins. That beast had been ripping, tearing, and snarling at the cage I kept him in. But now, he was freed. Sterling could surely subdue him if things got out of hand.

I unbuckled my leather belt and slid it from my pants. Both Emily and Milo focused on the quiet slide of the material. Sterling echoed my movement and took off his belt at the same slow pace. Emily shifted in her seat.

"Bind her hands behind her back," I instructed Sterling. He obeyed instantly, making her stand and turn.

Milo looked up at me and quirked an eyebrow as if to say, "Well, here we go." I smiled cruelly down at him. "Stand."

He stood and turned around to face the island. I kicked the stool out of the way, and it fell to the tile floor with a loud cracking clatter. I placed my hand flat on his back between his shoulder blades and pushed him until his face was pressed against the counter. He put his hands behind his back like he was being arrested and I bound him tight with my belt.

I moved without thought, without feeling, without planning. I was pure instinct as I reached around and fumbled slightly to undo Milo's belt. He hissed in a breath and jerked against the granite as I brushed against the bulge in his pants. It had been unintentional, but his discomfort was my doing, and I liked it. His belt undone, I undid his fly and pulled his pants down to his ankles. I roughly removed his pants and his socks before yanking down his boxer briefs and removing them. I stood up and examined him. Sterling had Emily stripped similarly and bent over the counter next to Milo.

Their pale asses were a blank canvas for my rage. I let them anticipate my next move while I stood and admired their submission to me. It was addicting. Being naked from only the waist down gave an added element of humiliation. They anticipated my move for minutes before I gave a sharp slap across Emily's ass. She squeaked out a little shriek before she bit it off and closed her mouth tightly. A pink handprint bloomed across her pale skin. Sterling moved to stand behind Milo and raised an eyebrow at me, like he was asking if I wanted to spank Milo.

I scoffed. Of course, I wanted to hit Milo. It didn't matter if it was on his ass. The man had gotten on my last fucking nerve multiple times in the past few days. His body was stronger than Emily's. He could handle more of my rage. I laid a searing slap onto his ass, and he groaned in pain. Sterling cupped himself through his pants next to me. I repeated the smacks on both of them until my palm was burning and their skin was rose-colored and warm to the touch.

With a nod to Sterling, I stepped back. I wasn't ready to be done punishing them, so I allowed Sterling to step in to give them a reprieve. "Don't let them finish," I snarled.

While I wiped sweat from my brow, Sterling got to his knees and turned Milo and Emily toward him. Emily's eyes streamed with tears as she straightened up and Milo looked calmer than I'd ever seen him. I cracked my neck and rubbed my raw and stinging palms on my jeans. Sterling alternated between using his hands and mouth on them, trading sensations when they moaned or gasped. Emily's legs trembled as wetness trickled down her soft thighs. Her pleasure was not mine. Her pain was solely mine, and it was delicious. Without the pain from me, she would never know bliss from these men. Milo's hips bucked, and he tipped his head back to the ceiling as Sterling gave a strong suck.

Sterling stood up, leaving them both trembling and whimpering. He had left them on the edge and desperate. I could see it on their faces. His eyes were wild with desire as he looked for the next direction. I looked over the trembling and obedient bodies before me. I wanted to see them tied up and writhing on my bed. Ropes were necessary. I had a beautiful navy cotton rope set that would look perfect on Emily's skin. And an emerald green set that would complement Milo's auburn beard. Their agony and bliss would be beautiful art. My body itched with the urge to get them bound and dripping in my bed.

"My room," I said, my voice hoarse but commanding still.

Sterling shoved Milo along on weak legs, and I lifted the shivering Emily into my arms. She nestled against my chest like I was a comfort to her. I let her have this minor reprieve. In my room, I got out my ropes while Sterling removed our belts from their hands.

"Naked," I growled as I opened the satin bags that contained my ropes. Sterling was a prompt and helpful assistant. Both of my submissives were soon naked and waiting on their knees for me.

I put Emily in a simple bondage belt, with a strap that went through her legs and a knot right over her clit. She watched me through hooded eyes as I worked. The belt I had her in pinned her wrists to her hips, unable to touch. She bit her lip and relaxed into the ropes as I created a harness around her full breasts. Watching her fall softly, sweetly into sub space as I tied her up would have warmed my heart if I had one. She submitted beautifully to the ropes, and the navy blue complemented the soft pink tone of her skin.

When it was Milo's turn to be tied up, I hesitated. I'd never tied a man up before. At least not shibari, certainly. Sterling breathed a laugh from where he was leaning against my dresser, watching our movements like a ballet. "I did the same thing. Here, I'll show you one I've done."

Sterling moved to kneel next to me on the bed and we worked together to tie Milo into a hip harness that was braided over the top of his ass and on the sides of his hips. Our bodies brushed as we worked and it felt comforting and supportive instead of inciting the beast. Sterling mimed for me that it was a harness with handles for taking Milo's ass. This left Milo's arms free, which was unacceptable. I bound him into a similar harness to Emily, though with considerably less emphasis on breasts. Once the ties were done, he shifted around, and his breath hitched. He wasn't relaxed, and if he wasn't relaxed, he was going to freak.

"Hey," I said in a low and soft voice. I ran a hand over his neck softly and made him look into my eyes. His blue eyes were wide and shockingly bright in the dim light of my room. "Deep breath, Milo," I directed. "Sterling is here, and I will not cross your boundaries."

Sterling lightly shoved me out of the way to kiss Milo softly, reverently. I had seen them kiss. Hell, I'd seen them fuck. But I was up close now. I was a few short inches from them and could see how they melted into each other. I felt jealous of their closeness and how they comforted each other. I turned that jealousy over to the beast of rage inside me. Milo's muscles relaxed as he sank back into submissiveness.

I got off the bed and moved to my drawer of blades. I'd recently cleaned the one I chose, and I admired the blood red enameled steel. The knife had been dulled specifically for play and wouldn't cut skin, but my submissives didn't know that. I unsheathed it and tossed it with a spin in my hand. Both Milo and Emily's eyes were zeroed in on the blade as the handle slapped into my palm.

"The two of you," I began as I prowled toward

them. "Have done nothing but provoke me. You've been bratty, you've been contrary, and you've been *disobedient*. It's time you see what happens to people that defy me."

I slid my blade across Emily's stomach and over to Milo's. Their muscles jumped as my cool blade met their skin. I didn't push hard enough to even scratch, but the idea of a knife in my hands should have been enough to get their hearts pumping. Emily gave a breathy moan as she shivered in the ropes, her nipples peaked and wetness was visible between her thighs. Milo's abdominal muscles clenched and unclenched as he breathed through the sensations of my knife, his impressive dick bobbing in front of him.

While I taunted them with the knife, everything seemed to fall away. Nothing else mattered outside this scene and our bodies. As I slid the knife over their throats and down their backs to their pink asses, nothing existed outside of this space. I was aware of my breathing just as acutely as I was aware of and monitoring theirs. I had complete control over their bodies and my raging, screaming need for domination quieted.

Their pale bodies bound by dark rope, their closed or hooded eyes, their relaxed and open mouths,and their every breath was art. Their submissiveness deserved to be in an art gallery to be worshiped and devoured by anyone who dared to look upon them.

Once they had fine, blush red lines over their exposed and unbroken flesh, I stepped back for Sterling.

He dove in, his hands and mouth everywhere on my two submissives like he was a man starved and I'd just set him loose on a feast. Their bodies moved like a dance as he brought them both to the edge with his mouth, alternating one lover to the next. Milo's panting breaths and the flush that crept up his chest and neck had me clued into his impending climax. I pulled Sterling away from Milo just as Milo's abs clenched. Sterling chuckled and wiped his mouth as Milo gave a pained groan at his missed orgasm. Emily sniffled in her ropes. Crying while being tied up wasn't uncommon, and she'd not said her safe word, so I didn't comfort her. Instead, I licked the tears from her cheeks and murmured "Delicious."

I got off the bed and prowled around the room, looking at them. Their bodies were heaving for breath and shaking as they leaned together to hold each other up. As Emily shook, the knotted rope against her clit touched her, causing her to jerk and moan. I watched as she discreetly tried to get herself off.

When her hips began moving more obviously and her eyes screwed shut, I jumped onto the bed and shoved her onto her face. She squealed at the movement, and I ripped off my clothes. Sterling also shed his clothes. He palmed his cock as I thrust into Emily in one hard movement. She cried out at the intrusion, but she was soaking wet. I felt her pussy pulling me in, hungry for more. The rope that went between her legs was pushed to the side, the cotton rubbing my skin. I took only a few seconds to revel in the feeling of her around me.

"Look at this pussy taking my cock," I demanded of Milo, gripping him by the back of his neck. I shoved his face to rest against Emily's ass. I wanted him to see me fucking her. I wanted him to see that she was mine. "Look how perfect her pussy is for me."

Milo's glasses had been lost at some point, but I knew he saw my cock glistening with Emily's arousal well and good. Sterling let Milo's face remain pillowed on Emily's ass as he adjusted Milo for his enjoyment. I wasn't finished with Milo, so I kept his head in place as I fucked Emily. She screamed against the mattress and her pussy fluttered like she was close to coming.

"Hmm," I hummed. "You like him watching you get fucked, don't you?"

Emily gave a moan in answer, and I let my head fall back in pleasure. She was tight and wet and throbbing around my cock. I wanted to paint her with my come. Mark her as mine. I wanted her *covered*.

Something warm and wet met my balls, and I looked down. I had let go of Milo's head and he'd moved to be on his back below Emily. Milo was licking from her clit to opening and when I thrust into her, he licked me, too. I almost kicked him away, but then I recognized the submission and service in his act.

Sterling was fucking into Milo with the same rhythm. I hadn't even noticed him lube up and enter Milo. The visceral need to paint them with come overwhelmed my senses, erasing and replacing all the other plans I had for my submissives.

That beast in my chest had me gripping Emily's rope belt roughly in one hand and Milo's hair below her in the other and fucking her hard. The need to come was hot in my veins like an inferno and sweat dripped down my back.

"I'm going to paint your faces. You're mine," I growled almost incoherently. "Mark you both. Perfection."

I let go of Milo just so I could flip Emily over onto her back. I wanted to paint her face and her chest. Roughly, I shoved Milo's face back down to her pussy, where he continued to lick her and me after flipping over to his stomach. His body twisted to pleasure us and his muscles rippled with effort. Sterling groaned at the different angle, and he fucked Milo hard and deep. Milo whimpered against Emily's clit before dipping down to pull my balls into his mouth. I would have normally been disturbed by his action but in this state, I didn't care. I needed more. *More.*

Emily's back arched as much as she could in the ropes, and she came with a rush of wetness and a scream. Milo didn't let up on his oral stimulation, but his eyes screwed shut as he shouted out his own release. Sterling sounded like he was right behind them in climax, but he pulled out with a groan.

Sterling flipped Milo over to be on his back with his head next to Emily's. Even without the oral from Milo, Emily cried out again as another climax had her shaking and soaking the bed under us. I quickly turned her to rest on her back next to Milo. Her body had been shaking so hard I wanted her safely on her back to breathe. Sterling gave a long groan while pumping his cock in his hand and kneeled between Milo and Emily's torsos. His other hand clapped onto my shoulder as he held himself up as he came. Rope after rope of come covered their faces and chests. When he was finished, he moved out of the way, and I pulled out of Emily with a roar. I took his space between them and wrapped my hand around my cock. It was two strokes until I came. Black spots had taken over my vision and I couldn't see, but I felt someone holding me up. It had to be Sterling, because of the ropes on the other two.

It was the biggest and most intense orgasm I'd ever had. In that climax, the beast I'd given over control to had disappeared. My mind was quiet, and my rage was still. I no longer wanted to brutalize my chosen family. In their submission, they had given me their trust for their safety. They had given me complete control. The feeling of acceptance and understanding filled me as I was gently placed between the warm, wet bodies of Emily and Milo.

Aftershocks of my orgasm still wracked through me when I could open my eyes and see straight again. Emily giggled, high and girlish, next to me. Milo chuckled on the other side, breathless and deep. I looked over at Emily and saw her trying to wipe come from her eyelashes. Milo was no better. Sterling appeared above us, nude, half hard again, and holding three wet cloths. He plopped two down on my chest and gently moved to wipe Emily's eyes. I wasn't exactly emotionally prepared to give Milo aftercare, but I realized my responsibility. I couldn't be a leader if I wasn't even willing to wipe my own come from my friend's eyes. A realization I didn't know I needed but was apparently due.

Once our faces were clean, and our breathing was even, a sense of calm fell over me. It was foreign, but not unwelcome. I swallowed around a lump in my throat, feeling the sweaty skin of my chosen family pressed against mine.

"So, that was fun," Sterling said to break the silence.

Everyone laughed.

Chapter 17

Devon

I sat in front of my mother in her rose garden. It wasn't often she allowed a male presence other than the occasional professional gardener in that space. It had always been her sanctuary. Her domain.

My father only ever invited the men in the family and the business to his cigar patio. The patio was certainly less floral than the rose garden, but hedges separated the spaces and ferns decorated it. A metal awning covered the area, making it the perfect place to have a smoke and listen to the rain. My father and I had spent many evenings silent and listening to the rain on the roof while enjoying a glass of bourbon and a good smoke. Thinking back to that time fondly made my stomach sour and my heart ache.

Being in this house at all made me feel that way. He was everywhere. Memories of him, good and bad, were around every corner. It was to be expected when any family member died, but this... this unsettled me. The awareness of what he'd done to so many people tainted every good memory of my time with my father. It curdled any fuzzy feelings I may have had when remembering the man that made me who I was today.

My mother had invited me there alone one afternoon for coffee after I expressed I had wanted to speak with her. I needed to know what her wishes were for the family business. She was the heiress, and it was her blood that remained. While she had long before given up her remaining shares to me and had retired, I wanted to know what she had thought the business should do after my father's death.

"How are your... lovers?" Mom asked me with a quirk of her lips over her cappuccino mug.

I rolled my eyes. "They're not all my lovers. Only Emily."

Mom opened her mouth to say something snarky, but I cut her off. "Please, that's not what I'm here for."

"Oh, and I thought you were just here to see your dear old mother," she drawled.

"You're not old," I said dismissively. "And I'm here because I'm having difficulty deciding on the direction I want the family business to go."

Her eyes narrowed, and she sipped her coffee meditatively. "Are you thinking about leaving?"

I sighed. "I don't know. The others... they aren't as married to the business as I am. We're running this new gang out of town, but after that, they don't care to stay the same way I do."

"What would they rather be doing?" Mom asked. "Only Emily has a career outside of this family."

"Sterling's been doing well managing our forward facing businesses. Milo could probably work in IT anywhere that doesn't require a background check. And you're right, Emily could go teach anywhere. They want to stay local for Marie, but... I don't know how long that will be a deciding factor," I explained.

"I would prefer the business to be in family hands, but it wouldn't be the end of our world if it wasn't," Mom said softly.

"Why in family hands?" I asked. "To keep earning?"

"No, I could live the rest of my days with what I have," she said and waved dismissively before continuing. "There will always be people buying and using drugs. If it's ours, it's clean because we made sure it was clean. There are always going to be gangs. If they're ours, they're paid and have constructive work. People will always buy and use weapons. If they're ours, we control who gets them."

"You make our family sound noble," I laughed and sipped the velvety cappuccino.

"Not everything we do is good, sure. But not everything we do is bad, either," she reminded me.

"We're a mafia, Mom," I chuckled.

"*Pshhh,* we're a family business. Look at Harold and Veronica. They're practically your grandparents. And the people in the gangs you run? You know everything about them. I've been paying for three different college educations just this year! Marie's salon does everyone's hair, and Harold practically cooks for every event we have. We're a *family*, Devon."

"What Dad did–"

"Was done in secret because it wasn't what our family believed in," Mom cut me off. "There was a reason Matthew had limited knowledge, and I knew nothing. He became evil."

I nodded.

We were quiet, listening to the distant traffic and the birds waiting for us to clear out before visiting a bird bath just outside the gazebo.

"You say he was evil, but he taught me everything I know," I said, almost in a whisper.

She smiled.

"What?" I asked, irritated and embarrassed.

"That Emily of yours had a feeling you'd be worried about that," she said.

I laughed self-deprecatingly. "That might be because I've had a few... meltdowns about it."

"You confide in her," Mom said. "In all of them."

"They're... mine," I said with a shrug.

"I think that as long as you keep confiding in them, you won't lose your way," she said. "They have the potential to balance you. And you need it. You have a big head."

I laughed at her words, but she was right. After our night all together, I'd felt closer to the three of them. Not just physically, as there had been plenty of contact, but it was like they were accepting of me. They met my raging need for control and aggression with submission and pleasure in that scene. My control over them didn't need to extend past the bedroom, because they were there to balance me.

"They were all together first. I'm an extra and on the outside," I said. This was the most I'd opened up to my mom in years about anything not business related. It made me itchy.

"And there you will remain if you don't show them vulnerability and connection," she said. "You need to show them that you can reciprocate emotionally. You can't be their leader in your home, you have to be their equal. But, well, I'm not an expert on relationships. My husband was a sociopath, after all. And I certainly don't know about... three, er, four-somes-"

"I get it, Mom," I groaned. She had it backwards in our situation. I could only be their leader in the house and their equal in the business. Her meaning was understood, nonetheless.

"Now, if I make a bouquet of roses for you to take home," she said and gestured to her pruning shears. "Do I need to make three? Or is just one for Emily sufficient?"

"Just one," I grumbled. "I'm only with *Emily*."

Chapter 18

Emily

The greenhouse was hot that morning as I checked on my plants. I had enlisted Milo to help me plant yesterday, and we'd gotten a lot done. There were tidy rows of little plants waiting for sunlight and water. He hated the dirt and the bugs, but I loved it. It felt productive and positive. It was proof that I could choose to do something good instead of terrible when given the opportunity. Maybe I wouldn't grow anything worth eating, but I was doing my best. There were even a few flowers starting on some plants.

I was alone in the sunny greenhouse until Sterling appeared in the doorway. "Oof, it's hot in here already." He was holding a fresh mug of coffee for me. The guys had taken to meeting me in the greenhouse or garden pretty much every morning with a new mug of coffee. "Should have made an iced coffee."

I took the coffee for him after wiping off my hands. "I'm done in here. We can go outside."

We sat in the new wooden chairs I'd convinced the

guys we'd needed last week. "Are the others awake?" I asked.

"Devon was in the office on the phone with Randy and Milo was in his room doing something on his computer," Sterling replied.

"Always working," I sighed. It was a Friday morning, so I was already thinking about the weekend. It was a habit from working in the school that had never left me.

"No kidding," Sterling exhaled and looked out over the garden, his gray eyes narrowed in thought. "We should take a vacation."

"Us? Now?" I laughed. "We're in the middle of a fight with Lucifer and Eden. Now is probably not the best time for a vacation."

"Maybe just a weekend trip, then," Sterling reasoned. "We could go up to my new cabin."

"Good luck convincing Devon and Milo," I said.

"Eh, we just have to bribe Milo with sex and tell him we'll watch Star Wars. Devon is even easier. Just bat your Bambi eyes at him and ask nicely. Tell him you *need* it, and he will pack your bag for you," Sterling chuckled.

"They will not be that easy," I giggled.

"Wanna bet?" Sterling asked with a mischievous grin.

"Yeah, I bet you oral that it's not that easy," I said.

Sterling held out a hand to shake on our deal. His hand was warm from his coffee mug as we shook hands. I wanted to curl up on his lap and relax, but it was hard to relax, knowing the next confrontation with Lucifer and Eden could be at any moment. Sterling was right, a vacation was exactly what we needed.

Devon was in the office chair, leaning back and slowly spinning while he was on the phone. He looked at me and Sterling as we entered the room and raised a questioning brow.

"Milo has the security feeds live and I'll send you the access codes. Keep it only amongst yourself and your second. Don't tell anyone about the cameras. I don't want anyone outside of us to know about them. I know your guys have a good relationship with the prostitutes in your area, but we believe this new gang deals with skin. The women might join their gang and talk. Remind your guys to keep quiet," Devon said before sitting up in his chair. "Alright, Randy, tell the girls Marie found that glitter hairspray they were talking about. She'll bring it for the birthday party. Yeah, bye."

"Good morning, Devon," I said in a light voice, almost a whisper. I looked up at him through my lashes. "Um, did you sleep well?"

Devon's eyes bounced from me to Sterling, like he was worried something bad had happened. Honestly, I didn't blame him. I was laying it on thick. "I did, actually," he replied. "Did you?"

"Yeah, um, I was just wondering. Well, it's silly, really," I said and tucked my hair behind my ear and shrugged shyly. "I had the worst dream last night about you being taken away from me. And I woke up and went straight out to my garden. Being by nature was so soothing to me."

"That sounds like a scary dream," Devon said, and his jaw twitched.

There was no freaking way that this was going to work, right?

"Oh, it was," I said and looked at him through my lashes again.

"I'm glad the garden is helping you," Devon added.

"Me, too. Well, I was wondering if maybe we could take a trip this weekend to Sterling's cabin. I just feel like being around you and all the ... trees would really help me," I said with a slight pout.

Devon winced. "Emily, we're in the middle of something kind of big here."

"Emily was just telling me how much she *needs* to get out of the city," Sterling added from behind me. "You know, she's from the suburbs and all."

I wanted to roll my eyes.

Devon looked at me for a long time. I bit my lip and fluttered my lashes. The Full Bambi.

"Fine," he said with a long exhale.

Wait, what?

Sterling pinched the back of my arm.

"Really?" I asked.

"Yeah, if you think you need it to feel... better or more secure with us, then absolutely," Devon said and turned his chair to the computer. "I'll arrange it with Harold to oversee anything that pops up this weekend. Should be slow, there's only two smaller shipments happening."

"Thank you, Devon," I said. "I'll pack your bag for you."

"No," he said sharply. "I'll pack my own bag. I've seen your style choices."

"Emily always looks good," Sterling defended jovially. "I've seen pictures of her when she was a teacher and lemme tell you, when I say, 'hot for teacher,' I'm not kidding."

"He's right, I had a great wardrobe," I said with a pout.

"Where did you get your clothes?" Devon asked with a sneer.

"I was a Kohl's Cash aficionado," I said proudly.

"I rest my case, your honor," Devon said and turned back to the computer.

Sterling snorted and pulled me from the office. Once in the hallway, he asked, "Do I get oral for every win? Or just once when Milo caves?"

"We only agreed on once," I said as we went up the stairs to Milo's room.

"I'm immune to Bambi eyes if I know they're coming," Milo drawled as we entered his room.

"Fuck, I forgot about the cameras," Sterling said as he jumped onto Milo's messy bed.

I opened the dark curtains to let the sun in. Milo groaned and tilted his multiple computer monitors away from the sunlight.

"I'm not going to squat around a fire in the woods

like a fucking caveman waiting to get rabies from a racoon," Milo derided.

"No need to squat. There's furniture," Sterling said dismissively. He was clearly used to negating Milo's complaints.

"Hm, no comment about the racoons," Milo countered.

"I didn't think dramatic stupidity warranted a response," Sterling said and scrolled on his phone.

Milo glared at Sterling, who wasn't looking at him.

"Milo, I really think it could be fun," I said and tried a Quarter Bambi. "We could watch Star Wars."

Milo turned his glare on me.

"Listen, Milo, we're all up to date on our tetanus shots. We don't have to be outside at night when the animals are out, and we can wear bug spray. I'll check you for ticks however often you need. We need a break. *You* need a break," Sterling said and sat up.

Milo sighed. "Fine. But I'm bringing a laptop."

"Only for emergencies or I snap it in half," Sterling said seriously. "Remember the Blackberry incident of 2009?"

Milo glowered. "Only for emergencies."

"Great!" Sterling said brightly. "Now, Bambi, you owe me a blow job."

"Hm, our agreement was specifically that Milo would say yes if we bribed him with sex and Star Wars. We had to negotiate more than that. It seems like I also won the bet," I countered.

"Sixty-nine it is. Let's go!" Sterling said and pulled me from the room.

Later that afternoon, after Stephanie agreed to water the garden and the gangs resolved their extra security, we were browsing a camping and outdoor supply store. Sterling pushed the cart while we threw in bug sprays, bedding, cookware, s'mores supplies, hiking boots, backpacks, water bottles, hats, sunscreen, and an emergency battery pack.

"There's no taxidermy, is there?" Devon asked as he stared down a mounted goose near the check-out lines.

"No, you saw the pictures," Sterling said.

"Yes, but I can never tell when you'll commit to a bit and go full mountain man on us," Devon replied.

"I didn't decorate it. I figured either you or Emily could give it a womanly touch," Sterling said. Devon punched him in the side.

We checked out and were walking back to Devon's car when shots rang out. I instinctively ducked, and Milo pulled me close to his side.

"Finally, I'm here for this shit!" Sterling shouted as he unholstered his gun from his hip.

It was afternoon on a weekday, so there weren't many people or cars in the parking lot. Considering this was a shopping trip before we were supposed to go to Sterling's cabin, I hadn't brought any weapons. The guys always had at least one gun and a knife on them. I needed to remember that we were always in danger, and I should carry a weapon. But there was no time for regrets now as Milo tried to run me to the car. Devon and Sterling had been just behind me and Milo as we walked to the car, and I turned back to look. Milo saw me move, and he grabbed my head and pulled me forward. I hadn't been able to see Sterling or Devon.

"Milo!" was all I could screech in a panicked voice.

"Get in the car and stay down!" Milo shouted over the sounds of gunfire and glass shattering. "There's a gun in the glove compartment if you need it."

It didn't sound like there were many people shooting at us. There would be a burst of gunshots and then a short, quiet period like they were reloading a pistol. It had to be two or three people based on the sound. I wasn't an expert, and it could be an echo, but it certainly wasn't over three people.

Milo opened the backseat of Devon's car. Devon had to be close as he unlocked the car with his key fob. Milo shoved me in, and the door shut with a slam. The sound of my ragged breathing filled the car, and I sat up and scrambled for the front seat and the glove compartment. My sweaty skin skidded along the leather interior as my shirt rode up and my stomach rubbed the center console. I located the gun and checked it. It wasn't loaded, but there was ammo in the compartment. I fumbled as I loaded it with shaking hands and looking out the windows.

The gunfire had slowed, like there was only one person shooting now. The return shots were limited, like my guys had little ammo on them. Or were they down and not able to shoot back? I gagged at the thought and my hands shook as I finished loading the gun.

I knew Milo had intended for me to wait in the car and use the gun for self-defense if someone approached. But I was not very good at following directions when the lives of people I loved were in danger. I jumped out of the car and crouched behind the cart return corral. It wasn't a great hiding spot and hid almost nothing, but I had to try. The gravel crunched under my sneakers as I crept along with the gun in my hands. I saw Sterling, crouched behind a pickup truck with a middle-aged man who was also holding a handgun. He had a big, round belly, and was wearing camo shorts and a baseball hat. They were both aiming over the truck bed, cluing me in to where at least one attacker was. I looked further down the line and saw Devon, who looked back and saw me. He tipped his head back as if to say, "You've got to be kidding me" and gestured for me to get back in the car. I was about to point in the direction Sterling was aiming, but Milo fell to the ground near a van that was parked in the handicapped spot up front. A young man had landed a punch to Milo's face, but Milo was back up on his feet quickly. They grappled for barely two minutes before Milo had him unconscious on the pavement.

Milo spit blood on the ground and then picked up his gun from under the van. The remaining attacker must have seen his odds in getting out of there alive and ran. Squealing tires sounded as they left the parking lot. Police sirens rang in the distance and store employees and customers were standing at the window, phones to their ears.

"Get in the car, Emily!" Devon shouted as he made his way back to me.

Sterling shook the man's hand that had helped them. They were talking, and the guy had wide eyes as though Sterling had just said, "Sorry you got caught up in a mafia shoot out. Here's two grand to pretend like we weren't here." And I knew that's exactly what had happened based on the guy's outstretched hand, like he was holding a wad of cash.

At a jog, the guys came back to me and the car. "Is everyone alright?" I asked them.

"All good," Sterling said brightly, like nothing bad had just happened. He located our full cart and started loading the truck.

"Fine," Devon replied. "Milo?"

"I'm okay. He got one punch in. It was a fucking kid. I hesitated to shoot him. This had to be his first job," Milo said and wiped at the blood coming from his nose.

"The other one was a kid, too. Or at least very young. I only got his arm before he left," Sterling said.

"If that's all Lucifer and Eden have, then I'm not worried," Devon said as we buckled into the car. "We have to get out of here before the police show up."

Devon sped away, and the guy in the pickup truck was right behind us. He turned in the opposite direction and sped off. He understood the assignment, that was for sure.

Milo pulled out his emergency-use-only laptop from his bag, sparing only a warning glance at Sterling next to him before getting to work. There were five minutes of silence as we let Milo work, typing away.

"Alright, I cleared the video surveillance from the parking lot AND inside the store. The guy who helped us had paid by credit card and I wiped it from their register app. It won't even process with his card company. And it looks like... yeah, the physical descriptions given to the police in the 911 calls were vague enough that we're in the clear. None of the calls stated our car or plates," Milo said.

"That was quick," I said, impressed.

"I'm offended that you haven't learned that I am a genius yet," Milo drawled and sniffed up the slowing blood flow.

Sterling and Devon exchanged glances in the rear-view mirror.

"You're lucky you give good head," I sighed and sat back in my seat.

Chapter 19

Emily

Milo informed Harold, Randy, and the other gangs about the attack at the store as we drove to Sterling's cabin. The guys were convinced that the two kids that tried to hit us were all that Lucifer and Eden had to deploy. Something about it didn't feel right, and I was antsy the entire three-hour drive to the cabin. When we had met with Lucifer and Eden, they were in expensive cars and had multiple men with them as security. They had to have the means to pay for their own gangs, and surely we didn't control all the gangs in the city. When I brought it up to the guys, they dismissed it and said the couple was probably paying those guys everything they had. The minor attack today seemed halfhearted, or it was meant to make us see them as weak. Either way, maybe getting out of the city was safer than staying.

We pulled into the driveway of the cabin and stared at it through the windshield. It was a well-maintained property and looked as though it used to be a vacation rental for the state park nearby. Sterling pulled out his keys and was first to hop out of the car.

"Home sweet home," he said, gesturing widely.

He seemed genuinely excited to have the new property and to show us, so I pasted on a smile.

"Ugh, I already feel my allergies acting up," Milo grumbled as we exited the car.

"Shut up," Devon hissed at him. "Let Sterling be happy."

"Oh, I let him be happy all the fucking time. I don't need to be in the fucking *wilderness* to do it," Milo snarked back as we opened the trunk to get our bags and the new stuff we had picked up from from the store.

"Give me attitude again, and I'll make you walk naked through the tall grass," Devon growled.

Milo was about to retort when Sterling came around to the trunk. I had remained quiet throughout their exchange, knowing that interfering just gets me in trouble, too. Sterling happily layered bags on his forearms, ignoring the tense air of his fellow campers. "Let's go inside. I can't wait to sit in the hot tub and have a beer."

"Ew, you got beer?" Milo asked and opened the cooler that Sterling had stocked earlier.

"Yeah, I figured 'when in Rome,' you know?" Sterling said as he carried almost all our bags into the cabin.

"See? This is why I questioned him about the

taxidermy," Devon murmured to me and grabbed an armful of bags of food.

I giggled and carried the remaining bags while Milo hefted the cooler out of the trunk. The cabin smelled like pine and had evening sunlight streaming in. It looked warm and inviting, if not a bit dusty. Sterling gave us an excited tour of the building, beginning in the living room and kitchen, then to the two bedrooms, the bathroom, and then outside to the patio with the huge hot tub. It was truly livable, and an even better vacation home. Even Milo shut up his grumbling when he saw how clean and well maintained the interiors were.

Devon and I sorted the kitchen supplies from the rest of the stuff and explored the cabinets and drawers. The place already had plates, cups, silverware, basic spices, and some cleaning supplies stocked. The bathroom had packages of toothbrushes, toilet paper, and other essentials that were probably for the convenience of previous vacation renters who had forgotten something. Near the washer and dryer, there were laundry supplies and a box of emergency snow supplies. Inside a box labeled "For cold emergency convenience," there were four sets of ski masks, gloves, scarves, a fire starting kit, maps of the area, and glove and boot warming packs.

Sterling was walking Milo through an explanation of the well and water filtration system when we finished unpacking. Devon joined their explanation, but I felt like I didn't have space in my head to hear about it. I stood in the kitchen, a bottle of wine on the counter, and staring out at the trees through the window. I didn't know if having a glass of wine would be helpful to relax or make me impaired if there was an emergency. The road outside was gravel and not heavily traveled, so I knew that we'd hear a car if it approached. But if one did, and I was drunk? That would be detrimental. I'd be dead in a minute. Maybe one glass would be good.

Someone touched my shoulder, and I gasped and swung around. Devon held his hands up with wide eyes. "It's only me."

"Sorry, I'm still anxious after earlier," I said and tried to will my heart to stop pounding.

"Bambi, we're in the middle of nowhere. Nobody is going to get us out here," Sterling said as he cracked open a beer from the fridge. "Let's grill some burgers, have a drink, maybe an edible because you're strung so tight right now, and *chill*. We're on vacation, baby."

"I don't know. What if someone shows up in the night and we're all drunk and high and not able to fight back?" I asked. There was a tense line of anxiety in my voice, and I tried to swallow it down.

"She's not entirely wrong," Milo said as he sniffed Sterling's beer with a wrinkled nose.

"Milo," both Sterling and Devon said in matching warning tones.

"I'm just saying." He shrugged.

"Ugh, fine. I didn't want you to obsess over it, but

here-" Sterling said and showed Milo his phone. "I have deer cams set up."

"Deer cams? What the fuck?" Milo asked and peered at the screen.

"Yeah, they ping my phone when something is nearby," Sterling said.

Milo inhaled and exhaled, like he was trying to calm himself down. "What service does it use?"

"I don't know, its own, I guess," Sterling said and sipped his beer.

"What's your privacy settings on the server?"

"It's cloud based," Sterling said dismissively. "I don't manage the server."

Milo closed his eyes and repeated his slow breath. "What's their retention and privacy policy?"

"No clue."

"Give me the phone. You're an absolute idiot," Milo snapped and ripped the phone from Sterling's hand.

Sterling grinned fondly at Milo and drank more of his beer.

Devon rubbed at my shoulder, and I closed my eyes at his gentle touch. I let out a shaking breath, trying to calm myself. This was probably the safest place we could be, but the gunshots from earlier still echoed in my ears. The blood that was dried and stained on the neckline of Milo's shirt had me remembering the blood that had dripped down Gregory's hand as I tried to cut off his finger. Simultaneously, I remembered the fear of not knowing where my men were in the parking lot while I was in the car.

I forcefully shook my head to rid myself of the flashbacks.

"I have an idea," Devon said in a silky tone.

"What's that?" Sterling perked up at Devon's statement.

Devon left us quickly and returned with the winter emergency box. He handed each of the guys a ski mask and pulled one over his head. He winked at me through the opening. "Run, *Bambi*."

Sterling shoved the black knitted material over his head, covering his smile. Milo looked up at us all, Sterling's phone in his hand still. "Hold on, give me two more minutes."

Devon shoved Milo's mask on for him, careful to keep his glasses on. "You have a head start until Milo finishes."

"Really? Right now?" I asked with a nervous chuckle.

"I think a good run through the woods would be a good way to get rid of some of this energy," Devon said, and tapped on my bunched shoulders.

He wasn't wrong, but....

"I don't know," I said and shrugged.

"I'm almost done," Milo taunted with a sly look.

Devon and Sterling crowded around me. I backed up, edging to the back door. They slowly crowded me towards the door. Their eyes crinkled at the edges like they were grinning roguishly under their masks. I was at the door and peeked behind them to where

Milo was slowly moving to set the phone down on the counter, his eyes on me.

As soon as that phone hit the countertop, it was going to be game over. I squeaked and turned to open the door. I had made it down the stairs of the back patio and hit the grass when Milo said, "Go!"

Their boots thundered on the wooden patio and I heard whoops of excitement as I ran, laughing, for the woods.

Chapter 20

Emily

Growing up, I had a friend down the road who had a German Shepherd Dog. The dog's name was General, and he would get bored and dig up my friend's mom's flower beds. This happened for a long time until her parents got one of those puzzle toys that dispensed food. It kept General occupied and not tearing up the yard. Apparently, some dogs need to work or hunt for their food.

These men were kind of like General in that way. It was a realization that made me laugh, even though I was supposed to be hiding and running through the woods surrounding Sterling's cabin.

I jumped over a log, thankful to be wearing shoes this time, and landed in a puddle of water from a recent rainfall. I could hear the guys trampling through the leaves and sticks behind me, and I pushed harder and faster. There was no way I'd outrun them for long, but it felt good to try. Devon was right. The running helped with my anxiety and loosened my muscles.

Endorphins flooded me as a hand grabbed my shoulder and fell away almost as quickly. I heard Sterling bark out a breathless laugh. "No, Milo! Get up!"

Running consumed my focus, leaving me unable to laugh with him. I chanced a glance back and in the dimming light of evening, three masked men were chasing after me. It felt wild and exciting. It felt dangerous. But these men would allow nothing truly bad to happen to me. They were doing this *for* me. I trusted them.

The look back had cost me, and I tripped over a branch. My knees skidded and my jeans tore as I fell. I had just enough time to take in a deep breath before I was flipped over onto my back. Three masked men with heaving chests and bright, excited eyes stood over me, blocking out the last of the sunset.

"Got you, Bambi," Sterling said in a breathless, menacing voice. While the other two followed, Sterling scooped me up and carried me over his shoulder. I went limp and worked on catching my breath. When I wasn't seeing spots from oxygen deprivation, I tickled Sterling's sides.

"That's it. I was going to take you back to a nice bed, but after that, I'm fucking you right here," Sterling growled and went down to a kneel before throwing me on my back on the ground.

"Wait," Devon said, his voice gravelly. "Get her naked."

Sterling and Milo roughly stripped me until I was

naked on the forest floor. Leaves and sticks dug into my back, but I didn't care.

"Milo, lick her pussy. Get her to come," Devon directed.

Milo pushed Sterling out of the way and kneeled before me. I opened my legs with a smile as he lifted his mask just enough to uncover his mouth. He dove and found me already wet and wanting. With a swipe of his tongue, I let out a cry. Birds fluttered out of the branches above us and a few leaves floated down. Milo's tongue was skilled even though he had the least experience out of the three of them. But he knew exactly what he was doing. Too quickly, I was at the precipice of coming, but I looked up at Devon.

"W-wait. Dev- oh- Devon has never, oh God," I panted and tugged on Milo's hair through his ski mask.

"Devon's never eaten your pussy?" Sterling asked, shocked.

"No, I haven't," Devon drawled in a voice like he was going to make me regret telling everyone.

"Well, get to it," Milo said and sat back while wiping his mouth and beard.

Milo moved over so Devon could take his place. Devon was glaring at me, but I smirked at him and opened my legs further. He lifted his mask like Milo had and bent down, his eyes on mine.

I was already so worked up. I knew it wouldn't take much to have me coming on his tongue. But Devon knew that, too. He didn't go straight for my clit.

Instead, he licked a gentle and slow circle around my sex. It made me shiver and whimper in anticipation. Ever so lightly, he sucked and lifted my outer labia- one side and then the other- into his mouth like little kisses, making me throb for more. I moaned his name, and he smiled around me. When he finally flicked his tongue over my clit, just once, I screamed. I didn't come, but the shock of it had my back arching and my legs trembling.

"Hold her down," Devon pulled back to say before going back to lick a flat tongue over my entire pussy.

Milo quickly got behind me and held my back to his chest and locked my legs open by slinging them over his own. He held both of my wrists in one of his and wrapped the other hand around my throat. I writhed against his body as Devon licked me again in another slow, flat line. He peppered me with more little sucking kisses. Whimpers fell from me with every breath, and I felt Milo's warm, big hand around my throat with each inhale.

"I'm going to come," I whined.

"That's it, baby," Milo crooned in my ear. He kissed my neck and the sensation of two mouths on me at once was overwhelming. I didn't think I could ever get used to that. Or wanted to, for that matter.

Devon nibbled at me, and pain bloomed with my pleasure. I gasped and almost choked on the lungful of air. He was all teeth and tongue and rough, wet sucking. My breath stalled in my chest as I shook and shook in Milo's arms.

Milo chuckled behind me, his chest rumbling against my back. "His name is one letter off from 'demon' for a reason."

I would have laughed, but I was too busy screaming. Just as I crested the top of my climax, something warm and wet landed on my face and body. I looked down to see it land on Devon's face and mask, too. Milo laughed again, and I realized, mid orgasm, that it was Sterling coming all over us. He stood over us, mask still on, cock out, and spraying us with his release. It only made my orgasm heighten to see him.

Devon licked and sucked me through it and then sat up. He ripped off his mask, leaving his hair disheveled, and wiped Sterling's come from his face. "Fuck you, Sterling."

Sterling laughed breathlessly and leaned against a tree with wobbly legs.

"Get her home. I need to fuck her," Devon said as he stood.

Sterling lifted me over his shoulder again and Milo gathered up my clothes from the ground. I was naked over Sterling's shoulder with my ass right near his face. He spanked me on each cheek before trailing his fingers down the cleft to my soaking wet pussy. He braced my legs with one arm while he sunk two fingers in with the other hand. I gasped and my back straightened, and I clenched my fists in his shirt.

"Fuck, it's difficult to walk through a forest with a raging hard on," Milo muttered as he watched me.

We weren't far from the cabin. I hadn't wanted to

run onto a neighbor's property while being chased by three masked men, so I'd run in an arch back towards our place. Sterling broke through the last of the brush just as I came on his fingers.

"Bedroom," Devon barked out as we thundered up the wooden stairs. Sterling carried me into the room I'd put my bags down in earlier and flopped me onto the bed. I had already come twice. I didn't know if I could handle having sex with all three of them. With a gulp, I looked at them, wondering who would be first.

They stripped off their clothes and I watched as their skin was slowly revealed to me. It was amazing and wild to think that every inch was *mine*. Every inch of skin, every muscle, every tattoo, every piercing. Wait, Devon had a tattoo? I realized I'd never seen him naked or even shirtless much. I must have not noticed it while he was in the ring fighting Giovanni and Taz's guy. Maybe it was new? Feeling deprived, I sat up and looked him over eagerly as he gently placed his clothes on the dresser. Milo and Sterling had dumped their clothes and masks on the floor and were climbing onto the bed. Devon's upper back had a tattoo of an animal skull with curling horns. A ram? A goat? I wasn't sure, but the narrowing of the skull's jaws accentuated the tapering of his back. He'd built up more muscle recently, I'd noticed. But seeing him fully naked was an unfamiliar experience. Lean muscles, soft chest hair, warm skin, and undiluted power.

"Milo," Devon said in a cool, demanding tone.

"Yeah?" Milo replied.

"Fuck her."

"Wait, he ate her out and now he gets to fuck her?" Sterling complained.

"I'm sorry, is this not your jizz in my eyelashes?" Devon spat and gestured irritably to his eye.

I giggled and trailed my fingers over my sticky skin where Sterling's release had mostly dried and gotten rubbed in.

Milo wasn't listening to their squabble and was lining up between my legs. I met his blue eyes, and he smiled before sinking into me. His smiling eyes fluttered and rolled in pleasure as his grin fell to an open-mouthed gasp. He settled his hips against mine and rested for a moment, like he was simply enjoying the fact that he was in me. I gave a few pulses of my internal muscles and he opened one eye to peer suspiciously down at me. I couldn't help but smile at my sweet, grumpy Milo.

Sterling shifted so that he was leaning against the headboard, and he pulled me up between his legs. It was like how Milo and Devon had me earlier, but this time, Milo was slowly thrusting into me. My back met Sterling's chest, and he kissed along my shoulder. Every thrust Milo made pressed me against Sterling's body. I felt his leaking hardness against my back, and I wondered if I'd ever have them both inside me at once. I shivered and a whimper escaped me.

I looked over to Devon and saw he was stroking himself and watching us together. He was long, and I watched him turn his wrist when he was near the tip of his cock. Taking note, I watched him closely. I saw the bead of pre come almost drip from the end and I swallowed hard.

"Fucking hell," Milo groaned and his voice ended on a whimper that told me he was close. Sterling roughly reached around and grabbed Milo's hips and helped him drive hard and fast into me. Their chests smashed me, making it impossible to draw a consistent breath, but it was perfection.

Devon approached me just as I was reaching my peak. Sterling turned my head to face Devon, who promptly slid between my open lips. I sucked him hard, swallowing him down. Milo's hips stuttered in their rhythm as he came with his lips on my neck and a low groan echoing in the space.

Devon's climax was not far behind. He stroked back my hair in a gentle caress and his eyes rolled back as he came. His gentle touch and reverent whisper of my name had me coming as Milo's thrusts slowed inside me. Devon pulled out of my mouth, and I relaxed back against Sterling's chest.

Milo rolled off me to lie on the bed. Devon sat in a slouch at the bottom of the mattress, and Sterling chuckled. "Sorry if your back is wet. I came on you."

Instead of answering him, I spit into my hand. Devon looked at me sharply as his release made a reappearance on my palm. He was still panting, his abs flexing and relaxing, but he looked wounded at my action. I grinned at him as I turned slightly in

Sterling's lap before wiping my hand on his cheek. Sterling jerked away from my hand with a scowl.

"Emily! What the fuck? Ew!" Sterling shouted and shoved me off of him.

Devon and Milo both laughed with me as Sterling wiped his face with someone's discarded shirt. "That's payback for coming on me," Devon said. That kicked puppy look gone and replaced with a prideful sneer.

Chapter 21

Devon

Friday evening found us lounging around a fire at Sterling's cabin. Everyone was freshly showered and still damp after our run through the woods. Sterling and Emily had made burgers for dinner. I had started a fire in the fire pit outside while Milo put in some garden solar lights around the property. Emily was impressed by my fire starting abilities when she came out with ingredients for s'mores, and I discreetly hid the lighter fluid so she wouldn't see that I had used it.

That giddy feeling I'd had after the intense sex we'd had returned this evening. A little less potent than last time, but it was still there. There were crickets chirping in the distance and fireflies were blinking in and out around us. A scent of pine, wood smoke, and burger grease hung around the property. The atmosphere was calm, satiated, and exactly what I knew Sterling wanted when he bought the cabin. I even had a beer that Sterling had brought while I watched Emily toast a marshmallow.

"I like them a little burned," she said with a giggle as the marshmallow turned into a ball of flame. She pulled the stick up towards her face to blow it out. Milo was sitting next to her, but scooted away with a scowl at the flaming wad of sugar.

She carefully made a perfect s'more and took a bite. We all watched as her eyes fluttered and she moaned. "Do you guys want me to make you one?"

"I'll make my own," I said. It had been a long time since I'd eaten a s'more.

"Make me one like that," Sterling said and gestured with his beer towards her s'more.

"Milo, do you wa-" she began.

"No," we all chorused.

"Ookay," she said with wide eyes. "I'm gathering that there's a story here?"

"Milo hates sticky foods," Sterling said with a casual shrug.

"Nobody likes to be sticky," she laughed.

"I hate foods that make you sticky and then you can't get it all off no matter how hard you wash your hands. Marshmallow is the work of the devil," Milo droned.

"Speaking of the devil, what do we think we'll do about Lucifer and Eden after that attack?" Emily asked, changing the subject.

Milo and Sterling looked at me. I sighed and set down my empty beer in the gravel at my feet. "I don't believe it was an organized attack. I believe those kids heard we were the enemy and wanted to make themselves important," I explained. "It's not likely that Lucifer and Eden endorsed the attack."

Emily's brow furrowed. I know she was worried that I was wrong, and that the attack was bigger than it was. Experience told me there would have been more men and better artillery if this had been a genuine attack. It was a pale shadow of what we'd dealt with in the past.

"Eh, I think that was all they had to fight. I think those kids were their only fighters. We control most of the gangs in the area and most people join ours because they get paid for their jobs more reliably than unaffiliated gangs," Sterling countered.

"That's option B," I said with a gesture to Sterling.

"Or option C, and it's something else entirely," Emily said.

Sterling and I exchanged glances. "Right," I said. I would not tell her she was wrong and ruin our nice evening, so I let her believe she was on to something. "Maybe."

"Have you thought more about what you want to do after this job is done?" I asked her after she finished her s'more and was making Sterling's.

"I miss teaching," she said with a sigh.

"We figured as much," Milo said.

Emily looked down with a blush and bit her lip.

"If it makes you feel any better, I like managing our legal businesses better than I liked being the attack dog for the mafia," Sterling said as Emily passed him his s'more. He kissed her cheek in thanks for the dessert.

"Really?" Milo asked.

"Yeah, I like our employees and I enjoy helping them. Yesterday, I was literally trying my hand on some plumbing at Marie's salon. Can you believe it? *Plumbing.* They had a busted sink, and I was able to get it working again. It was... cool to do something normal and get a positive reaction. Everyone was so happy."

"So, you have a praise kink?" I snarked.

Sterling laughed. "I don't know, man. It was just... nice. Oh, and then last week some bitchy Karen was complaining at Harold's deli while I was there and she asked to speak to the manager. Harold was right there, obviously the owner, but he made me come out of the office. That bitch shut up so fast you would have thought I'd barked at her!"

"I'm sure you flashed her a little 'pain' and 'gain,'" Milo chuckled, referring to the tattoos on Sterling's knuckles.

"Nope, I just came through the doors and looked at her," Sterling said proudly. "But really, I like that I haven't had to hit anyone outside of our training and that one time with Devon."

"Milo, have you changed your mind about the business?" I asked him, ignoring Sterling's reference to our fight.

"No," Milo said with a shake of his head. "I want to

stick around. I want to be near Marie and be a good uncle."

Milo's job was typically less violent than Sterling's job or my job in the family business. If anyone was going to feel most comfortable and sure about continuing the job, it was going to be him. Which was good because he'd built so much of our technology infrastructure and security from the ground up, and I was unlikely to find anyone as skilled as he was.

"How are you feeling, Devon?" Emily asked.

I opened a fresh beer. The hoppy flavor was growing on me, and I needed something to do with my hands.

"I met with my mom recently and talked over the business with her. She was the heir before me, and I wanted to know where she thought the business should be. I had even brought up the idea of us retiring. She said that she had always stood by our life because there were always going to be drugs on the streets. But when they were on our streets and being sold by us, we could be sure they were clean. And the people selling it were being paid. There would always be gangs and violence, but if they were our gangs, they would be supported and working. There's less inter gang violence when the gang members have a job to do. And we give them a job."

"I never thought about it that way," Emily said thoughtfully. "Does that mean you're staying in the business? Like the whole thing, illegal and legal?"

I picked at the label on the beer bottle. Condensation

had made the glue loose, and I easily peeled it off and threw it into the fire. "I'm staying. All of it."

Part of me wanted to look up and see their reactions to what I'd said, but the biggest part of me wanted to remain protected from their glances and nonverbal communication. I didn't want to see the moment they decided this life wasn't worth their time or their efforts. When they decided *I* wasn't worth their time and their efforts.

"I'll stay with you," Emily said finally. "I'm not the most knowledgeable about this stuff, but I'll do my best."

My head shot up to look at her. She smiled softly. My heart thudded almost painfully in my chest. It was like I'd just run a mile dash.

"I'll stick around for now," Sterling said with a grin.

Milo gave me a firm nod.

My shoulders fell, and I realized the tension I'd been carrying as it melted away. They were outright choosing me. Not the business. Not the money. Me.

Fuck.

I needed to get my shit together if they were all organizing their lives around me. I couldn't be an asshole all the time anymore. Fuck. I needed to be *nice*.

"I don't think you'll be able to teach if you stick with the business," Sterling said with a wince. "From a security standpoint, you'd be putting your class in danger."

"I understand," Emily said and sat back in her chair. "It's not a deal-breaker, honestly. I'm not sure what part I miss. Safety in the routine? The kids? I don't know."

"This job won't be safe or routine," I informed her.

"I know. I've been thinking lately that sometimes routine can be stifling," she said. Her eyes were on the campfire and slightly glazed over, like her thoughts weren't here with us at all. I imagined she was thinking of her ex-husband and her life before us.

"Um, speak for yourself," Milo, the most routine dependent fucker, interjected.

Chapter 22

Devon

A phone ringing woke me. I sat up with a start, jostling the person in the bed next to me. Emily mumbled in her sleep and turned over to lay her head on Milo's chest. Sterling blinked up at me from the other end of the cramped bed. I grabbed my phone off the nightstand and looked at the number. It wasn't one I recognized, but it had a local zip code. "Hello?" I rasped into the phone.

"Is this Devon Bilal?" a frantic woman's voice asked.

"It is," I said and slowly got out of bed.

"This is Jim's wife, Linda," she said.

"Jim? Oh, Doc," I said as my brain cells finally woke up.

"Right, Doc," she said. "He never came home last night."

My stomach sank with dread. I snapped my fingers impatiently at the people in the bed to wake them up. "Do you know where he was when you last spoke to him?" Sterling and Milo sat up quickly. Emily rubbed her Bambi eyes and looked worried. I turned away from them as I listened to Linda.

"He was home for lunch and then went out again. I didn't ask him where. We- we don't talk about it so that I- I know nothing in case...."

"I understand," I said as I roughly pulled on a pair of jeans. "You don't track his phone or anything?"

"No, I don't," she said regretfully.

"It's alright, Linda. I understand he didn't want you in trouble. We'll do some digging and I'll call you back as soon as I find anything," I soothed as I shoved Milo's computer in front of him.

He gestured with an irritated shrug to say he didn't even know where to start. Sterling put Milo's glasses in his hand and Milo put them on.

Emily slipped out of the bedroom, and I heard her running water in the kitchen.

I hung up with Linda and sat on the edge of the bed. "Doc's missing."

"What?" Sterling and Milo chorused.

"He never came home yesterday. That was his wife," I said and stifled a yawn and pulled an undershirt out of my bag at my feet.

Milo opened the computer and started his lightning fast typing. Sterling leaned over to watch him work and kissed Milo's bare shoulder. "She doesn't know where he was going?"

"No, they don't talk about his job to protect her," I said, and guilt flooded me.

Doc was practically a parental figure for all of us. I had taken a strong interest in medicine at a young age and he had been the only one to encourage my learning. I'd attended a lot of his procedures before my father put a stop to it. The man had been the one to attend all our mothers' births and cared for all of their pregnancies. He mended all our wounds and was the one to oversee our growth and development into adulthood. My stomach was sick, thinking about his disappearance almost more than when I found out what my father had been up to.

"He was at Stephanie's yesterday at about four. It looks like he stayed there for... forty-five minutes. Mrs. Golding waved him off at the door and he pulled out and went... South," Milo narrated as he watched the footage. "Hold on for a minute and I'll have traffic cameras."

The smell of brewed coffee wafted through the cabin, and I inhaled deeply. Emily padded back into the bedroom and opened up a few duffle bags on the floor. She handed the guys their clothes and found her own before heading to the bathroom. She didn't look any of us in the eye. Was she upset?

Then it occurred to me. No, she just didn't want to gloat. That brat. She may have been right in believing that the minor incident at the camping supply store was bigger than I'd thought. If something had happened to Doc after leaving my mom's, then it would have happened at the same time as our attack at the store.

I pulled on my shirt and finished getting ready in the bathroom while Milo worked. Emily and Sterling had dressed and were packing up our bags while Milo remained in the bed typing and with a furrowed brow.

"I followed him to a grocery store. He was in there for approximately thirty minutes. I'm watching him come out with a cart now... he makes it to his car... oh, there. Fuck," Milo said, and we all rushed to gather around his laptop.

He replayed the video footage. Doc was barely visible in the security camera frame, but he could be seen going to his car and loading the trunk before a black SUV pulled up and two men jumped out. Doc was then shoved into the SUV before they drove away.

"See if you can get a run on those plates and then follow where that SUV goes," I directed as I turned to my bag. I zipped it up and Emily handed me a Styrofoam coffee cup. "You can say it," I told her.

"No," she sighed. "Someone's life is at risk. It's not fun."

"I'll say it," Milo piped up. An image of my hand cracking down on his ass permeated my thoughts. "Emily told you so."

"I know," I said and cracked my neck.

We had the car packed up and the cabin appliances unplugged and turned off in less than ten minutes. I was thankful nobody offered to drive because I needed to do something. I needed to be actively doing something with my body so I wouldn't go insane.

Guilt tore through my guts, shredding any bit of relaxation I'd gathered in the twelve hours we'd been able to stay at the cabin. I should have been there. I should have been able to protect Doc from whatever had happened to him. If I was a better leader, this wouldn't have happened at all.

I called my mom to let her know what had happened and to make sure she was alright. She said she would have Marie and Brendon come over with Veronica and Harold. Harold had been in the life long enough to know how to protect everyone in the house. I had faith in him, they'd be just fine.

Not long after a quick swing through a drive through for a greasy breakfast and more coffee, Randy was calling my phone. I had Sterling answer for me.

"Hey Randy, it's Sterling. Devon's driving, so I'll put you on speaker."

"We had another shipment get taken last night," Randy said, sounding tired. "It never made it to the stockyards, so it didn't come up on our security feeds."

"Fuck," Sterling groaned.

"Yeah, no kidding," Randy huffed. "Listen, some of my guys say that our drugs are coming up tampered with. The bags have our mark on them, but they're not clean. There were a couple of deaths of a few regulars in the early hours."

"Wait, tampered with post production?" Milo asked.

"I'm not sure. We're working with the idea that

these are drugs we lost and they're popping back up with our mark on them. One of my guys said he didn't see these regulars once or twice last week and he was worried back then that they had OD'd. I think they came across someone else selling with our name on it," Randy explained.

"They're tampering with our shit to give us a bad name," Sterling said.

"That's what I'm thinking," Randy said, and yawned.

"Sorry to be the bearer of more bad news, Randy, but Doc got picked up last night," I said.

"Fuck. The cops or these new shit heads?" Randy asked.

"The new gang, we think. Still working on it," I replied.

"Plates on the SUV were stolen. I lost track of them going through a residential area on the East Side," Milo informed us. "Doc's phone got smashed at the grocery store where he was picked up, so I don't have tracking on him."

Emily reached over the center console from the passenger's seat and squeezed my thigh in support. I rubbed her hand in acknowledgement.

"Shit. I'll get my guys out looking. The East Side is not our territory, but we'll get everyone on it," Randy said.

"Should you throw out the drugs that you have that maybe came from shipments around the same time?" Emily asked.

Randy made a sound of hesitance. "Well, not all of it was taken from the shipments that got jacked. I'll track that shit down and assume it to be trash."

"That's probably best. We'll eat that loss. Spread the word to the others. I can't have our customers dying from dirty drugs," I said and took Emily's hand in mine.

We hung up with Randy, and everyone was silent.

"Fuck," I sighed.

"What do you think they wanted with him? Information?" Emily asked in a soft, sad voice.

"He was probably just an easy target," Milo explained. "If they'd been watching us, they would have seen him leaving our house and Stephanie's house regularly. And Marie's. So when they saw him out alone, they took him."

"Yeah, but if they were going to send us an easy message, wouldn't he have been found dead somewhere?" Emily asked.

"Milo, check the cameras at our house," I said in a rush.

"On it," Milo said while Emily gagged. "None of my perimeter stuff went off, so I think we're good."

"He better not be in my greenhouse," Emily groaned.

"Why would you even think of that?" Sterling asked with a horrified and disgusted look.

I snorted a laugh. "Because she's been with us for too long. We've corrupted her."

"Whatever." She rolled her eyes. "But does Doc know enough to be useful to them?"

"Yes and no," Sterling said. "He knows a lot, yes, but I don't know what info would even be useful to them."

"Gang affiliations, addresses, names," Milo droned. "That's all he'd really have, other than our health information."

"So, a lot that could put many people in danger," Emily said. "Do we still think they're a small operation?"

"I don't know about the size of their operation, but they're smart. I'll give them that," I said and rested my head back on my seat as I drove.

Chapter 23

Emily

As soon as we got home, we dropped our bags in the hearth room while Sterling did a sweep of the house and property for Doc's body. Milo was certain nobody had been on the grounds or in the house, but Sterling wanted to be cautious.

Devon had been tense and shifty ever since he'd gotten the call from Doc's wife. I knew Doc had been a mentor to Devon and they were close. Devon's anxiety as a new leader had already been high even before someone near and dear to him had gone missing. I made a fresh pot of coffee while the guys scattered to do their jobs. I didn't know what to do other than text Marie to check on her and shuffle around in the kitchen.

Devon came up behind me while I was pulling mugs out of the cabinet and wrapped his arms around my waist. He buried his nose in my hair at the nape of my neck and inhaled deeply. "I'm making coffee," I said needlessly. The aroma of the fresh brew surrounded us and the machine beeped to signal its completion.

"Thank you," he murmured against my skin.

I spun in his arms and looked up at him. "You okay?"

"I have an idea and it's not one I like," he said by way of a response.

My heart sank. "What do you need?" I asked, offering to meet him in whatever hell he was headed to.

He winced slightly at my offer. "We have another shipment tonight. I'm going."

"Just you?" I asked, horrified.

He shook his head. "I'm going to ask Sterling to go with me. Milo will watch on the security feed."

"Will- will you go with Randy's guys?" I asked and bit my trembling lip.

He gave a slow nod, but it seemed like he was hiding something from me.

"Spit it out. You can't keep secrets from me if you expect me to be in this with you," I said and pushed on his chest lightly.

"I'm taking a skeleton crew. I don't want to risk too many men," Devon replied hesitantly.

"But you would be at risk then," I whispered.

He nodded.

I closed my eyes. "I don't like it."

He pressed his forehead against mine. "I can't risk my men."

"No, you'll just risk mine," I said with as much

venom I could muster. Which wasn't much. I sounded like a petulant child.

He breathed a laugh, and I opened my eyes to see him looking fondly at me as he pulled away. "You'll stay with Milo in the van. I don't want you alone in the house and I don't want to drop you off at my mom's."

"No," I said. "I'd be pissed if you just dropped me off somewhere like I needed a babysitter."

"I know," Devon said and poured himself a cup of coffee.

"Wait," I said as it occurred to me. "You're going with a skeleton crew? Shouldn't you have a ton of guys there to reduce the risk?"

Devon shrugged and leaned against the counter. "I don't want to risk everyone."

"Why? Isn't it, like, kind of their job?" I asked. "Why not have the usual guys there, but a bunch more hiding and waiting for an ambush? Haven't these guys been going to work every day knowing there'd been attacks on shipments?"

Devon only stared at me and sipped his coffee. I couldn't read his shuttered expression.

"Why not assume this is a trap, and have guys hiding and ready to react?" I asked.

Devon was still silent, and he set his coffee down. I noticed the tremble in his hands. "My father would risk-"

"Your father would probably have sent guys in to die but stayed safe at home," I said and waved my hand dismissively. "He wouldn't have felt the way you do about risking your men."

Devon let out a long exhale and hung his head.

"You are not your father," I reminded him sternly.

"You're right," Devon said and looked at me intensely. His eyes were laser focused on me and his jaw clenched.

"What?" I asked with an awkward laugh. "Why are you looking at me like that?"

"I love you," he said in a rush.

I smiled. "I love you, too. So, please be careful tonight. You may have to delegate to the gangs and that's alright. That's not disregarding their lives, that's having them do their *jobs*."

He cupped my jaw gently and pulled me to him. Devon kissed me softly, pulling away after peppering my lips with little pecks. I giggled against him. "Be a good boy and go to work," I said and smacked him on the butt.

He looked at me incredulously. I wasn't sure if anyone had ever spanked Devon. I wanted to fix that oversight.

"Hey, so what are we doing about tonight?" Sterling asked as he came into the kitchen, lured by the smell of fresh coffee. "The shipment of weapons at the stockyard is due at eleven."

"We're going," Devon said and tore his eyes away from me to look at Sterling.

"All of us?" Sterling said and glanced at me.

I glowered.

"You and I will go. Emily here had the idea that we should pretend to only have a small crew until Lucifer and Eden's guys show up and then more of our men come out of hiding. She and Milo will wait in the van," Devon explained.

"Nice work, Bambi." Sterling said with a wink at me.

"We should tell Milo," I said.

"I HEARD," came a distorted, excessively loud, mechanical echo of Milo's voice.

We all jumped in reaction. "Jesus, fuck!" Sterling shouted and spun around towards the doorway.

"Where the hell are you?" Devon asked, looking around.

"MY ROOM. I'M TALKING THROUGH THE CAMERA SPEAKERS," came his response. I cringed and covered my ears.

"Well, stop it. You're making my ears bleed," Sterling snapped.

Later, Milo and I were waiting in the van we'd used before the confrontation with Anthony and Gregory. We were quiet and watching the security feeds of the stockyard. Sterling and Devon stuck together, trying to look casual. They conversed with the stockyard guards who received regular payment to keep quiet about their observations, inspected the stacks of shipping containers, and mingled with Randy's crew. There was no movement on the road, but I knew there were about twenty men hiding, waiting for the cue to come out.

A train sounded in the distance, and Milo sat up straight. "Here comes the train. If they're going to show up, it would be now."

We watched in sharp-edged silence as the train slowed to a stop. The yard workers worked on unloading the shipment they were scheduled to unload, while our guys met with a man who slid open a cargo door near the back. The man hopped out and greeted Sterling and Devon. Devon's phone was in his pocket and connected with Milo's on the little desk in the van. I heard them casually greet this man from the train and engage in small talk.

A vehicle pulled into a frame on one of the cameras. "Milo," I muttered and pointed.

"Yup," he said to me and started typing out a message for Sterling.

Through Devon's open phone line, I heard Sterling's phone chime with a message.

"We have movement," Sterling muttered to Devon.

Two more trucks and an SUV pulled onto the street from the other direction. Milo typed another text to Sterling.

I didn't want to watch. I didn't want to see my men get hurt. My heart was in my throat and my stomach simmered with nerves as I watched the alert get sent out to all of our hidden men. As soon as the new vehicles came to a stop, our men jumped out of hiding.

Everything moved so fast, but with an organized type of chaos. Everyone had a job and moved with efficiency. We had successfully trapped the trap. Before

I knew it, there were bodies on the ground and Devon and Sterling were hefting a man into the van. He thrashed about while being beaten and bound.

"Milo, you drive us home. Emily, up front," Devon directed smoothly.

I obeyed his demand immediately and buckled into the passenger's seat as Milo drove us home.

My heart felt sick hearing my men keep their prisoner subdued. But I was never under the impression that this was anything out of their ordinary business proceedings. It had been a few months since the basement torture cell had been used, but it was ready for us when we got home.

They left me in the office while they worked on getting information from the prisoner. I didn't want to take this man's life, but I didn't want to be separated from the work they were doing, either. I had voluntarily stayed in this life and would not be a passenger princess to the work. With a deep breath, I knocked on the metal door and Devon opened it.

"You don't have to be here," he said earnestly.

"I do. I'm a part of this family. I need to be here," I said stubbornly.

He quirked an eyebrow at my tone but stood to the side for me to enter. The room was dark except for the spotlight shining on the bloodied and naked man hanging from the ceiling by his wrists. The space smelled like urine, blood, sweat, and death. Our prisoner was groaning in pain as Sterling sliced a thin line between two of his ribs with a large knife.

"Let's try again," Sterling spit. "Where's Doc?"

The guy shook his head.

Milo reached for my hand and had me sit in a metal folding chair next to him. We were in a dark corner, not visible to the prisoner. Milo had the man's criminal records pulled up on his tablet and showed me. He was not a good man. He had a list of crimes a mile long. I *tsked*.

"Old man. Harmless. Travels without a fucking weapon other than a scalpel in his doctor bag. Taken from a fucking Whole Foods parking lot. Anything ringing a bell?" Sterling listed as he poked shallow holes into the guy's stomach with his knife.

"I don't know. I don't know everything they do, I promise," the guy said, tense pain threading through his voice. He let out a howl as Sterling poked his knife into the guy's navel.

"Well, what do you know then? Tell me," Sterling said like he was waiting for gossip.

"I only know one building. They sleep there," the guy said as he struggled to pull in a breath.

"Who is 'they?'" Sterling asked as he held out his hand to Devon for another weapon.

Devon handed him pliers. The guy's eyes went wide as he saw them.

"Lucifer and Eden. They sleep at this warehouse," he said in a rush. "Please, don't kill me. I haven't seen the old man, but I know where they sleep. That's all I know. Please!"

"Address!" Milo barked out from our dark corner.

The man told him the address and Milo typed it into his tablet.

"Abandoned for two years. Previously owned by a food bank. Electricity was never fully turned off, and... it has racked up a bill the last three months," Milo said as he flipped between multiple windows on his tablet.

I watched, impressed, as he mobilized Randy's guys to meet them there in an hour.

"Anything else for us?" Sterling asked the guy brightly as he tossed the pliers in his hand.

"No, I just started working for them. They're psycho, man," the guy groaned.

"Milo?" Devon asked.

Milo tilted his tablet so the light would illuminate his face as he nodded once to Devon.

"Take him out," Devon said in dismissal to Sterling.

"Emily, please leave," Sterling said calmly as he crouched in front of the prisoner. The begging, crying prisoner was strung up before a demonic gargoyle.

"I'm here with you, Sterling," I said in a choked whisper.

"I don't want you to see me like this," Sterling said, not looking back.

Devon stood next to Sterling's crouched form, his shoulders tense and face scowling. He spared me one warning glance before he focused back on the prisoner. He was there with Sterling. He wouldn't let Sterling bear this man's death alone.

Milo gently took my hand and pulled me from the

room. The metal door swung shut behind and all was silent.

"I think he gave us their headquarters. If they're living there, then that's probably it," Milo said as we went upstairs.

"Will they be okay?" I asked him distractedly. Milo knew I was talking about Sterling and Devon.

"No," he said honestly. "But they have us. And if we get Doc back, it'll be worth it."

Chapter 24

Devon

"What are you planning?" Milo asked when he entered the office.

I was standing behind the desk, staring at the pile of paperwork we'd taken from my father's office in the past few weeks. The only thought in my head was a memory of when he blew up a house where a rival gang had been staying when I was thirteen. Eight people had died, all of them senior members of the gang, but the news had considered it a local tragedy. Even as I stood in the office, there was a memorial out in front of the lot where the house had once been.

Emily had taken Sterling to bed after he'd killed our captive. My stomach had felt sick knowing he'd just hours before been talking about how happy he was that he hadn't needed to hurt anyone in weeks. And, at my direction, he'd had to break that streak of nonviolence. It was my fault. I could have done it. Hell, Sterling could have denied me. But he hadn't. He'd taken my orders and done his job. It was my fault he needed Emily to remind him of his humanity. I needed to finish this.

"How many bombs do you have on hand?" I asked him.

"Um, none," he said slowly, like I was an idiot. "I don't exactly keep them on a shelf in the cupboard."

I exhaled and hung my head.

"You're thinking of blowing up their headquarters?" he asked and plopped down into the chair that was still pulled up at the desk.

"If I blew it up, we could be done," I said evenly.

"We could kill Doc in the process," Milo replied sharply.

"Come on, he's dead," I spat and shoved over a stack of my father's paperwork from decades ago. "There's no reason they'd keep him alive."

"You don't know that," Milo insisted.

"Would *we* keep anyone alive?" I said and gestured to the basement that had recently housed a corpse. Sonny and his guys had left an hour ago after removing the body.

"Devon, you don't *know* that he's dead," Milo replied. "Could you live with yourself if you thought you killed Doc?"

"Haven't I already killed him?" I snapped. "Aren't I already responsible for every single life touched by this business?"

"No."

"Milo," I said, defeated. My hands fell to my sides, and I felt so very tired. The kind of tiredness that ached down to the marrow of my bones. It sucked me dry.

"No," he repeated. "Nobody is here against their will."

"Anymore," I scoffed.

"Right, anymore. You gave her and Doc the choice. You're not your father," Milo said slowly.

"No, but he taught me everything I know and I'm planning on blowing up their headquarters like he would," I said.

"I was taught by Matthew, who really was just as ruthless in this business as your dad. He wasn't his co-leader for nothing, Dev. He was just as much of an asshole," Milo explained. "And I'm telling you we don't have to blow it up and risk Doc."

I sighed and sat in the desk chair, feeling defeated. My cuticles burned from where I'd been clawing at them all night.

"Doc is your mentor. Why wouldn't we try to rescue him?" Milo continued.

"We'd be risking more men to swan in and drag out a corpse," I argued. The mention of my respect for Doc had my blood acidic and sweat beaded at my temples.

"Or we'd catch them unaware and rescue Doc," Milo insisted. "They're cocky and stupid. They've attacked our men over and over again, thinking they would see no type of retribution from us because they had us beat. We need to move quickly before they realize we took one of their guys, though."

He was right. If we were going to end them, we needed to move quickly. Saving Doc or not, blowing the place up or not, we needed to act fast. If they realized that someone with knowledge of their headquarters had gone missing and had not died at the loading docks with the others, then they were sure to clear out.

I nodded and looked at my phone on the desk. I needed to make calls to Randy and the other gangs if we were going to do this.

"You balance me, Milo," I said, thinking back to my conversations with my mom. She was right. I needed him. I needed him, Sterling, and Emily to remind me I wasn't a monster like my father. I wasn't evil.

Milo considered me for a time. His lack of judgment and ridicule at my statement made me realize the fear of seeing it was what held me back in the first place. "I think your dad and Matthew could have balanced each other, too. In the beginning, at least."

"And we saw how that ended up," I said darkly.

"It doesn't have to," Milo countered. "You don't have to kill everyone and make shitty decisions behind everyone's backs."

I snorted.

After some silence, I said, "I wish I would have made the kill tonight."

Milo stared at me. His expression was open, but blank. He was waiting for me to explain, but not arguing with me or judging me.

"Sterling was just talking about how he enjoyed not

having to hurt or kill anyone. And here I come along, not twelve hours later, and make him torture and kill a man," I grumbled.

"Respectfully, Devon, you're an idiot," Milo said carefully. "He would do anything you ask of him because he respects you and loves you. Not because you *made* him. All of us would. And I think that goes both ways."

The beast of rage and violence that lived in my chest whimpered, but I remained stoic.

"If he had asked for you to do it instead, would you have done it?"

"In a heartbeat, yes," I replied. "But not out of a space of love. It needed to be done."

"See, that's where I think you're wrong. You love us just as much as we love you," Milo said with a grin.

"Ugh, we're so fucked up," I groaned. "We're talking about killing a man as a sign of love."

Milo shrugged. "I expect nothing less from us."

"How can I... show that I love you guys with the plan tonight?" I asked awkwardly.

"Flowers, chocolate, and shibari" Milo droned and pushed his glasses up his nose.

I rolled my eyes.

"We delegate," he said simply.

"Delegate to the gangs?" I clarified.

"Yeah, honestly, it'll save our asses. If Lucifer and Eden have two brain cells to rub together, they'll be waiting for us or gone," Milo reasoned. "If we send in some men first to clear us a path, we can go in at the end and finish it. Hopefully, we'll find Doc in there, too."

"That's risking our men," I reminded him.

"It's their job," Milo said. "Besides, what's riskier? One last confrontation where we potentially catch them off guard? Or continued attacks on our day-to-day operations?"

Again, he was right. I spun idly in the desk chair.

"I think your problem is you're trying so hard to not be like your father that you're fucking yourself over in the meantime," Milo said, his brow furrowed in thought.

I considered what he was saying and groaned.

"It's alright," he said in a cocky, bratty tone. "That's why I'm here. To be your voice of reason."

"The reason I bend you over this desk and spank you black and blue," I threatened.

"Sure. Explain that one to Sterling and see how fast he has your balls in a jar in his room," Milo snarked back, unaffected by my threat.

"Wait, I have an idea," I said and sat up suddenly. Milo, being a brat, had me thinking. What was something my father and Matthew would have never thought of? Subterfuge. They would have gone in guns blazing every single time. What if we got sneaky? What if we tricked them?

"And that is?" Milo asked.

"Which of our members do you think could pass as us from a distance?" I asked him, a smile creeping over my face.

Chapter 25

Emily

I awoke to the scent of baking cinnamon and the sound of Mrs. Golding talking to Devon in the foyer. I left a soundly sleeping Sterling in the bed to go listen.

"Tonight?" Mrs. Golding asked, irritation in her tone.

"Yes, please, this is important," Devon was saying as I looked down over the railing.

"Doc is missing and you're planning to throw a party?" She exclaimed.

"Not a party," Milo said from somewhere out of sight. "It's a meeting that will look like a party to anyone watching us. We're going to be planning to get him back."

Mrs. Golding gave a long-suffering sigh before throwing her hands in the air, defeated. "Sure, I'll get a lavish party planned, catered, and bar tended on a moment's notice. Nothing strenuous about that!"

"I'll pay you-" Devon said, but was cut off.

"Devon Anthony Bilal!" she scolded. "Of course

you will pay me more! You will also hear me complain about this stupid plan of yours!"

"It was actually Milo's plan," Devon argued, sounding more like a teenager fighting their mother enforcing a curfew than like a mafia boss.

"I don't care whose plan it was. You're going to hear me complain," Mrs. Golding said and pushed past them into the kitchen.

Milo and Devon stared at each other in a heavily communicated silence as I descended the stairs. "We're having a party meeting?" I asked. I kissed them both on the cheek in greeting.

"We want to gather as many of our people as we can to plan our next action. It's going to take all of us and communicating would be much more effective and quicker if we could have them all here at once," Devon explained.

"How's Sterling?" Milo asked. I noticed the dark circles under his eyes. He must have been up all night planning and working. "I checked on you both on the camera a couple of times, but neither one of you moved an inch."

"He's alright," I said and looked at a very guilty looking Devon. "What's wrong?"

"Oh, he feels bad he made Sterling kill again," Milo replied.

Devon glared at him.

Milo shrugged. "It's true. We talked about it for a while last night."

"Social skills, Milo," Devon said through his teeth.

"He's not mad at you, Devon," I said. "Honestly, he didn't really talk about you. He just needed a gentle touch to remind him he is good. I thought you knew that."

Sterling had told me that Devon knew about his difficulty coming back down after the high of aggression and violence. He said that Devon had been the one to put in the sauna for Sterling and used to hire massage therapists to help after fights.

Devon nodded solemnly. "I still want to apologize to him."

Milo's eyebrows shot up, and I elbowed him in the ribs.

"Him, too?" Milo asked.

"What do you mean?" Devon asked, looking confused.

"You have a crush on him, too?" Milo clarified.

Devon looked horrified. "No! Why would you say that?"

I stifled a laugh and bit my lip.

"Because you have a crush on Emily and me. That's why you apologize to us when you fuck up," Milo said simply.

Devon's horrified expression remained. My resolve not to laugh lost out to the peal of giggles that came out like a snort.

"I only have a crush-" Devon said before closing his eyes and exhaling slowly. "I only have feelings for Emily. Milo, I don't have feelings for you. At least nothing soft."

"You're hard right now?" Milo asked, his eyes wide and shocked.

"No! Fuck, Milo," Devon groaned. "I meant 'soft' like...."

"Lovey dovey heart eyes," Sterling said from where he was leaning on the railing upstairs.

Milo looked mildly disheartened as he understood. "Fine. Lick your own taint while you fuck Emily."

"Milo!" everyone shouted.

After hours of work, an ungodly amount of coffee, and four very rushed showers and wardrobe changes, we were holding court over the gang members. The thrones had been set up just the same as the New Year's party, but now I had my own. Mine had roses tangled in with the chains and a soft cushion. When I saw it, I'd almost gotten emotional. I'd been a few minutes behind the guys in coming down to the meeting and they were all lined up and grinning lasciviously at me in their own thrones. The only thing that stopped the tears was the realization that I was in the center with Devon. At his side. I took my seat with pride.

No music was playing, and everyone was passing around plates of food and bottles of liquor. Men and women were dressed for a party, but they were sitting and standing, prepared for instructions. Mrs. Golding had worked tirelessly to get food and drinks catered for the party meeting, but all the staff had cleared out immediately. Our business was too sensitive to have anyone else in the building.

"Alright, thank you all for being here tonight. You

all know the trouble we've been having with these two newcomers. They've damaged our merchandise, sabotaged trusted relationships with our customers, and even taken one of our own. On Friday, someone took Doc from outside of Whole Foods and he is now missing. Our maneuver last night found us their headquarters. Our informant told us that is where they live and sleep. We believe this is where Doc is being held," Devon said, his voice strong and clear. The way he spoke demanded attention and respect. It was a marvel to witness as it came naturally to him. I was mesmerized.

"Is anyone here familiar with the area around this location?" Milo asked as he displayed a map on the TV that had been set up behind us. Two side-by-side windows displayed the building Lucifer and Eden were using. One was street view and one was the map.

A few people murmured their knowledge of the area. Milo gathered information on area businesses and who our members knew in the area. At least one addict that had died over the weekend bought from our people near there. This further solidified our knowledge of that being where Lucifer and Eden operated.

Devon led the meeting, Milo gathered information, Sterling talked strategy, and I mediated a few fights. Within two hours, we had a plan. A really great one, too. I was impressed with the cooperation of everyone in the room, despite the fact that many of them often fought each other outside of this house. But when it came down to outsiders and threats to our way of life, everyone worked together.

We dismissed the meeting and everyone transitioned to the party. The music was turned on and the liquor flowed. Lights dimmed and strobe lights shone in the den. I leaned back on my throne, remembering the last party fondly. I watched over the dancers like a queen watching over her subjects. Devon leaned over to me, a sly look on his face. I leaned to meet him to hear what horrible thing he was probably about to say.

"Much better this time, right?" he asked.

"Yeah, I'm not watching you come down some random girl's throat," I snarked.

He recoiled like he'd forgotten, and I had reminded him.

"Oh, well, if it makes you feel any better as soon as you looked away, I couldn't come," he said regretfully.

"It actually doesn't make me feel any better. But sorry to hear about your blue balls," I droned.

"I could come down your throat right now, if you want," he taunted. "Stake your claim in front of everyone."

"No, no, no," I said with a laugh. "That would be *you* staking *your* claim. If I wanted everyone to know who was mine, I'd have all three of you on your knees while I sat pretty and spread on my throne."

Devon's eyes flashed dangerously. His jaw worked as he watched me, his nostrils flaring as he breathed. I gave an innocent smile and looked back out to my subjects.

"Just say the word, Bambi," he said, his low voice just barely audible over the sound of the music.

"Hm," I said in a considering tone. "They all know. Look, I even have my very own throne. They all know you're mine. Besides, someone recently told me I was soft with the wrong people in the past. I will only be soft with the right men now that I've learned my lesson. And nobody else in this room has earned my gentleness. Not even a glimpse."

Devon's jaw unclenched and his eyes softened. He took my hand and kissed along my knuckles. "In that case, let's visit the office. For old time's sake."

Chapter 26

Emily

Devon led me through the dancing people. Their bodies swayed to the sultry beat of the music. Their lustful movements fed me as I followed Devon, hand in hand, to the office.

He opened the door with a key and let me in first. When he shut the door behind him, the volume of the music outside the room was dulled just enough to shout a conversation.

"You know, we can go upstairs," I laughed.

Devon smiled and shook his head. "I've been thinking about this since I found you that night."

"Oh?" I asked. "The weapons cabinet gets you hot?"

Devon shrugged. "You touching the weapons does."

I hummed and turned to look at the cabinet. He didn't let me get far before he picked me up and turned to sit me on the desk. He swiped an arm over the desk, clearing it, just like last time, before he pushed my legs apart. My legs dangled over the desk and my shoes clunked to the floor. As he opened my thighs to accommodate him, he pushed my tight black dress up to my hips. He got down on his knees before me and slid my panties down my legs. He kissed the skin on my thighs as he moved, and I sighed in pleasure.

We had been talking about staking our claim, about showing dominance over our people. And here he was, the devil on his knees before me. Ready to worship. Shivers ran down my body as bumps arose on my skin. The room took on a charged, electric feeling as he peered up at me. His lashes were thick and dark, framing his amber eyes beautifully. His stubble and tan skin made the skin of my thighs look like snow. I whimpered in anticipation.

He didn't hear me, but he knew I'd made a sound. He grinned up at me wickedly before he blew cold air over my now heated and soaking pussy. I shivered again. He licked over my entire pussy with one slow stroke. I felt my walls clench around nothing as I groaned. He blew cold air again. I shuddered. Another long, slow lick. Another gust of cold air. I was shaking now, almost rattling the desk.

"Please," I moaned, but not loud enough for him to hear me. He knew, though, and didn't listen.

I was over sensitive at the simplest of touches and I was surely dripping down the back of the desk. With a desperate groan, I grabbed his hair and held him to me. He nipped at me, and I shouted out in pain and shock. I wanted to kick him but also knock him on his back and ride his face. Instead, I pushed his face harder against me. I felt him laugh, the rumbling against my skin like a vibration.

He licked and sucked at me until I was just at the edge of coming. The door swung open, and we both jerked away and looked up. It was Sterling and Milo. They were grinning ear to ear as they shut the door behind them. I smiled at my two other men and wondered if I could fit them all between my legs to worship.

Devon must have communicated something to them, because they both nodded. Sterling shoved Milo against the door and dropped to his knees. Milo and I made eye contact as Devon's mouth landed back on my pussy. My eyes fluttered, but there was so much to look at. I needed to keep them open. Sterling made quick work to undo Milo's belt and zipper.

I couldn't hear Milo moan over the music, but I saw his throat move with it and his jaw drop open. Sterling was on his knees, sucking Milo in the same spot where they shared their first kiss. It was wild to think that was barely six months ago. Love for these men consumed and overwhelmed me, causing me to reach out a hand to Milo. I wanted him near me. Milo looked down and tapped Sterling's jaw and said something to him. Sterling stood up and Milo leaned next to me on the desk. Sterling got to his knees next to Devon and took Milo back into his mouth. Milo leaned down and kissed me lightly. I felt his gasps fan over my face, and I clutched his hand in mine.

The warmth of his hand in mine was steady and

reassuring. Tonight we were embarking on a huge mission. In more than one way, truly. We were confronting Lucifer and Eden in two waves. One was a distraction and one was the real takeover. Both endeavors were heavy with the lives of our gang members. There were so many people involved from so many of our gangs. But their respect for my men, and me, went so deep that they were ignoring their own fights and wars to work with us.

This was the first major incident with my men as leaders. This was their first time proving themselves. It was their first time demonstrating what they had been trained to do all their lives. Devon, Milo, and Sterling had always been part of the army going into these confrontations. The soldiers on the front lines. Now they were behind the scenes, directing and delegating. In a way, they were itching for more action. But they were also grateful for the reprieve.

Our adrenaline and anxiety were better worked out through sex, anyway.

Devon latched onto my clit and slid two fingers into my soaked center. I felt a shout claw from my throat as I kissed Milo. I was going to come. My thighs trembled on either side of Devon's head, and his mouth worked faster and harder on my clit. His fingers were pressing that spot inside of me that had me seeing stars, and I broke the kiss with Milo to tilt my head back and shriek. It felt like electricity coursed through my body as I writhed on the desk. Devon was incredibly skilled at this. It was almost unfair.

As I came down from my orgasm, Devon slowed his movements only slightly. He gave me enough of a break to catch my breath and watch Sterling and Milo. Sterling sucked Milo down until his nose brushed Milo's lower abdomen. I watched as Milo's abs clenched and unclenched over and over as he panted and moaned. His hand in mine shook as he approached his peak. I lifted his hand to my lips and sucked his index finger into my mouth. His head turned to me and he watched as I suck and swirled my tongue around his finger.

"Fuck," he mouthed to me.

I grinned as much as I could with my mouth full.

Devon took that as a cue for me being ready for more. His fingers curled inside of me and his mouth suctioned over my clit again. It was quick to get me to the top of another orgasm, but I breathed through it, wanting to wait until Milo came. I wanted to come when he did.

Milo rolled his hips, seemingly subconsciously, and his eyes closed. I gave one more hard suck on his finger before my brain ceased functioning and I opened my mouth and moaned. Milo thrust into Sterling's mouth. Sterling pulled back to gag at the aggressive intrusion and I saw jet after jet of Milo's come as it filled Sterling's waiting mouth. It sent me over, as well. I felt myself clench down on Devon's fingers as wetness coated my thighs. My body shook and trembled with the release and my vision blurred.

When I became aware of my surroundings again,

Devon was standing before me and kissing my neck and jaw. I returned the kiss and then looked up at him from under my lashes. He smiled softly at me, something I'd never seen from him before. I wanted to take a picture and get it framed. The soft smile was almost loving and sweet. It suited his dark-lashed and golden eyes more than the angry scowl I saw most often. I cupped his face in my hands and stared at him, taking it all in. While our mission tonight wasn't as dangerous as our past ones, it still carried risk. I didn't take our relaxed position for granted. He tipped his forehead against mine and I pushed lightly on his chest to make him back up. I wanted to return the favor.

I pushed him until he was far enough for me to slide off the desk and stand on shaking legs. With very little effort, I spun him, so he was the one leaning on the desk. Getting on my knees, I realized I'd only had him in my mouth once before and the other guys had distracted me. Now it was my turn to give him all of my attention. I unbuckled his belt and undid his pants before shoving them down over his ass and around his thighs with his boxer briefs. I wanted nothing in the way.

He looked down at me with hooded, soft eyes as I licked him from base to tip. His chest rose and fell deeply. Swirling my tongue around the tip gave me a taste of him before I took him into my mouth all the way. I took him as far as I could and sucked. He wrapped his hand in my hair and held it tight at the base of my skull. Not so hard to be painful, but enough to give a delicious pressure on my scalp. I bobbed my head up and down on his length and watched his beautiful face. I watched the ticking of his jaw before he gave up and let it hang open. His eyes never left my face, other than to roll back when I did something he particularly liked.

Movement caught my eye next to me. I saw Sterling and Milo swap places like Devon and I did, with Sterling leaning against the desk next to Devon while Milo matched my pace in sucking Sterling's cock. Sterling winked down at me and reached over to caress my face.

Devon gripped my hair harder and thrust into my throat. Tears sprung to my eyes in reaction and I held my breath while he used me.

"Fuck, fuck, so good," his lips mouthed as he thrust into me. He said something else, but I couldn't read his lips.

It wasn't long before he came down my throat. I looked up at him. I wanted to see his face as he came. His mouth was open, and his eyes rolled back and fluttering. A small smile curled the corner of his mouth. He ended his orgasm with a bite to his bottom lip to contain his smile as he looked down at me again.

I smiled up at him and licked my lips, his come bubbling over my tongue and lips messily. A fire flashed behind his eyes, and he snaked the hand not tangled in my hair out to snatch at my jaw. He leaned down to get closer to me, his eyes narrowing with a glare.

"Swallow it," he snarled.

Instantly, I obeyed. He still had my face squished in his grasp, and I felt my chin bob with my swallow. He pulled back a little. "Open," he demanded and loosened his grip.

I opened.

He smirked at my empty mouth. "Good girl."

I wanted to roll my eyes at him to be a brat, but Sterling and Milo caught my attention. Sterling was gripping the desk tightly in his hands and had his head tipped back in pleasure. Milo pulled off Sterling in just enough time to watch him come. Milo worked him with his hand as Sterling came jet after jet onto Milo's glasses, their clothes, and the floor.

The pattern over Milo's glasses made me giggle, and I pulled them off his face. Devon and Sterling pulled their pants back into place while I cleaned Milo's glasses with a tissue from the desk. They were all talking to each other while Sterling wiped his come off the floor with a tissue. Or, rather, they were shouting to each other over the music and having a hard time understanding each other. We should have gone upstairs.

They had serious expressions, so I knew they were talking about the job tonight. I looked at the clock. We were fifteen minutes before the music was going to be turned off and some of our party guests would be leaving. We needed to get some sleep, or at least try to, before we were set to leave early in the morning.

"I'm bringing you to bed," Devon said and stroked over my arm.

"Are you staying with me?" I asked, my eyes wide and hopefully Bambi-ish.

He smiled. "I shouldn't. I need to be with my people."

"But I am one of your people," I pouted. I wasn't just being ridiculous without a reason. Devon needed to sleep. I wasn't sure if he had gotten any sleep since before Doc was taken, and even then, his sleep was interrupted. Dark circles had formed under his eyes, and I was sure he'd benefit from at least a couple of hours of rest.

He considered me for a moment and swallowed. He knew what I was doing. I was taking care of him in a way that gave him the control. It was the only way he could accept my help right now. He gave a brief nod before looking at Sterling and Milo. They both gestured to the door with approving looks at me. They knew what I'd done, too.

Devon took my hand in his and pulled me towards the door.

"You two should get some rest, too," I said as I passed them.

"I'll be there soon, Bambi," Sterling said and pinched me on the ass.

This time, when we made it to the stairs, the big security guard didn't stop me from going up. It was the same guy as last time and tonight he only nodded in greeting before looking back out over the dancing mass of people. I wanted to stick my tongue out at him, but instead let Devon, in view of some dancers

in the hearth room and foyer, whisk me up to his bedroom with a slow, lazy smile on his lips.

Chapter 27

Devon

The sun rose on our house party to find us ready to mobilize. We had had members of our gangs pretending to trip over themselves as they left for their cars throughout the night. Milo had noticed that we were being watched sometime around two in the morning. We had thought it was inevitable that they not only found our home but also would watch us closely. Our meeting, disguised as a raging party, was intentional and successful.

We left in the van at around eight. The last of our members had exaggeratedly stumbled out thirty minutes before us. Everyone was in place except for us. We armed ourselves to the teeth, caffeinated ourselves well, and were ready to end this stupid war.

Milo was in the back of the van, already booting up his computers and gadgets. "Everyone is where they should be. We're ready to go in five," he said as he checked in with the security cameras and text chains.

This was the first time we'd delegated our operations

as leaders. The first time we truly stepped into our roles as bosses. This was it. This was what I had been training for my entire life. I wondered if my father would have been proud of me. Shaking that thought away, I focused on the task at hand.

Sterling drove us to our planned location, and I was sure there were no followers. The person who had been stationed to watch the house left just a few minutes after the last car had vacated our driveway. Sterling parked us, and we all turned to Milo to wait.

"There are no cameras near their headquarters, so we'll need to rely on the reports of our guys," Milo said as he typed. "Unless... let me see what their internet is like."

We waited in well-trained silence as Milo worked. Behind his glasses, Milo's brow furrowed as he typed with lightning quick speed. "What's the name of that gas station on the corner?"

"It's a Sunoco," Emily said.

"Alright, they have an unsecured public Wi-Fi network. I can get into their cameras. Very stupid of them. Should have had professionals set up their rig and not some Joe Shmo who has only ever plugged in an Xbox. And that means this other network is... aha! It's Lucifer and Eden's. Password was Cheryl dot 1992. Fucking dumb. See everyone? This is why we have two factored authentications and a secure network. The next time someone whines about not having easy Wi-Fi access at our house, please remind them of this moment," Milo droned.

"Do they have cameras?" I asked, used to Milo's rants.

"No. But they have their phones connected to the network. They're on Wi-Fi calling so I'll see if they call for help," Milo said.

"Give the signal for group one," I directed him.

He nodded and picked up his phone. "Done. That group I have cameras on."

The second monitor flickered to life with the security camera feed of the train station of a local distribution center. We'd pretended to schedule an early morning shipment and had some of our guys talk about it out on the streets last night while we were partying. We were confident that someone would hear them and launch an attack on our fake shipment. Out in that yard of shipping containers were four people who had dressed in disguise to look like us. I couldn't help but grin at the four people pretending to be us. The woman dressed like Emily was wearing a long wig and was holding the hand of the man playing Sterling. The two of them hated each other. They were in rival gangs. I had to pay them a considerable amount to be on the same job. It was worth it, though, to watch them successfully trick our opponents.

The man pretending to be me was standing tall and kept brushing his clothes. I frowned. He looked like he had a stick up his ass and didn't want to be there. Did I look like that?

"Milo looks submissive and breedable," Sterling said and peered at the screen.

Emily giggled.

Fake Milo stood with his shoulders in and kept messing with his glasses and flicking his hair out of his eyes. All very Milo. I rolled my lips into my mouth. I was not about to piss off the computer genius.

"Shut up. At least I don't look like that Devon," Milo grumbled.

"He looks... prissy," Sterling agreed.

"Oscar winning, I think. So close to the real Devon, I had to do a double take," Milo said.

"Ha. Ha," I grunted.

As we watched, a troupe of men descended on our group.

"I knew it," I murmured.

A group of our men came out of hiding and the fight began.

"Go for group two," I said, and Milo sent the text.

We waited in heavy silence as we watched Milo turn the gas station camera to face the building that housed Lucifer and Eden on the first monitor. We watched as our people stormed the place. Milo opened another tab, and it looked like he was monitoring emergency services calls as they came in at the local dispatch.

There had yet to be a solid estimate of how many people Lucifer and Eden had on their roster. We had made the decision to separate them by having two different operations at the same time. It was the same way that Lucifer and Eden had us occupied at the store while they took Doc.

There were no calls to 911 regarding shots fired at either location. Business continued as usual at the gas station. It was close to the highway and, likely, the sound of the cars on the road covered the sound of gunshots inside the warehouse. I felt more settled without the interference of the police. We had known that moving during the day brought that risk to the forefront, but luckily, both operations were in loud areas.

It wasn't long before our disguised people at the distribution center sent messages to us. They'd been successful in taking out the people that had attacked them. Their next phase was to meet us at the warehouse and wait to be called for more action.

Milo centered the warehouse on the monitor, and we watched it remain still. Nobody went in or out after our men initially entered. It was a long fifteen minutes before we got a call from Randy.

"Yeah?" I answered.

"All ready for you, Boss," Randy said, slightly breathless but happy.

I hung up, and we scrambled from the van. Emily squealed excitedly, and I gripped her hand tightly in mine. I would not squeal and giggle like her, but the feeling was mutual. We hurried to the warehouse, and the doors opened for us. Two of our people were grinning ear to ear as they opened the doors with a flourish. A successful operation always felt euphoric. I couldn't blame them for their excitement. It had been a long while since they'd had a leader that wasn't trying to pin them against each other or use them indiscriminately. And being one of those leaders as we walked through without a threat was... indescribable. I felt god-like.

"In here!" Randy said from a room down the hallway.

Sterling pushed to go first. He had his gun drawn, just in case. There was no need, though. Our guys had pajama clad and bed headed Lucifer and Eden cornered.

Chapter 28

Devon

We entered a room that looked to have been an office at one point, but was now being used as a bedroom. Tapestries and blankets adorned the walls with twinkling lights. A messy bed stood centered in the room.

"Where's Doc?" I asked and wrinkled my nose at the mess of the room. Food wrappers and bottles littered the place.

"Who?" Lucifer asked. Both he and Eden were standing in front of the bed with their hands up. Randy and another guy had them both at gunpoint.

"The man you took while he was doing his shopping," I bite out through clenched teeth.

"Oh, he's a doctor?" Eden asked, her breathy voice high and wavering.

"Where is he?" I demanded.

"Got him!" A voice shouted from down the hall. "He- uh, needs some help! He's bleeding!"

Doc needed medical attention. I was the only one

with the knowledge and experience to help him. While I was someone with the power to end Lucifer and Eden, I was the only one with the power to save one of our own. As I made my way down the hall to my mentor- to a man who was more of a father to me than the man who raised me- I realized my true power and leadership ability lie with the people around me. My heart pounded in my chest and blood rushed in my ears. I left the room where Lucifer and Eden were cornered, fully confident that Milo, Sterling, and Emily would handle it. Everything clicked into place as I rushed to where I was being called down the hall.

Loyalty was power. And loyalty was reciprocal. I had to show my loyalty to Doc by choosing him over the glory of the win. The realization felt both simple and staggering at the same time. It took my breath from my lungs. This was what my father had under-estimated his entire career. This was what my father missed in his lessons. I was nothing without these people. I was not a leader without people to lead, and I would not lead through fear and retribution. I would lead with loyalty.

My boots skidded to a halt outside of what looked like a utility closet. One of Randy's men, Lucky, was pointing inside. "He was like this when I found him. He opened his eyes and recognized me. He said my name, but then passed out again."

I touched Lucky on the shoulder in acknowledge-ment. I couldn't speak as fear seized up my chest. Doc had been handcuffed to a radiator and was unconscious. I could smell urine and sweat and... singed skin. Fuck. I went to my knees before him while I pulled out my wallet. I had a handcuff key inside, and my hands shook as I unlocked the metal cuffs. Doc's arms fell limply to his sides.

"Come on, old man," I grumbled and pulled him away from the steaming hot radiator.

I felt his pulse and checked his breathing. He was alive, but fading. I looked him over quickly, assessing his needs. He had lost a lot of blood, judging by the staining on his clothes and the cement below him. Multiple stab wounds dotted his body. They weren't deep, but they were dangerous. Fuck. Fucking fuck fuck. He'd been tortured. For what?

There was a medical kit back in the van and I shouted for someone to go find it. Doc was wearing a pale blue button-down shirt and khaki pants. His clothes were littered with holes from the stab wounds and blood was slowly pouring from some of them. How he was still alive was beyond my comprehension. They must not have stabbed any crucial organs, which was good for Doc. But they were letting him die slowly from blood loss while chained to a hot radiator. I opened Doc's shirt to see that his wounds were almost closed. A breath caught in my chest just as someone came barreling in with the medical kit. Doc had tried to cauterize his own stab wounds on the hot metal radiator.

Emily appeared at the door as I ripped open the kit. "Is he alright?"

"He should make it. I'll get him stable, but he will need to see a doctor. Lucky! I'm getting him partially patched and then I want you to drop him off at the hospital. Say you found him while looking for your sister in a crack house."

"My sister isn't-" he started to say.

"Lucky, I don't care. I just need you to not get arrested for bringing an abused senior citizen to the ER with obvious torture wounds," I snapped.

"Why do his wounds look like that?" Emily asked as she crouched next to me.

"He was trying to cauterize them on the radiator. He was successful enough that it probably saved his life," I said as I covered the visible wounds with gauze and tape.

Emily gagged and apologized. I didn't gag in echo. I was too focused on the task.

We got Doc patched up enough to move. As I was directing Lucky to carry him out to a car, Doc opened his eyes. He looked old. Older than I'd ever noticed him appearing before. He reached for my hand, and I lunged to him so he didn't strain. "Doc, you're going to be alright," I said, my voice choked up. I would not cry in front of everyone in this room. I couldn't.

"Son," was all Doc said before his eyes closed again and his hand slipped from mine.

"Go!" I said with a desperate, pleading look at Lucky.

He rushed Doc from the room, and I leaned against the wall. Relief at finding him warred with the fear of losing him all over again. It had a cold sweat forming on my skin and my breath was not full enough.

"Devon, he's going to be alright," Emily said and gripped my hands in hers. "We did it. We got Lucifer and Eden, and you saved Doc. You saved him!"

"I know, I know," I panted and wiped my forehead with my sleeve. "Baby, I know. I just... holy shit."

She laughed. "Let's go see what the guys decided."

"Torture and humiliation, probably," I said as we went back to the makeshift bedroom.

Sterling and Milo had Lucifer and Eden on their knees in front of the bed with their hands zip tied behind their backs. Sterling, Milo, and Randy all had their hands on their hips and disgusted scowls on their faces.

"What's going on?" I asked.

"How's Doc?" Sterling asked.

"Lucky is taking him to the hospital. He should be alright," I said and looked over the couple on the floor. They were in ratty pajamas and looked more normal than the overly made-up picture they presented at our last meeting. Eden was whimpering, and Lucifer stared at me with his chin up and jaw firm.

"What did you try to get out of him?" I asked Lucifer.

"Nothing," Lucifer spat at my feet.

"No, I know you *got* nothing. But what did you *want*?" I asked, ignoring his insult. I brushed at the dust that had accumulated on my shirt just from being in this place. Ignoring Doc's blood, I was filthy.

I ruined these clothes after kneeling on the ground only once.

"Your suppliers and connections," Eden sniffled.

Lucifer shot her a glare.

"Oh," I scoffed. "Yeah, Doc knows none of that."

"We, uh, told Cheryl and Jared here that we were going to call the police and get them turned in," Milo said and scratched the back of his neck. Both of our captors visibly winced at the use of their legal names.

A gift of mercy, if I was being honest. I had figured they would be dead by now. Certainly, if my father or even Matthew were still alive, they would have turned these sad sacks into rat food as soon as they found them.

"I choose death with my woman," Lucifer- Jared said with a dramatic bow of his head.

I recoiled with disgust. Emily snorted next to me.

"Death over prison?" I asked to clarify.

"Kill us both," Jared said like he was in a stage production of a Shakespear play. "For there is no life without my woman at my side."

"Mmkay," Sterling said and turned to me. "I want to burn them with fire, but I feel like it would just be bullying at that point."

"I'll do it," Randy grumbled. He pulled his gun out of his holster.

"Nah, they want to die. Let's not give them what they want. Let's get them locked up," I said and gestured around us. "Trespassing on private property. This place is owned by a bank. Let's drop some unregistered weapons in here and a couple of grand in drugs. Let's get them put away for a good long time. Separated."

Lucifer and Eden wailed and screamed, and we hauled them out of their bedroom. I directed some of our guys to set up a scene. A simple scene for the cops to come in and make the arrests. We didn't have to bring in any weapons or drugs. They had a few shipments of ours hidden away, anyway. That included what they were using to tamper with our supply, which killed people over the weekend.

One of Randy's quickest guys was in charge of cutting their zip ties as the police showed up. Leaving a scrambling Jared and Cheryl amongst their contraband. Even if they screamed that we were there and set them up, they were still caught amongst their own crimes. We'd wiped our fingerprints and deleted the security footage from all our locations.

The job felt... anticlimactic in a way. It was the first time I wasn't part of the team going in, guns blazing. I was the man behind the curtain. Or, rather, the man in the stifling hot box truck watching on security cameras. But walking out of the building with all of my people unharmed and happy was a different type of win. A better one.

Chapter 29

Emily

It was late afternoon by the time we got home. We had picked up Doc's wife and brought her to the hospital and she'd let us know he was alright and awake. We checked in with Randy's men and also had Devon treat the minimal injuries sustained by our people during the fights. It truly had been a successful mission. I couldn't help feeling proud of the leadership skills of my men as we walked through the front door of our house.

I was smiling, but Devon was chewing the corner of his bottom lip and had a furrow in his brow. "Hey," I said soothingly. "What's wrong?"

He shook his head dismissively. Sterling and Milo exchanged glances. I took Devon by the hand and took him to the kitchen for a drink. "Wait, I need to watch over our headquarters on the cameras."

"Why?" I asked as he tugged out of my grasp and went down the three steps to the den where our party equipment was still set up. The thrones looked extra ridiculous in the humbling light of day. They looked like party center props. I would have snorted a laugh if I wasn't so worried about Devon.

"I'll get drinks," Milo murmured to me as I followed Devon.

In the office, Devon was already sitting in the creaking leather office chair and typing on the keyboard. He didn't look up at me as I entered. "Why do you have to watch them?"

"I need to make sure they're not planning a takeover of their own. The most likely time for any of our gangs to plan an attack on us of their own accord is just after one set up by us. Whether we win or lose, they can see our injured or relaxed state as a weak point and take advantage," he explained blandly.

"Do you suspect any of them would try? I have seen nothing other than total respect and love for us," I said and rubbed his shoulders over the chair.

He shrugged me off.

"Hey," I scolded softly.

He exhaled and leaned back for me to put my hands on him again. He let me massage the tense muscles as he pulled up the security feeds. I looked at them as Milo and then Sterling came into the office. It didn't look like much movement or talking was happening in their gang headquarters. A few had people sleeping, one looked like they were all playing video games on a console, and more were empty than inhabited. Most of the gang members had probably gone home, honestly.

"Looks pretty normal and sleepy," I said lightly.

Milo poured some bourbon, neat, into a glass for Devon and slid it on the desk. Sterling opened a bag of potato chips, crunching happily. Devon didn't take the glass, his eyes still on the cameras.

"Dev, chill. It's done, and it went well," Sterling said between chewing. "Beat it and meat it."

I glared at Sterling over my shoulder, and he grinned and shoved a handful of chips into his mouth. "Devon," I murmured and turned the chair so he faced me. I straddled his thighs to see him eye to eye. "Tell me what's bothering you?"

"It was too easy," he said in a rush, like he'd just convinced himself to say something. "We didn't lose anyone and had only minor injuries. Doc was still alive, for fuck's sake! I'm waiting for the other shoe to drop. For the next hurdle to show itself. There's no way our first war as leaders was that successful!"

His eyes were pained and manic. Like it hurt him to say this out loud. Like it was a struggle to be this vulnerable, even after everything that had happened. I wanted to smack sense into him but also hold him tight.

"Maybe you're just that good," I tried to reassure him.

He snorted sardonically and rested his head back against the seat. He hadn't put his hands on me like I thought he would have. I looked down and saw his bloodied hands on the armrests of the chair. He didn't want to get his blood on me. I picked up the glass of bourbon from the desk and took a sip. The burn I felt all the way down emboldened me. Lifting one of his hands, I sucked a bloodied finger into my mouth. His eyes snapped to me and he hissed in a breath. Part in pleasure and partly in pain from the sting of alcohol on his torn cuticles.

I felt his dick twitch in his pants and I smiled slowly. I let his finger slowly slide from my mouth. The metallic taste of his blood coated my tongue as I licked clean all of his wounds. Salt of his skin, iron rich blood, and woody bourbon danced on my taste buds. Sweat and cologne hung in the air. The room was dimly lit by one lamp across the room. Dark and heavy curtains covered the sliding doors to the small patio. I slowly lifted my black shirt over my head, leaving me in a lacy black bra.

His hands were on me now. Clean of their blood and free to touch my heated skin. He caressed over my torso light enough that bumps rose on my skin, and I shivered in reaction. I reached behind me and unclasped my bra, letting my breasts fall free. His hands slid up to cup them gently. His eyes were on me. Warm like molten caramel as he watched me. I grabbed the glass of bourbon again. Devon needed a drink.

Gently, but firmly, I guided his mouth to rest between my breasts. I tipped my head back and poured the bourbon over my neck in a small stream. He eagerly drank the liquid from my skin and licked up my chest and neck when I stopped pouring. His smirk was firmly on his lips as he swallowed and leaned back in his seat. The chair creaked beneath us as he massaged my breasts, his hips rolling beneath me just the slightest bit. Like he couldn't help it. I cupped his chin in one hand and said, "Open up," in a soft, lustful voice. I couldn't help it. These men brought out the best and the worst of me.

He obeyed and opened his mouth. I poured the liquid over his pink tongue until he swallowed. His throat bobbed against my hand and I wanted to bite it. So I set the glass down and did just that. He hissed a breath of pain before exhaling with a growl. I gripped his shirt and rolled my hips against him, enjoying the friction against my core.

I heard a deep chuckle behind me, and I turned to see both Sterling and Milo watching me. Their blue and gray eyes were intense and bright. Their expressions were full of lust and care as they watched me and Devon. I reached out to them, too. They both approached us in the chair and Devon spun us so that they could come on either side of me. Hands caressed up and down my bare torso, and I tipped my head back and closed my eyes. The feeling of multiple sets of hands on me was overwhelming in the best way, and I loved it. I would forever cherish the feeling.

"I want you all," I whispered. "In my bed."

"You want us to fill you up, baby girl?" Devon asked.

I hummed in response.

"Bambi," Sterling crooned. "Can I tie you up so pretty?"

"I want to be able to touch you all," I whispered. "I want to make love to you."

The guys all stopped their movements for a second and I thought maybe they were not pleased with my words. I closed my eyes against the rejection, but lips were on mine. I felt the bump of Milo's glasses against my cheeks, and I smiled into the kiss. Another set of lips kissed my neck. A third set sucked a nipple into their mouth and flicked it with their tongue. I squealed in reaction.

Hands lifted me off Devon's lap until I was suspended enough for him to undo and rip down my jeans and panties. I giggled into Milo's lips just as they left mine. Sterling and Milo held me so my pussy was at Devon's face. I wanted to laugh, but Devon's lips and tongue were toying with my pussy like he'd done last night. Devon rolled back in the chair and stood up, his mouth never leaving me. His hands gripped and supported my ass and Sterling and Milo adjusted their grips on the top half of my body. I wrapped my legs over Devon's shoulders. Sterling took over, holding my top half while Milo grabbed the bourbon and glasses.

"D-Don't drop me," I giggled breathlessly.

"I mean, no promises," Sterling replied, since Devon's mouth was busy. "You're kind of precariously balanced."

Devon gripped my ass even tighter as they walked. My heart leaped and skipped a beat as I realized they were walking out the door with me suspended between them. I looked up at Sterling's slyly grinning face. He didn't look like he was straining under my weight, so I guessed I trusted him.

Ascending the stairs, held up between two men, while I orgasmed was certainly a novel experience. I tried to hold still and not wiggle too much as I came, but I couldn't help the trembling. Their grips shifted, and Devon chuckled against my skin as we entered my room.

I was placed gently and trembling on my bed. Milo was quick to take Devon's space between my legs and I shrieked at the sensation of him ferociously licking and sucking me while his beard rasped against my damp skin. Sterling placed his cock at my lips. The metal of his piercing was warm from his skin and smooth against my lips. I opened immediately, slowly and rhythmically sucking as I was brought to the edge of a second orgasm.

Devon stood next to the bed, stroking his cock while watching me reverently. I reached out a hand and wrapped it around his base. I stroked him with the same slow pace as Sterling in my mouth, and they both moaned in unison. Idly, I wondered if I could get them all to moan at the same time. A flood of wetness between my thighs suggested that I *really* liked that challenge.

I pulled away from all of them. "Devon, sit against the headboard," I directed. He obeyed with a challenging look, like he wasn't a fan of taking so many orders from me today. Too bad. I was a woman on a very important mission. "Milo and Sterling kneel on either side of us," I continued as I straddled Devon.

A moan escaped me as I sank down slowly onto Devon's length. His hands rested on my hips like he wanted to slam me down hard, but he resisted. His abs clenched with the effort of restraint, and I praised him. "Good boy, letting me set the pace. You're so pretty when I'm on top."

Milo let out a wheezing huff of air like he had been punched in the stomach.

"You good, Milo?" Sterling chuckled, just as breathless.

"I think I just fucking died," Milo practically whimpered. His huge cock bobbed next to me. He looked like he needed some attention.

"Look at this amazing cock, just waiting to be sucked," I said in a husky, authoritative tone.

"I would be blind not to notice it," Devon muttered as it was bobbing in his face, too.

I giggled and licked my lips before taking Milo into my mouth. While settling on Devon's hips, I sucked Milo up and down a few times. Rocking on Devon, I pulled off Milo and looked at Sterling. "And that decorated dick, waiting so patiently. So good," I said with a hoarse voice.

Sterling smiled proudly and jerked said cock in his hand. I wrapped my hand around him and flicked his piercing gently. He grumbled a moan before removing my hand to spit down on his length and returning my hand with a wink and a smirk.

Now, to reach my goal to get them moaning in unison, I needed to work in a rhythm and not get distracted. I settled my knees better around Devon's hips and returned my mouth to Milo. Up. Down. Squeeze and suck. Two moans and one hiss. Not enough. Up. Down. Up. Down. Squeeze and suck. One moan. Damn. Up. Down. Small squeeze and suck. Up. Down. Up. Down. Squeeze and suck. A chorus of three moans. Goal accomplished. Perfection. I let out a shaky laugh as I felt myself get wetter. My pussy clenched around Devon, and I sucked hungrily at Milo.

"What's so funny, Bambi?" Sterling asked in a growl.

I pulled off Milo to reply. "I wanted to see if I could get all three of you to moan at the same time."

"Oh, little Bambi here was playing games!" Sterling crooned in a voice that suggested I was in trouble.

"No! I love you three equally and I wanted to make love to you in a way that you all felt pleasure equally," I scrambled to say. It sounded nice-hopefully they believed it.

Milo scoffed. "She played us like instruments, not games."

"And your moans are music to my ears," I said before I returned to my efforts with extra vigor.

I rode Devon until I was stuttering in my movements, and he needed to lift me and fuck up into me. Milo's grip on my head prevented me from slacking on my oral work. Sterling's hand was wrapped around mine, guiding my hand up and down. I lost myself to the sensation. My eyes closed. All three of them had their mouths on me in some way now, and I only knew who was who based on their angles. Milo was kissing the palm of my hand that wasn't wrapped around Sterling's cock. Devon was kissing my shoulder, and Sterling's mouth panted and kissed against the middle of my back. So many hands, so much touch.

An orgasm crept closer and closer as I relaxed into their hands and mouths. Milo tapped my cheek to signal he was coming. I gave a long, hard suck, and he shouted his release. His hips tilted up in his thrusts and I fought against a gag as he filled my mouth. I swallowed most of him down, but some dribbled over my chin as I gasped and pulled away. I came hard around Devon. "It's so good, I love it!" I whimpered.

Sterling kissed my come covered mouth as he coated my chest, and Devon's, with his release. "Oh, come on," grumbled Devon breathlessly. His grip on my hips tightened as he fucked up into me at an almost brutal pace. Someone touched my clit, rubbing back and forth quickly, and had me rocketed into back to back orgasms.

The world around me ceased to exist. I could barely hear the soft praises of my men or Devon's shout of release below me. It felt like the atoms making up my body separated and then snapped back together, making me wobbly and boneless. When I came back to a solid state, I heard the end of my cry of pleasure and Devon was growling on every exhale as his own release slowed. I still felt him pulsing within me.

"That's my girl," Sterling murmured and stroked back my hair.

Milo kissed my forehead. "Beautiful. So beautiful," he whispered.

Devon sat up from where he had slouched against the pillows and buried his face in my neck. He inhaled long and shaky. "I love you," he said against my sweaty skin.

"I love you, too," I said sleepily. They laid me down next to Devon on the bed, and I was asleep in seconds. Happy, loved, and thoroughly sated.

Chapter 30

Emily

Marie lifted her swollen feet up and rested them on the stool Milo had lovingly placed near her chair. She leaned back and let the sunlight bathe her skin. We were sitting out by my garden in the backyard and the sun was heavy on us. I didn't mind the heat if it made Marie relax like that. Milo had greeted his sister and checked in with her before he was sent away so we could catch up on girl talk.

"I know it's cliche, but you've changed them," Marie said and cracked open an eye to peer at me.

I sipped my lemonade. "Well, they've changed me, too."

The jury was still out on whether that was for the better. Sitting in the sun next to the garden that I grew, and with three men who treated me like a queen not far away, I was leaning toward gratefulness. I was hesitant to say I was a better person now. I was hesitant to say *they* were better people now. But we'd surely changed.

"How have they changed you? I didn't know you before," Marie asked.

I thought of a good way to explain simply to my new friend. "I was a pushover. Too trusting. Too... submissive to the wrong people. I let my husband and my parents mold me and decide almost everything for me."

"These guys could bowl you right over if they wanted to," Marie said with a shake of her head. "What makes them different from your ex?"

She wasn't wrong. Three bull headed and dominant personalities was a lot to go up against. But... she was also wrong about them. "I've proven myself to them. But I had to fight for the opportunity. We've all come out the other end learning about our own actions and how they affect others. Good and bad. I think they've learned that they need to give people the opportunity to be worthy of their trust and loyalty. And I've learned... well, I've learned a lot," I said and looked over the garden.

"Like what?"

"When I had tasted the freedom of choice for the first time, and a few times after that, I found that I... moved toward cruelty rather than self defense. It was like all the poor decisions I had never made throughout my life came out at once. And it typically came out violently," I said, still not looking at Marie.

"That makes sense. Like bottling up anger," she said casually and shrugged.

"I guess. I was so angry, too. Honestly, I still am.

But the guys help me be more constructive with my energy," I said.

"Ew, I don't want to know," she laughed.

"That's not entirely what I meant," I laughed with her. "This garden is one. Then they give me jobs within the business that they think will help me learn more about how it runs. Next week I'm helping Harold while he has an employee out on vacation. He's going to show me how some of our banking operations work and tell me more about the origins of our business."

"Harold's history lessons are a *bore*," she groaned. "I'm happy you're staying. It's weird how you got here, but I guess Stockholm Syndrome could be hot."

I snorted a laugh, and she giggled. "You know they only held me against my will for like a month."

"I don't know if that speaks more about you or them," Marie laughed. "And I think a month is an ample time to be traumatized."

"I like to think I traumatized them more than they did me," I said.

"Mutual traumatization and mutual masturbation are the keys to long lasting polyamorous relation-ships," Marie said in a tone that sounded like Milo's sarcasm.

"You say that as a joke but-"

"Stop it! Those guys are my brothers!" Marie wailed and covered her ears.

We laughed again and settled into our seats. The sun was scorching, and I was wishing for more ice in my drink. Marie seemed to enjoy the heat like an incredibly pregnant lizard on a rock. So, I kept quiet.

"You know, you probably had enough control and autonomy in your classroom that you didn't notice you were missing it," Marie said after a few minutes of quiet.

I shrugged. "Maybe. I was typically so exhausted by the end of the day that even the decision of what to cook for dinner was better made by Gregory."

"I knew his girlfriend," she said, like she was waiting for me to get angry. "I did her hair. She used to date one of Randy's gang members."

"I figured she had an in somewhere. She was the one who got him started on the path to working with Anthony and Matthew," I said.

"She's not welcome back in the salon. Just so you know," Marie said.

"Thanks," I laughed.

"Speaking of Randy, though," Marie started and sat up. "I was talking to him while I did all the girls' hair at his daughters' sleepover. He wants to homeschool his girls. Apparently, they were exposed to some nasty stuff on the school bus and the school didn't respond the way he thought they should have."

"What a tough way to make that decision," I said empathetically.

"No kidding. And then I was talking to Brendon's sisters, and they both have little kids and want to homeschool. They're nervous that someone will target them because of their family. What if you became the teacher for our family? You could teach my little one when he or she grows up, too," Marie listed.

Tears welled up in my eyes. "I really loved teaching."

"You are great at it, too. I had Milo pull all of your employee files from the school," Marie said.

I snorted. I didn't find it shocking at all.

"We couldn't exactly call your previous employer as a reference," Marie joked. "But I really want you to teach my kids. And I know a lot of other people would love it, too."

"I- I don't even know what to say. Or even where to begin!" I said, overwhelmed by the feelings in my chest. I felt seen. Seen for my love and talent for teaching children. Understood for my strengths and my weaknesses. Accepted despite all of those weaknesses. Fulfilled and loved in every way.

"You'll still be a leader of the family business, co-owner of our legal businesses, and all that. Resident Bad Bitch, if you will. But you'll be Ms. Emily to a bunch of kiddos who want to learn from you, too," Marie explained.

"Where would I do it? Here?" I asked. I looked out to the yard. We could totally have a little schoolhouse built back by the woods.

Marie grinned. "Stephanie and I already talked about it. She has agreed to open her home to it and will completely fund all the school's needs and your salary."

"Oh my God, the guys are going to freak!" I exclaimed.

"Milo kind of already knows. He wouldn't release your work information until I told him what I was planning," Marie said and rolled her eyes.

"Of course not. He's very nosy," I said.

"So, is that a yes? It's okay if you're not feeling it. I get it you've changed and maybe you changed your mind about teaching," Marie said hesitantly.

"It's a yes! I would love to be a teacher again," I said excitedly. Tears rolled down my cheeks now.

This was the best of both worlds. I couldn't have asked for more of a balance of my desires in life. I could still have the gentleness of teaching *and* the excitement of the family business. Now, I didn't have to give one up to maintain the other. It was like my conversations with Devon. He had said that there was nothing wrong with my gentleness, my softness. I had just given it to the wrong people. He, Sterling, and Milo gave me that safe space to be soft and then cut-throat when I needed it. I didn't have to stifle any part of me to appease those men.

"Now, what about nannying?" Marie continued. "I'm having this baby in like two months. When do you start?"

I giggled through my tears. "I'll babysit but call me when he or she is potty trained and is ready to start preschool."

Chapter 31

Devon

Emily was outside in her garden, leaving Milo and Sterling somewhere in the house. I tracked them down and had them come with me to the office.

"Is Doc alright?" Milo asked as he sat in one of the pulled up chairs.

"Yeah, he'll make a full recovery," I said with an exhale. "He'll have some nasty scars, but he will be just fine. He's going home this afternoon. They only kept him because he was dehydrated, and that's dangerous to the elderly."

"Don't call him elderly to his face," Sterling scoffed and leaned back in his seat.

"Actually, that's part of what he talked to me about," I said and tucked my hands under my thighs on the chair to prevent myself from nervously picking at my skin.

"His age? Is it his birthday?" Milo asked.

"No, he is aware of his age and fragility. He was

telling me he and Linda had always wanted to retire and move to Arizona."

"Arizona? I thought all the Ohio geriatrics were shipped to Florida," Sterling said.

"Something about the dry air," I said dismissively. "The point is that he wants to retire."

"Do we have... a pension?" Milo asked hesitantly.

"Not officially, but I'm sure we can figure something out," I said. "I've known of no one who retired from our business."

We were silent for a time while we all considered this.

"No... everyone just died," Milo said matter-of-factly.

"Yeah, I think that may have been by design," I said regretfully through my teeth.

"Huh, I wonder who designed that rule," Sterling said sarcastically.

"So, we need a new Doc," Milo said. "Doc was acquired similarly to Emily. How do we hire someone to be the mafia's on call doctor without advertising the job as such?"

"That would be a weird listing on, uh, what is it? Zip Recruiter or Indeed," Sterling laughed.

"He wants me to take over," I said, interrupting their laughter.

"Oh, shit. That's cool," Sterling said, but shifted in his seat like he was uncomfortable.

"He says that ninety percent of what he treated when my dad and Matthew were in charge were injuries inflicted by my father and Matthew. They led with more threat of violence than we thought," I explained. I cleared my throat to hide the tremor there.

"I knew that," Milo said. "I watched it happen on the cameras more than once."

"You never said," Sterling scolded.

Milo shrugged. "I thought it was common knowledge."

"It wasn't," I said. "But Doc said that he believes my current medical knowledge would be sufficient for most of our needs day to day."

"Dude, it's been years since you shadowed him," Sterling said carefully.

"I know," I sighed. "He has some connections with a school that will let me in, no questions asked to finish up some training. Really, just the basics and some stabilization."

"What about after stabilization? If I need an appendix removed, I want to know you know what you're doing," Sterling said.

"You had your appendix out when you were fourteen," Milo said with a squint at Sterling.

Sterling stared back at us wordlessly. His steel-gray eyes were expressionless and bounced between me and Milo.

"You only have one and it doesn't grow back," I deadpanned.

"Oh, cool. But that doesn't answer my question," Sterling continued.

"Doc said he would assist in anything more serious

until he moves away. And he'll help me find another doctor or a hospital that would be willing to look the other way when we come through. Apparently, he's had a few contacts over the years that get him blood and access to imaging machines or more complex tests," I explained.

"When my appendix was taken out, he had Stephanie bring me to an urgent care after hours to use their X-ray or whatever. I didn't pay too much attention, but I remember it was dark," Sterling said.

"So, you remember your appendix," Milo muttered.

"If you're off in med school and patching up boo-boos, who is leading here?" Sterling asked the million-dollar question.

I leaned forward in my seat and rested my elbows on the desk. The wood of the desk had become marred from years of use. Lines and scratches, a few gouges, littered the surface. To avoid unintentional errors in writing, we had placed a desk mat made of marble over top. I ran my fingers over the scratches still visible now as I gathered the courage to speak.

It felt like I was going against everything that I was. Or, rather, I felt like I was going against everything I had been trained to be. I knew once I said it, once it was out in the air, I would feel better. The decision felt right in my heart, but so very wrong in my head. The rescue mission for Doc and the takedown of Lucifer and Eden had cemented my awareness that I was not alone in this business. Because without the people around me, there would be no business.

For the first time in decades- no, for the first time *ever*, this was a family business. And I needed to lean on that family.

"Milo, are you willing to take over as the leader of our business?" I asked, and my voice didn't tremble one bit.

Milo's eyes widened behind his glasses and his eyebrows disappeared into his unkempt hair. Sterling reached over and slapped Milo on the shoulder in congratulations. Sterling whooped with joy. Milo froze.

"I was under the impression that Matthew had trained you just as much as my father had trained me to lead. He thought you were just as worthy of leadership as I was. And you are. You both are. We should have always been equals in this," I said in a quiet voice.

"He did. He was so angry," Milo muttered.

"Do you want the spot or no?" I chuckled.

"Yes!" Milo shouted.

I grinned and stood to shake his hand. Both Milo and Sterling stood, and Milo shook my hand tight and enthusiastically.

"Our IT budget just got exponentially bigger," Milo said excitedly.

I laughed.

"Can I still work with our legal businesses?" Sterling asked once we sat back down.

I looked at Milo and raised my brows. It was his decision.

"H-how do you think you have grown or benefitted

our businesses?" Milo asked, like he was interviewing Sterling.

Okay. Maybe Milo needed a bit more guidance. Good thing I was not going anywhere.

"*Previous management* neglected requests for upgrades and repairs to the buildings, and I've helped them fix that. I've even helped them organize finances to allow for significant raises and hiring abilities. I'm kind of weirdly good at it."

"What are your plans for future management?" Milo asked.

"Well, I'm thinking we need a coffee shop and a burger place. But that's down the line. Really, we need new chairs at the salon. Harold needs a new register, and a whole digitized banking system. Oh, and our club needs a better DJ," Sterling listed.

"You really have been busy," I said thoughtfully.

"Where do you think I've been every day?" Sterling asked.

"Getting free massages, free drinks, free lunch…" I listed.

Sterling scoffed. "Maybe it started out like that, but it's not anymore. I'm… important there."

"You're important here, too, dumbass," I snapped at him benignly. I looked at Milo. "You both are."

"Aw, that's really cute," Milo crooned insincerely. "But can we get back to me being the new leader?"

"Sure," I said and gestured to open the floor to him.

"Okay, so we need all new servers. I've been keeping them together with digital bubblegum and dental floss. We're running on outdated hardware and software. We're not *un*safe by any means because I'm good at my job, but we need upgrades like very badly," Milo rambled and only stopped to breathe and push up his glasses.

As much as he drove me insane, I loved that some things about Milo never changed. "Milo," I said and cut him off. "You're very right. You and I can look over some financials another time and see if we can do it all up front or if we need to space it out."

"Okay," Milo said with an eager nod. "I'll build a quote and scope of work."

"Perfect," I said and curled my lips into my mouth to keep from laughing.

"Everybody's got new jobs, I love it," Sterling said and leaned back in his seat again. "Devon is the new Doc, Milo is the new Devon, I'm regional manager, and Emily is the family teacher."

"Regional Manager?" I asked with a laugh. "How very Michael Scott of you."

"Yeah, it was easiest to explain to staff and customers. I couldn't say 'owner' because most of them know you as the owner," Sterling said.

"Speaking of..." I said and pulled a folder out of the desk.

I flipped open the manilla folder and spun it for them to look at. At the bottom of each page on the signature line was the loopy, feminine signature of Emily Ambrose.

When they saw the signature, there was an almost

collective sigh of relief. It was stupid that a simple signature was what we needed to see to feel secure. We were businessmen through and through. Even in matters of the heart. *Especially* in matters of the heart, as much as we've learned- I've learned- to let go. She had said it with her words and her actions and her body for months. But now, it was official. She was staying. *Staying* staying. Invested. Deep-rooted. She was *ours* and we were *hers*.

Chapter 32

Epilogue- 2 months later

Emily

The late July buzz of insects and the evening haze of heat came back into focus as the guys approached me. I was in the garden, holding a basket of slightly odd-looking zucchini and a bundle of green beans. An entire bushel of tomatoes stood ready to be brought in and turned into marinara. Sweat beaded down my spine under my grungy gardening clothes and the dirt under my fingernails was drying and flaking. I'd zoned out, staring at the line of sunflowers I'd planted in the spring. Now, their heads were full and heavy with seeds and petals. I was marveling at the number of seeds that each bloom held when I heard the brushing footsteps of all three men as they approached me.

"Are you alright? You've been standing here staring forever," Milo said, an edge of concern in his voice.

I looked back at them and gave a small smile to reassure them. Milo was wearing a crisp suit, having just got back from a meeting. His hair was neatly combed and styled, and his beard trimmed. Sterling was wearing his self-appointed work uniform of khaki shorts and a polo shirt. He wasn't carrying his briefcase now, but he loved carrying it to work and thought it made him look official. I happened to know that it contained two coils of shibari rope, some lube, a pack of cinnamon gum, a ridiculous amount of gummy candy, and a handgun. Devon... Devon took my breath away. The setting sun shone bright on him, clean shaven, hair slicked back, and wearing his scrubs. He was taking some nursing courses at a local college as a refresher for what he'd already known, and for some added skills. The long nights of helping him study had us all looking worse for the wear, but he wore it best. He wore it with pride and confidence. But most of all, he wore it with a sense of purpose each day.

"I'm fine," I said and looked back out over the garden. The setting sun illuminated the sunflowers, and I could hear the impatient birds in the distance, waiting for their supper of seeds.

"What are you doing?" Sterling asked, the concern that was in Milo's voice was also present in his.

"Have you ever heard of heliotropism?" I asked.

"Is that on my test?" Devon asked, sounding exhausted and stressed.

"No," I giggled. "Sunflowers are heliotropes. They move in response to the sun. There have been multiple theories over time about what exactly causes them to move, but the general thought is that sunflowers follow the sun. See how they're turned to face the sun as it sets? Tomorrow morning they'll be facing the other way to get that morning sun. But if you tie down a sunflower to get a straight stem or hold the bloom longer, it won't be able to get to the sun and it won't grow as large or as bountiful."

"That's really nice, Emily," Sterling said in a kind voice. His eyes edged over to Devon as if to share a Look, but Devon was watching me intently.

"Do you feel like a sunflower?" Devon asked, his honey eyes fixed on mine.

I nodded. "Before I came here, I wasn't allowed to follow the sun. I couldn't follow what fed me. Now, of course, not every person or flower would feel stifled in the position I was in, I know that. Different flowers have different requirements, just like people. That tomato plant over there needs to be supported, otherwise it will topple over, for example," I said and pointed. I sighed. "With Gregory's job as mayor and my job as a teacher, so much perfection and performance were required. My parents were very strict growing up on what I could say and do and think and wear and aspire to be. They thought they knew best. Later, Gregory inadvertently did the same. And, like a gardener wanting to support their sunflower, I was tied and staked down. I had the perfect storm of ties and stakes. Where I could have probably overcome one or two, there were just too many."

The guys were silent while I set down my basket of vegetables. I could feel their eyes still on me. I had their attention and their love, so I continued.

"When I started killing with you guys, I undid my own ties and stakes. I think I mistook an artificial light for the real thing. I let violence and blood feed me until I was so heavy with rage that I broke my stem. Now, I think I'm learning what the actual sun is like. Here, with you guys, with the kids I'm teaching, and in our business," I finished. I knew it was cheesy and sappy, but it was as accurate as I could explain to them.

"Did you know that a mature sunflower will only face East and will not turn to follow the sun anymore? It also attracts much more pollinators than one that's been staked to face West," Milo added in his Well-Actually voice.

"Ehh, let's not call our woman 'mature,'" Sterling mumbled to Milo. They all looked warily at me.

I laughed, tilting my head back with it. "No, Milo is right. Sunflowers, like people, are more healthy and fruitful when they are allowed the space and the freedom to grow."

"I was alluding to us being pollinators attracted to- wait, Emily, are you pregnant?" Milo asked with a gasp.

I let out a loud, cackling laugh. Perhaps the flower comparison got muddled. "No! Hell, no!"

"Oh," Milo said, and his face fell.

Devon's brow furrowed, and he toed the grass with his shoe. Sterling had a frown marring his features.

Were they... disappointed?

Well, crap.

"You guys haven't even married me yet," I said in a bratty tone. It didn't really matter to me if I was married or not. I'd been married before and *that* didn't turn out well. But I wanted to change their moods from disappointed to... literally anything else.

"Pick a new last name, baby," Devon said, his voice smooth like satin.

"Excuse me, now that I'm leader of the family business, it should be my last name," Milo said with a seductive grin as he tugged on his suit jacket.

"Leader, my ass! I was first to claim her, so it should be me," Sterling argued while he winked and smirked at me.

"Oh, I'll lead your ass alright," Milo snarled at Sterling.

"Cut it out!" Devon snapped. He was still watching me as I took in the bickering.

"How about..." I led them on as I slipped on my garden shoes. I'd learned from my previous mistakes. Shoes were necessary. Even if they were dirty Crocs.

Once my shoes were on and I tied my hair up in a firm ponytail, I turned back to see my men waiting. Waiting like their lives depended on it. I hadn't seen them pay that much attention for that long to anything before. Feeling flattered, I gave them a saucy grin over my shoulder. "How about whoever catches me gives me their last name?"

Their eyebrows went up with understanding, and they pounced. And with that, I was off laughing through the yard. There was shouting and fighting behind me, but I didn't look back. It didn't matter who caught me; I was equally theirs in every way.

Exclusive Extended Epilogue Available to Newsletter subscribers!

Catausten.com/subscribe

ABOUT THE AUTHOR

Cat Austen is an emerging romance author based in Ohio. She lives with her husband and their two boys. She enjoys gardening and baking and is a voracious reader of romance novels.

You can find Cat on TikTok, Instagram, and Facebook. For updates on new releases, ARC opportunities, and pre-orders, subscribe to her newsletter at catausten.com/subscribe

TITLES BY CAT AUSTEN

Convergence- *August 2022*- a polyamorous, contemporary, romantic suspense. Forced proximity, bi-awakening, college aged characters.

Aisle 5- *November 2022*- a contemporary, erotic, romantic comedy. Small town, hetero couple, BDSM, adult characters.

Solace- *Aug 2023*- book one in a polyamorous mafia trilogy. Dark romcom, bi-awakening, morally gray adult characters.

Spite- *November 2023*- book two in the Solace series.

Strength- *April 2024*- book three in the Solace series.

Check out catausten.com, subscribe to newsletter at catausten.com/subscribe, and follow on amazon.com for all new releases.

9 7 9 8 9 8 9 3 8 7 3 4 2